"I am n... imaginatio... souls," Ma...

Leaning over the bed, she pro... ... ...e chest with one finger. "I escort the fallen to their next destination."

Adam appeared to find her anger amusing and pulled her closer. "I don't care what you do. Let's leave my brother out of whatever the hell is going on in my screwed-up head."

Squirming to break free of his hold, she was conscious of his superior strength.

His nearness was having the strangest effect on her. Although she was still struggling to escape, she was no longer sure getting away from him was what she wanted. A strange sensation was sweeping through her as the warmth of his touch seemed to seep into her bones. Adam drew her toward him, and she faced a decision: keep fighting or give in. His lips were inches from hers.

Slowly, enjoying the flare of surprise in his eyes, she lowered her head and kissed him.

"I am not a figment of your imagination, and I do not steal souls", Maja protested angrily.

ONE NIGHT WITH THE VALKYRIE

JANE GODMAN

First Published in Great Britain 2017
By Mills & Boon, an imprint of HarperCollins*Publishers*
1 London Bridge Street, London, SE1 9GF

© 2017 Amanda Anders

ISBN: 978-0-263-93019-1

89-0917

Jane Godman writes in a variety of romance genres, including paranormal, gothic and romantic suspense. Jane lives in England and loves to travel to European cities that are steeped in history and romance—Venice, Dubrovnik and Vienna are among her favorites. Jane is married to a lovely man and is mum to two grown-up children.

I love paranormal romance. It's a genre in which everything is supercharged—including the romance. Additional powers, other worlds, magic and danger... All those things provide both readers and writers with a minivacation from reality.

This story is dedicated to my fellow paranormal-romance lovers, who encourage me to keep building fantasy worlds and creating larger-than-life characters. Thank you for your support!

Chapter 1

Adam Lyon had dodged many bullets in his life. Until now, they had always been of the conversational variety. For the first time ever, the fire and fury being unleashed around him was not in a boardroom…and it was not of his own making.

He thought of his time in Syria in numbers. Two weeks. Seven towns. Ten uncomfortable hotel beds. Fifteen thousand dollars. One question his guide had asked over and over.

"Where is the American called Lyon?"

Despite its seriousness, the question had become a source of amusement between Adam and his guide, Yussef. Something to lighten the darkness of their mood. As they toured the Damascus bars with Danny's picture in one hand and a wad of American money in the other, Adam had joked that at least Yussef had made it clear they were seeking a Western mercenary, not a man-eating beast from the United States.

The answers—or half answers and hints—he got in one of those bars had brought him north to this desolate, shelled-out town called Warda. They were the reason he was now crouched in the corner of a half-ruined, empty office building with all hell raging outside. His arrival had coincided with an intense new outbreak of fighting.

Yussef had brought him to this building, the deserted workplace of one of his friends. The terrified guide had advised Adam to hide here while he attempted to negotiate a way out of town. He explained that Warda was the center of an ongoing battle for supremacy between ultra-hardline government fighters and radicalized rebels.

And you walked into the middle of this place before you checked that out. Nice going, Lyon.

That had been an hour ago, and Yussef had not yet returned. Adam might have known the guy for only two weeks, but Yussef didn't seem the type of person to run out on his responsibilities. Apart from anything else, Adam hadn't paid him for his services, and he knew Yussef had a young family to feed. No, he had a horrible feeling about the reason why Yussef had not come back. His only hope had been killed, injured or captured. Which left Adam on his own. Not a new situation, but not one he had ever faced with bombs and bullets going off all around him.

As an American in Syria, Adam had known all along he was kidnap fodder for both sides in the ongoing conflict. He hadn't entered into this trip lightly, and hadn't gotten into this country easily. It had been a question of weighing his own safety against the need to find his brother. In those circumstances, Danny would always come first. A year ago, Danny had volunteered with a medical charity and come to Syria. Now, as the ground beneath his feet shook in time with the explosions just outside the building, and his ears rang in protest, he realized that kidnapping wasn't his most immediate problem.

I am in so much trouble here. Now there are two missing Lyon brothers, and no one back home knows where either of us is.

The thought galvanized him and he got to his feet, pleased to find his legs were steady. There was no point sitting here waiting for death. May as well head on out and meet it face-to-face.

As he staggered toward what remained of the front door of the building, the shooting outside intensified. Something else happened at the same time. Everything got suddenly darker and a whole lot weirder.

Automatically assuming the change was caused by dust from the explosions, Adam rubbed his eyes to clear them. It didn't help. If anything, his vision darkened even further.

This is it, he decided. *I've been hit. They say you don't always feel pain.*

He was about to grope around his body for a bullet wound when the door flew inward and a black cloud filled the foyer.

"What the...?" *Chemical weapons. I am so screwed.*

The amorphous mass of darkness that had poured into the space began to shift. Within the quivering cloud, Adam could make out three winged figures. Although their features were indistinct, they were female and they were on horseback.

Hallucination. But what a way to go.

One of the figures moved slightly ahead of the others, materializing more fully. Her voice echoed in the small space. "I seek the American Lion."

Adam decided he may as well go along with his own delusion. That whole lion joke between him and Yussef had clearly taken a grip on his imagination. "That makes two of us. If you find him first, tell him his brother said 'hi.'"

Fascinated, he watched as the forms manifested themselves completely. His senses seemed to be heightened to the point where he could observe every detail of the illusion in front of him.

The horses' coats shone like satin as they plunged and reared with restless energy. Adam was only mildly surprised when each animal unfurled giant wings at the same time as it snorted steam and pawed the ground. This was all going on inside his head, after all, so why should anything that happened come as a shock to him?

The woman who had spoken dismounted and took a step closer to him. Adam took a moment to congratulate himself on the quality of this fantasy. Two weeks of enforced celibacy had clearly done wonders for his imagination. It also seemed he might have a previously unexplored warrior-princess fetish.

This tall, slender vision possessed silken skin, impossibly blue eyes and flowing, gold hair. She and her companions were dressed in identical silver helmets adorned on either side with decorative wings, and a tight scarlet corset over which was fastened a fish-scale breastplate. Each of them wore a cloak made of feathers so pure and white they could only have come from the breast of a swan. They carried shields and spears, and had short swords in sheaths strapped at their waists.

In other circumstances, Adam might have spent more time enjoying this visual feast. Since Armageddon seemed to be unfolding in the street outside, he didn't have another minute to waste. It couldn't be wrong to barge past a figment of your own imagination, could it? As he took a step forward, the woman placed an unexpectedly solid-feeling hand on his chest, halting him.

"I am Maja, Valkyrie shield maiden." She spoke clearly enough to be heard over the sound of automatic gunfire. The echoing note had gone and her voice sounded almost normal, although her accent was hard to place. "I must take the bravest of the fallen back to the great hall of Valhalla."

As Adam gazed into Maja's incredible eyes, trying to decide how his mind had endowed a make-believe creation with so much detail, one entire wall of the building collapsed.

Although his body was intact—there were no bullet wounds, after all—this shock-induced delusion hit him hard. Dark spots danced at the edges of his vision as dizziness overtook him and the dust scented floor rose up to meet him as he sprawled at Maja's feet.

The man facing her with an expression of bewilderment clouding his handsome features was not a warrior. He was clad in pants made from a faded, heavy-duty blue cloth and a lightweight, khaki jacket, under which he wore one of those garments she had heard described on other earthly visits as a T-shirt. On his feet were scarred and dusty boots. *Not combat clothing*, Maja decided. He carried no weapons. More importantly, he was alive.

Maja wasn't interested in living people. Her task was simple. Odin the Allfather wanted the souls of the bravest warriors who died in battle. They would join his army-in-waiting. The role of the Valkyries was to swoop into the scene of conflict and escort those souls to Valhalla, the great Hall of the Slain, within which Odin's elite fighting force lived.

This land called Syria had recently become a scene of such great strife that even the Valkyries had turned their attention in this direction. Although their chosen warriors were usually Norsemen, Odin wanted the finest for his army. If that meant widening their search, then his shield maidens must follow the Allfather's will. Brynhild, the Valkyrie leader, who was also Maja's older sister, had been at the end of her wits as she planned this mission. There was desperate fighting going on in two places at the same time and Odin's demands were becoming more difficult to fulfill.

"The American Lion." Brynhild had shaken her head as she pored over her charts. Finding the bravest warriors wasn't an exact science. Brynhild could predict where each fighter would be; she had an idea of the danger they would face, but she couldn't be certain who would die. Odin remained insistent. Only the best would do for his army.

"One name crops up over and over in the stars. The Allfather is determined to have the warrior known as the American Lion. The Norns tell me he will be here in the town of Warda—" Brynhild had pointed to a dot on her map "—and there will be intense fighting there today." She had moved her finger to another location, also in Syria, but many miles away. A frown descended on her face. "Yet there will be ten other warriors, all of whom Odin wants, in this other town at the same time. Each of them is less likely to survive than the American Lion. Do I risk the chance at ten warriors on the gamble that the American Lion will die today?"

"Why don't I go to Warda, while you take the other town?" Maja had said.

It would be a chance to prove herself. To step out from beneath the shadow of her older sisters. The skepticism in Brynhild's eyes as Maja had made the suggestion told her everything she needed to know.

I am still seen as the baby of the family.

It was always the same. Maja was the youngest of the true Valkyries. The twelve true daughters of Odin made up the group of female fighters whose job was to claim the finest souls for their father.

There was a hierarchy among the ranks of the Valkyrie. For many centuries Odin's daughters had been the only ones considered worthy to bear the title of shield maidens. As the population of the mortal realm grew and humans became more adept at finding ways to kill each other, Odin had widened the numbers of Valkyrie to include faeries, dryads and nymphs. Known as his stepdaughters, these new recruits were of lesser rank than Odin's own flesh and blood.

Yet I am treated like a new recruit! Like a stepdaughter, rather than a true daughter.

Maja knew she was seen as a problem to be solved. She was that unheard of a rarity...a disobedient Valkyrie. Most of her rebellion took the form of minor insurgencies, such as wearing her helmet at the wrong angle or arriving for training a few minutes late. Now and then, however, she had been known to use the worst word of all. She had asked why. There were regular how-do-we-solve-a-problem-like-Maja conversations between Odin and Brynhild. They didn't know what to do with their bad Valkyrie.

Maja had no idea why she was different. One of the

difficulties about being the daughter of gods was that her parents were not exactly approachable. Growing up, she did her best to conform, tried to fight the desire to question why the Valkyrie way was the best way and accepted her punishment when she inevitably failed.

She was never given the same level of responsibility as her sisters, even though she had demonstrated her capabilities over and over. It made her more determined than ever to show them what she could do.

After some intense debate, she had worn Brynhild down. Even as she mounted her great winged steed, Magtfuld, Maja got the feeling her sister was indulging her, allowing her to have her own way, but not expecting anything of her. It infuriated her that Brynhild might think she wasn't up to this simple task. She had arrived in Warda fired up and ready to take this American Lion back so she could lay his body in triumph at the feet of the Allfather.

It was intensely annoying to arrive at the location Brynhild had given her to be confronted by the wrong man. A living, breathing man. A man who, now that she looked more closely at him, dared to have a hint of amusement in his dark brown eyes alongside the perplexed expression he wore. It was as if he couldn't quite believe this was happening.

Those eyes made Maja pause. Maybe it was because she had never interacted with a living human being until now. Maybe it was because they were so incredibly beautiful. Whatever it was, she wished she had more time to spend looking into them.

When he fell, she experienced an unexpected dilemma. Her hand had actually twitched with the impulse to reach out and help him up. Luckily, he had hauled himself to his knees before she had forgotten herself and touched him.

"This has been fun." He had to shout to be heard above the chaos around them. "But I think it's time I was going."

As he spoke, a group of men wearing dark clothing and carrying machine guns burst in through the damaged wall. They carried a white flag that bore a painted image of a hooded, grinning skeleton carrying a scythe. Putting his words into practice, the man darted out the open front door and into the main street of the small town. His action left Maja with a scant second in which to react. Since the American Lion was not where he was supposed to be, she should probably leave Warda right now. That would be the Valkyrie way. But the man had mentioned his brother. Did that mean he had further information? Was his brother the American Lion?

"Go to Brynhild." She issued the order to her companions, ignoring their disapproving looks. She was the shield maiden in charge on this mission. They would not dare voice their reservations out loud. "Tell her I have been delayed, and that I will rejoin her at Valhalla later."

Obediently, the two Valkyrie departed. The fighters who had entered the house paused in astonishment to watch the winged horses rise into the air. Within seconds, the Valkyrie and their steeds had become a swirling cloud. Less than a minute later, they had disappeared. Maja's own horse would remain hidden in the shadows until she needed him.

Maja cast another glance around the damaged foyer. How could Brynhild have been so mistaken about this location? With a shrug and a swirl of her swan feather cloak, she ignored every prompting of her Valkyrie training and followed the man who had spoken of his brother out into the street. As long as she didn't interact with him, or—the Norns preserve us—interfere in his future, what could possibly go wrong?

* * *

Adam glanced left and right as he exited the office building. Although he'd believed he'd blacked out back there, he now knew he hadn't. In the same way, he knew his body hadn't suffered any physical damage. He had been fully conscious when he'd imagined the Valkyrie, clearly suffering the effects of shock.

This was a living nightmare, and his subconscious was clearly responding with a subliminal message. *Don't worry. We'll send a beautiful Valkyrie to the rescue.* Just as he had been coping with that little treat for his senses, the arrival of a group of armed men bearing the dreaded Reaper flag—probably the most feared symbol in the world—had brought him sharply back to reality.

The terrorist organization known as the Reapers had risen to prominence in recent years, spreading its brand of hatred and fear across the globe. The Reaper himself, the shadowy leader of the group, was the most wanted man in the world.

Captured by the Reapers, the most feared killers on the planet? I don't think so.

Now, Adam's heart pounded against his rib cage and the hairs at the back of his neck stiffened until they felt like pins being driven into his flesh. The car in which he and Yussef had arrived was ablaze in the middle of the street. The roar and crash of grenades and the staccato sounds of gunfire were deafening. As he tried desperately to find a way out of this living hell, a small figure caught his attention and he paused, his eyes narrowing as he followed its progress through the dust and smoke.

The boy—Adam decided it *was* a boy—was bent almost double as he ducked inside a drainage ditch at the edge of the road, clutching something tightly to his chest. As he drew level with Adam, with only the span of the street separating them, another grenade went off, throwing the fleeing child off his feet.

Adam moved swiftly, closing the distance between them, sliding into the ditch and crouching beside the boy to inspect him for injuries. The child seemed stunned rather than maimed, and he gazed up at Adam with wide, uncomprehending eyes. As he checked him over, Adam saw that what the boy was carrying was a small dog. Despite the mayhem going on around them and the strangeness of the situation, the bedraggled canine licked Adam's hand and wagged its tail.

Cradling the boy against his chest, Adam shielded him and the dog from the gunfire with his own body. From his size, he judged the child to be about eight years old.

"Where are you going?" He mimed a gesture to go along with the words.

"I speak English." There was a trace of pride in the words. The boy pointed in the direction of the road out of town. "I go to the mission."

Another grenade hit close by and Adam decided waiting around in a ditch wasn't the best idea for either of them. Scooping up both the boy and his dog, he stayed low as he broke into a run. He had gone only a few hundred yards when the bullet hit him. Even though there was surprisingly little pain, he recognized what had happened instantly. It felt like someone had punched him hard in the back of his left shoulder.

I've really been shot this time. There should be more pain.

Blood, hot and sticky, began to pour down his back. The pain did hit then. Like a demon digging its claws gleefully into his muscles and sawing on his flesh with razor-edged teeth. As his vision blurred, Adam staggered and veered wildly across the road. Determinedly, he kept going. Getting the boy to safety was all that mattered.

"Let me help you." The voice was cool, feminine and vaguely familiar. It sounded like the speaker was used to giving orders. As an arm slipped around his waist, he gazed into the clear blue eyes of the woman who had burst in on him as he sheltered in the ruined office building.

Her name came into his head through the mist of unconsciousness that was trying to claim him. *Maja.* Since leaving the house, she had disposed of the horse, helmet, cloak and weapons. Even without those items she was still the same unmistakable warrior princess.

Great. Just when I think I'm being rescued, it turns out to be a figment of my pain-filled imagination.

"Lean on me." For an apparition, she was surprisingly strong, and Adam was grateful for her support. With her arm around his waist, he could drag his feet along with her in something that resembled a walk. Somehow, he was still able to carry the child and the dog.

"This way." From within Adam's protective hold, the boy gestured to a large, run-down building, half-hidden behind a drystone wall lined with dusty olive trees. "The lady will help us."

The next few minutes passed in a blur. As Adam staggered into a tiled courtyard, Maja vanished. At the same time, a tall, gray-haired woman came out of the building and issued a few commands in English. Three men in local dress emerged and followed her instructions. One of them took the boy from his arms, then Adam was carried inside and strong hands lifted him onto a portable examining table.

Exquisite pain followed as the woman probed the wound in his shoulder. After that, he dipped in and out of consciousness. He was aware of her clipped English tones telling him how lucky he was. He tried to laugh, to make a joke about the sort of luck that had brought him to Warda on this day. He wasn't sure his voice had worked, but it didn't matter because sweet, blessed darkness swept over him once more.

When he regained consciousness, he was in a small room. He took a moment to assimilate his surroundings. He was lying on a narrow bed with a broken ceiling fan above his head and a window with cracked shutters painted a faded shade of green. Oh…and his shoulder hurt like a demon.

"Where am I?" Since he was alone, he had no expectation of a response when he tried out his voice. Sure enough, it sounded like he had gargled with broken glass.

"Tarek called it 'the mission.'"

Startled, Adam began to turn his head in the direction of the voice. The movement caused darts of sheer agony to shoot through his shoulder. He guessed the woman who had removed the bullet had done so without the benefit of anesthetic. He continued the movement of his head, slowly this time, and carefully.

Maja was seated on a chair near the window, her blue eyes fixed on his face. Her expression was one of mild curiosity. As if he was an interesting specimen she was studying and about which she was making mental notes.

"Who is Tarek, and who the hell are you?"

"Tarek is the child you rescued. And I have already told you I am Maja, Valkyrie shield maiden."

"Of course you are." Adam closed his eyes, too weary to pursue this strange alternate reality his mind appeared determined to force him into.

"Are you going to die?" The question had the effect of opening his eyes again. Fast.

"What sort of question is that?"

She got to her feet and he took a moment to appreciate the way the red corset fitted her curves. Who needed painkillers with that sort of distraction around? "What you did with the boy was brave. If you die, I can take your soul back to Valhalla and my journey will not have been wasted."

"Sorry to disappoint you, but I'm planning on sticking around." That was his ambition. Whether the government forces and the rebel opposition who were unleashing mayhem on the local area allowed him to fulfill it? That was another matter. Although sound was muted by distance, he could still hear the battle raging.

She bit her lip. "I was afraid you might say that."

With those words, the ultraefficient, ice maiden facade slipped slightly and he saw another side to her. Briefly, he caught a glimpse of a frightened expression flitting across her perfect features. The swift change intrigued him, and he made an attempt at getting himself into a sitting position. It wasn't successful.

"Can you lend a hand?" She might be something his mind had conjured up, but he seemed to be able to put her to use to get his body working. Sure enough, Maja slid an arm around his waist and, with some effort on both their parts, Adam managed to maneuver himself upright. "And some water would be good."

She reached for the glass at the side of his bed and held it to his mouth. "None of this is helping."

Adam took a long gulp of the lukewarm liquid. His shoulder was more painful than anything he could ever have imagined, but his head was clear. He still needed to know where Danny was, and Maja was a distraction he could do without. But she was looking at him with such wretchedness in her eyes that he found it impossible to ignore. "Helping what?"

"My defense." She placed the glass back on the table next to the bed. "By interacting with you, I have broken the Valkyrie Code." Her lower lip wobbled slightly. "By saving you instead of letting you die and securing your soul for Odin's army, I may have signed my own death warrant."

Chapter 2

Maja knew she was putting off the inevitable. Sooner or later, she would have to return to Asgard, the home of the gods. Once there she would have to confess all to Brynhild. Not only had she failed to find the American Lion, she had interacted with a mortal. Worse than that, she had committed one of the worst possible sins known to a Valkyrie. She had saved a man from death. A man who had likely been about to die in the performance of an act of great bravery.

This man had been a prime candidate for Valhalla. While he didn't seem to be a warrior, the courage he had demonstrated when he rescued Tarek had been remarkable. Maja was sure many of the so-called heroes of Valhalla would have abandoned the boy to his fate. Her heart had lifted with an emotion she didn't recognize as she watched him cradle the child in his arms and break into a run.

She didn't know what had prompted her to go to this

stranger's aid when he was shot. Maybe it was the wild streak in her nature that Brynhild had always deplored. Maybe it was those intriguing dark eyes of his. Whatever it was, she had acted without thinking. Thoughtlessness was not a trait that was encouraged in the Valkyrie.

The consequence of that action was that she was sitting in this box-like room, with its cracked plaster and concrete floor. The only pleasant thing to look at within its four walls was the man himself. Maja had never seen a man as handsome as this one. From his dark, wavy hair to his chiseled features and muscular body, everything about him was perfection. But it was those eyes that drew her attention over and over. Darker than the storm clouds that surrounded Asgard, they could appear soulful one second, then lighten with humor the next. Maja felt herself being drawn into their depths. Which was an unforeseen circumstance. She had been told humans couldn't weave spells, yet he seemed to be working a strange and powerful magic on her.

"I don't understand." The man's voice forced her to focus on what he was saying instead of the melting darkness of his gaze. "How could you be punished for helping me?"

"Because I am a Valkyrie." Why was he finding this so difficult to understand? Surely everyone knew what a Valkyrie was? "My mission is to take the souls of the dead back to Valhalla. By saving you, I have deprived Odin of a warrior for his army."

"Maja." Those incredible eyes fastened on her face.

What now? She had spoken to him, saved his life. According to the Valkyrie Code, the only thing she could do now to make things worse would be to have sex with him. If he asked her to do that... Maja felt a blush burn her cheeks. Was he going to ask her that? Surely not. She didn't know much about these things, but she'd have expected some sort of preliminaries. And just because she had broken part of the Valkyrie Code, that didn't mean she was likely to further, and forget her vow of purity. Not even for a man whose gaze did strange things to her insides.

"Yes?" She hoped the slight squeak in her voice hadn't betrayed the unchaste trend of her thoughts.

"Why do you seem so real? Am I going mad?"

Before Maja could answer, the door opened and the woman who had operated on the man's shoulder to remove the bullet entered. Maja promptly faded into invisibility. She was aware of the man looking around him in surprise at her disappearance, but he said nothing. Apparently, mortals were smarter than she'd been led to believe. Maja wanted to hug him to express her gratitude. Maybe even kiss those perfectly carved lips. The problem with that idea was that she would have to tell Brynhild about it on her return to Valhalla. Honesty was high on the list of Valkyrie values. Lying, or hiding the truth, never occurred to Maja. Somehow, she didn't imagine her sister would approve if she discovered kissing a human had been added to the growing list of crimes.

Maja had only ever heard of one case of a Valkyrie breaking the Code. On her first mission, Silja had become separated from the group and had asked a mortal man for directions. On her return to Valhalla, Odin had ordered her execution, but Brynhild had intervened. Silja was now locked away in a tower in Valhalla, forced to spend the rest of her life in isolation. Maja wasn't sure her own future held anything as lenient.

"Ah, you're awake." The surgeon had a hearty, clipped manner of talking. "You passed out while I was removing the bullet. Since we don't have access to anesthetic here, it's often a relief when that happens."

"Is this a hospital?" the man asked.

"No, although I am a doctor." The woman held out her hand. "Edith Blair."

Maja watched as he took the hand and shook it. "I'm Adam Lyon. Thank you. You saved my life."

"Tarek tells me of your own heroism. He said he would have died in a ditch if it wasn't for you. He has been talking of superheroes ever since."

Even though she was invisible, Maja held her breath. Would Adam—she wrinkled her nose at the strangeness of the name—give her away?

"Maybe Tarek has been reading too many comic books?" he said.

The frown on Edith's face eased slightly. "Maybe. It's very hard to provide a rounded education for these children. Even harder for Tarek, who has learning difficulties."

Briefly, a flash of pain crossed Adam's features. Edith appeared not to notice it, and it was gone as fast as it appeared. Maja wondered why those words had provoked such a strong reaction in him. Learning difficulties? What did that mean?

Edith shook her head. "I warned Tarek not to go out today, but that dratted dog of his escaped and he insisted on going out to find it." She pursed her lips as she studied Adam. "I would normally suggest rest, but these are not normal circumstances. I'm surprised no one warned you about the dangers of this region for an American, Mr. Lyon."

"They did." Adam's face was expressionless. "I'm looking for someone and it's likely he's in this area." With his good hand, he reached into the back pocket of his jeans and withdrew a photograph, which he held out to Edith. "This is my brother, Danny Lyon. Have you seen him?"

She studied the picture carefully before shaking her head. "I'm sorry." Her manner became brisk as she rose to her feet. "I'll have someone drive you to the border with Lebanon in the morning. The worst of the fighting seems to be over, so you should be safe tonight. You've had a lucky escape, Mr. Lyon."

Maja made sure Edith was gone before she reappeared.

"Invisibility is one of your more unsettling habits." Adam's expression was unreadable as he observed her.

"You said that was your brother." Maja pointed to the photograph. "Is he the American Lion?" Adam had said his own surname was Lyon. It was close enough. Perhaps all was not lost. It seemed safe to assume there was a connection.

Adam regarded her through narrowed eyes. "Maja, even if you are a figment of my imagination, I am not going to help you steal my brother's soul."

"I am not a figment of your imagination, and I do not steal souls," she protested angrily. Leaning over the bed, she prodded him in the chest with one finger. "I escort the fallen to their next destination."

Adam appeared to find her anger amusing, a fact that stoked her fury even further. Grasping her wrist, he pulled her closer. "I don't care what you do. Let's leave my brother out of whatever the hell is going on in my screwed-up head."

Squirming to break free of his hold, she was conscious of his superior strength. Despite his injury and the pain he must be in, he held her easily.

His nearness was having the strangest effect on her. Although she was still struggling to escape, she was no longer sure getting away from him was what she wanted.

A strange sensation was sweeping through her, a combination of lassitude and excitement. The warmth of his touch seemed to seep into her bones. As Adam drew her toward him, she faced a decision: keep fighting, or give in to the promptings of her body. His lips were inches from hers, the smile that flitted across them too tempting to resist. Slowly, enjoying the flare of surprise in his eyes, she lowered her head and kissed him.

Adam decided that, at some point, he must have floated out of his own body and into a trance. His theory wasn't finely tuned, but he had conjured up Maja back in the office building. Maybe out of shock or terror? A desire to escape the situation? Then, when the bullet was being extracted from his shoulder, it seemed he had developed the fantasy even further. He didn't care how it had happened. There was no point trying to make sense of it. As dreams went, this was the sort he needed right now. Even a truckful of painkillers couldn't have numbed the ache in his shoulder the way Maja's kisses did. Her lips met his with shy, sweet promise. He'd forgotten what this sort of kiss was like. First-time kisses. Nervous kisses. Not-quite-perfect kisses.

"I've never done this before." She raised her head, a blush staining the creamy perfection of her cheeks. "Am I doing it right?"

In response, he pulled her back down and took over. Adam had kissed many women in his life. As his lips met Maja's he realized with a pang of sadness that this had become a meaningless activity to him. It served a purpose only as a lead-in to sex. But kissing Maja took him on a whole new adventure. Possibly it was the circumstances, the danger, almost dying, the fact that she couldn't possibly be real…but this was the most erotic experience of his life. When he slipped his tongue inside her mouth, he sensed a moment's hesitation before she tentatively returned his caress. A soft groan escaped him as he tangled his good hand in the silken mass of her hair. Liquid fire throbbed through his veins, sending a hit of heat straight to his groin. He had never wanted anyone the way he wanted this woman, this woman who was a fictional character from his fevered imagination.

Maybe if I keep kissing her none of that will matter.

The weight of her body pressing down on his was perfection. He never wanted to return to reality. He inhaled her scent. She smelled like spring meadows. As out of place in a Syrian war zone as…well, as a kiss with a Valkyrie. And she tasted like honey. He wanted to lick every part of her to find out if the rest of her body tasted as sweet. As he slid a hand over her shoulders and dipped lower into the back of her corset, tracking her spine, he marveled at the satin feeling of her flesh.

Sometime later, he was never sure how it happened—to be honest, he didn't really care—she nestled into the crook of his good arm on the bed next to him, her tempting Valkyrie curves pressed up against him as the kisses continued. He marveled at the way his brain was feverishly finding release from the nightmare he had endured.

Since arriving in Syria he had witnessed the horror of shattered lives. This was a land of blood, pain and tears. And now he had come close to death himself. Was his resourceful mind creating this image of feminine loveliness to compensate for the hell of this place? Okay, if he was going to make her absolutely perfect, he might not have gone for the whole warrior-on-horseback theme. That was a kick in his psyche he hadn't seen coming. But as fantasies went, Maja was more than adequate. If she was here to compensate for the horror of the day just gone, she was doing a damn good job.

He had reached a point where the pain in his shoulder was nothing compared to the throbbing of his erection. The heat of Maja's body was driving him crazy with desire. How could a dream feel so deliciously warm?

"Maja, I need…" As he spoke, he fumbled to undo his jeans with his right hand.

Her eyes widened as she leaned on her elbow. "I have never seen a naked man before." Her voice was a husky murmur as she watched him free his rock-hard cock from the confines of his briefs. "Can I touch you?"

Not only was his horse-riding apparition a gorgeous, blue-eyed blonde, she was also a virgin. That was another unexplored side to his fantasies he hadn't anticipated. Reaching out a hand, she stroked it downward in a long, slow movement, tracing the long, thick length of his shaft. Any pang of conscience Adam may have had, any thoughts of discussing the implications of losing her virginity with her even though she was a figment of his imagination…all of those mixed-up thoughts flew out of his head.

He hissed in a breath as her other hand moved inside his clothing to cup the heavy sac between his thighs. Pure sensation ricocheted through him.

"So strong," she whispered, color staining her cheeks as she drew in a ragged breath. "So much power right here in my hand."

Adam used his good hand to tug her corset and the chemise beneath it roughly down. Her breasts were creamy and firm, tipped with delicate pink nipples. As his lips moved down her neck, she arched her back, squirming against him. Her hands continued to caress him, driving him into a frenzy. Moving lower, his lips covered her nipple, sucking her as she gasped. Pleasure threatened to overwhelm him. His cock hardened and throbbed with an urgency he had never before experienced.

What was it that made her so different—apart from the fact that she wasn't real? It was in her response to him. The way she quivered at his touch, her expression when she looked at him and the tiny sounds of appreciation she made. Adam wasn't a vain man, but he knew he was considered handsome. Cynically, he sometimes wondered if it was him or his bank balance his partners found most attractive. Those doubts didn't arise with Maja. It was clear she couldn't get enough of him and that, in turn, increased his own desire to furnace levels. His hand moved lower, finding the heat at the apex of her thighs. This corset hadn't been designed for a one-armed man to remove with ease. His creativity had deserted him when it came to the costume department. Luckily, Maja herself came to his aid, wriggling out of the offending article until she was lying naked in his arms. And as his fingers skimmed the soft curls between her thighs, the fantasy was back on track.

Maja wound her arms tightly around his neck, pressing her face against his uninjured shoulder as her legs parted to allow access to his probing fingers. She gave a soft moan as his thumb brushed her clit, and the sound was so incredibly erotic that Adam almost came there and then. He slid one finger inside her and she rocked against him, welcoming the intrusion. Adding another finger, he kept up the pressure with his thumb, circling the tiny, hard bud until he felt her shudder as her internal muscles clenched tightly around his fingers.

"Oh!" She tilted her head back, staring at him with a question in her eyes. "What just happened to me?"

He gave a soft laugh. "It's called an orgasm. Didn't they teach you that at Valkyrie school?"

The blush deepened further. "We are not taught anything about our bodies, and definitely not about sex. Since it will never happen to us, we have no need to know."

Although the words struck him as strange, Adam couldn't wait any longer. His injury meant there was no way he could do this conventionally, or gracefully. Using his good arm to lift Maja across his body so she could straddle him, Adam claimed her lips in a kiss and pulled her down onto his steel-hard cock. Even in the grip of a fantasy a brief, bizarre thought about protection flashed through his mind. He dismissed it. This was his imagination; the responsibilities of reality were not going to derail it.

No matter how much pain or danger he was in, his body was demanding more from this woman than he had ever believed it was possible to crave. Maja gave a little cry as he entered her.

"Is this okay?" A condom might be a detail too far, ensuring his partner's well-being wasn't. He was still the same person, even in a dream.

"It feels so good. Pleasure and pain at the same time. We were taught this is wrong…" Her voice was hesitant at first, then, biting her lip, she ground her pelvis against his. "But nothing ever felt so right."

Running his good hand over the luscious curves of her ass, he released a groan of male exultation. Nothing had ever approached the surging, blistering heat of desire that flamed through him. Would he ever be able to cope with reality again after such an incredible dream?

Stop overthinking. Your body is compensating for the trauma it's been through. Just enjoy it.

His lips found the hard, pointed tip of a nipple again

and drew it into his mouth. Maja's soft, feminine cries filled the air as her hands moved to his head, holding him tightly to her. As he sucked her sweet flesh—tasted her, *branded* her—he felt his desire spiral out of control.

Above him, Maja writhed with pleasure, moving in time to his rhythm. Encased in the satin confines of her tight muscles, Adam thrust his pelvis up, and she met his movements with perfect timing. They were both poised on a knife edge, ready to tip over. Adam felt his body tighten and wished he could make the feeling last forever. To keep these wild, searing sensations crashing through him, knowing he would never be able to recapture such perfection.

"God, Maja. I'm not going to last long." The words were a hoarse groan.

Each movement was like a white-hot surge of ecstasy building, tightening his sac and moving like lightning up his spine. Maja gasped, her muscles clenching and un-clenching around him as she panted her way through an-other orgasm. Pure rapture hit him, firing its way along his nerve endings in a series of ever wilder explosions. *Never like this.* This was the storybook orgasm to com-plete his perfect fantasy.

Maja lay very still on top of him, and when he had re-covered his breath, Adam smoothed a hand down the length of her hair. "I'm sorry. That was over way too soon." Was he seriously apologizing to the star of his erotic dream?

She lifted her head, a hint of mischief in her smile. "I might not know much about these things, but I don't know why you are saying sorry. That was very nice."

He laughed. "Maja, if I wasn't injured, and if this wasn't some sort of crazy delusion, I'd show you that we can do a hell of a lot better than nice."

The smile disappeared and a frown appeared in its place. "This can't happen again."

Since this was going on inside his head, surely he should be the one to make those decisions? Adam was too tired to ask the question out loud. Instead, he drew Maja back into the crook of his uninjured arm and closed his eyes. She felt good there. Warm and comforting. Almost immediately, he felt sleep begin to tug the edges of his consciousness. He needed to rest, but he wondered if slumber would drive away this wonderful, wakeful dream. It was a disappointing thought. He doubted if he would ever again conjure up an image as powerful and realistic as Maja.

Chapter 3

Warda was eerily quiet as Maja made her way back to the place where she had left her horse, Magtfuld. Most of the buildings were reduced to mere shells after the bombings, although some still smoldered in the predawn light. Several cars were blazing, and she guessed they would soon join the graveyard of abandoned vehicles that littered the side of the road.

Even in this scene of utter devastation, there were signs of life returning to normal. An old man drove a herd of goats down the center of the street, seemingly not noticing the strangely clad woman who passed the other way. A family huddled in what was left of a bullet-riddled house, pulling blankets around themselves as they watched Maja, who hadn't used her power of invisibility, with listless eyes.

I should do something. Try to help them. Even as thoughts of anonymous rescues that would remain hidden from Odin and Brynhild entered her mind, she dismissed them. *You have already done enough to secure your death sentence.*

How had this happened? How had she gone from being the ice-cool shield maiden carrying out her mission as Odin's representative here in the mortal realm, to a quivering mass of raw emotion? Adam Lyon. That was how.

The thought of him almost stopped her in her tracks. Instead of continuing in her determined stride, she wanted to find somewhere to hide away, to curl up tight and examine the whirlwind of feelings that were buffeting her body. The memory of his touch was almost too much to bear. Too intense. Too perfect. Just the thought of him made her internal muscles clench with remembered longing.

No one told me how much I would enjoy breaking the Valkyrie Code!

She had been taught only that sex was forbidden, not that it was pleasurable. Maja choked back a laugh. *Pleasurable? Try magical. No one told me how much I would want to do it again...and again.* But even in her dazed state, she knew this was not a reaction to the physical act itself. This was about Adam. He had changed her life. Changed *her.* But now she had to face the consequences.

Indulging in daydreams about her handsome mortal lover wasn't an option. After the storm of their lovemaking, she had allowed herself the brief indulgence of lying in Adam's arms and watching him as he slept. But she had done so knowing that she must leave him. It was time to go back to Valhalla and confess both her failure and her crimes. Her failure was bad enough. If the true American Lion had been in Warda during the latest outbreak of fighting, Maja had found no trace of him. But her crimes? They must surely be the worst ever committed by a Valkyrie. The only words they were permitted to exchange with their target must be relevant to the mission. The penalty for a Valkyrie who was found to have spoken unnecessarily with a warrior was imprisonment.

But Maja had done so much more. Not only had she spoken to Adam, she had saved his life. And then, as if driven by some inner madness, she had violated the Code in the worst way imaginable. *I lay with him in his bed. I took him into my body. All the things I have been warned against... Yet I cannot find it in me to feel shame. Even though I will admit my transgressions, I will do it with my head held high.*

There was no place in Asgard for a Valkyrie who had lost her virginity. On her return, Maja should expect her execution date to be set immediately.

With her usual disregard for convention, she had once asked Brynhild about the reasoning behind the rule about Valkyrie purity.

"Wouldn't it make more sense if, instead of recruiting stepdaughters, it was the descendants of the true Valkyries who enlarged our force? Our daughters and granddaughters could learn the shield maiden way from an early age."

Once Brynhild had recovered from the shock that Maja had dared to speak of such a topic, she had taken her sister's hand. Her expression had been the half-resigned, half-bemused one she reserved only for Maja. "You must never speak of this matter again. It is unseemly and unwise. The decree about virginity dates back to the very first Valkyrie ride. There was an incident that took place after the fighters were brought to the great hall—" Brynhild had shuddered as though the memory was still distasteful to her. "The warriors felt that the duties of the Valkyries included meeting their carnal needs. Sadly, some of our older sisters did not refuse their demands,

and the result resembled an orgy. It was so shocking that
Odin was forced to introduce the death penalty to ensure
there would be no repeat. The distance between the men
of Valhalla and the Valkyries must be maintained." She
shook her head. "We will not dwell on the past, but these
things are decided for good reasons."

The Valkyries lived a separate existence from the gods,
but Maja had caught glimpses now and then of pregnant
women. In addition to the scandal Brynhild had alluded
to, she supposed sex, childbirth and babies would interfere with the smooth running of Valhalla.

Now she had joined the ranks of those who brought
that look of horror to Brynhild's face.

*I have no defense. If I met Adam once more, I would
do it all over again.*

It was something she could never explain to Brynhild,
Odin or to anyone else, partly because she couldn't understand it herself. The magic of that all-too-brief time she
had spent in Adam's arms lingered in the thrill that trembled through her body. It really had felt like magic. As
if an incredible, heart-stopping spell had been cast upon
her. She would die as a punishment and as an example to
other Valkyries who might be tempted to stray from the
path of purity, but the brief life that was left to her had
been changed forever by the touch of a mortal.

The office building in which she had first met Adam
had not fared well. Only one wall remained in place and
that was leaning precariously outward. Twisted iron gird-
ers pointed skyward like gnarled, accusing fingers and the
entrance doors hung on damaged hinges. Maja, probably
the only individual in Syria who could not be harmed by
any of the warring factions, stepped into the deserted foyer
and felt a chill finger of dread track its way down her spine.

Magtfuld was gone.

* * *

When Adam woke some hours later, it was to the discovery that he had been right. Maja had disappeared and the room was in semidarkness. The light told him it was early morning. He lay still, wondering what, apart from her absence, had changed. Then he realized the bombing and gunfire that had continued intermittently throughout the previous day seemed to have finally stopped.

His shoulder throbbed unbearably; his whole body was tense and weary, yet at the same time he was experiencing a curious sense of peace. Aware that his zipper was undone, he attempted to fasten himself up one-handed. Feeling the evidence of his release on his body, he grimaced. What sort of fantasy had that been? While the imaginary sex had been better than anything he had ever experienced in reality, it had been over too soon. Shouldn't a man be the superhuman, lasts-for-hours star of his own dreams?

Just as well it was *a dream, since I didn't give a thought to protection.*

He spent a few minutes wishing he could summon her again. It was a foolish hope. Dreams like that came along once in a lifetime, and he supposed Maja had answered a deep-seated need inside him during a combination of terror and trauma. For someone who had always been rigorously in command of every aspect of his life, it was a strange sensation. *I lost control.* A smile touched his lips. *And I liked it.*

It was just as well that the corporate world would never discover that the bad boy of the boardroom had a weakness. Finding the time to leave the helm of his vast media conglomerate of newspapers, magazines, TV and internet news publishers, and publishing houses had been difficult enough. If it had been for anyone other than Danny it wouldn't have happened. Getting shot was an added complication. Hopefully, his injury wouldn't put him out of action for too long once he got home. Adam had built a global brand on the strength of his personal charisma. He couldn't spare even a minute to let that slide.

Struggling to his feet, he made his way to the curtained-off commode. With normality restored, he returned to the bed and propped himself against pillows that were as hard as bags of cement. It was impossible to get comfortable, so he settled for the best he could do...which was somewhere between discomfort and agony.

He would be leaving Syria today. For the sake of his battered body and his damaged psyche—anyone who needed the sort of illusion he had created for himself in the form of Maja had a few unresolved issues—it was time to go. He thought of the beautiful countryside he had seen on his travels, with its rolling hills full of olive and lemon trees. Everyone he encountered had been warm-hearted and helpful. This was a heartbreaking land and he would leave it with regret. For the first time ever, he felt the need to do something with his life other than make money. Although he had no idea what it would mean in practice, being here had unleashed a need within him that he intended to explore on his return home. The worst thing about leaving Syria was that he would be going without having accomplished what he had come here for. He still hadn't found any information about Danny.

Danny had battled with learning difficulties all his life. It infuriated Adam that some people couldn't figure out that didn't mean Danny was dumb. He was a whole lot smarter than Adam in so many ways; it just took him longer to learn things. Their father had died when Danny was a baby and their mother had remarried almost immediately. Although their lifestyle was privileged, their stepfather was not a warm man, and despite their age difference, the two brothers had grown closer than ever. When their mother died, Adam had been twenty-one. He hadn't needed her deathbed reminder to care for Danny. His eleven-year-old brother had moved in with him. Adam had found a school that specialized in helping students with Danny's needs. Even though the diagnosis of severe dyslexia had come late, the teachers had supported him well and Danny had thrived. He had graduated high school and, refusing Adam's offers of help, had found himself a job in a charitable foundation working with refugees.

Adam had done his best to talk him out of coming to Syria, but Danny had a stubborn streak a mile wide. Adam smiled. It was a Lyon trait. His own was several miles wider. His mind conjured up an image of his brother in the days before he'd left. So sure of what he was doing, so dedicated, so determined.

"That's where we differ, Danny. You have strong principles, and are prepared to stand up for them." Adam remembered his own words just before Danny left.

Danny had returned his gaze steadily. "Don't sell yourself short. You're the person who raised me."

Adam had given a self-deprecating laugh. "I have no illusions about myself."

Once Danny got to Syria, the brothers had maintained a regular communication. Calling, messaging, emailing whenever they could. Then Danny's attitude had started to change. He had always been upset about what was happening in Syria. Suddenly, instead of wanting to help in a humanitarian way, he began to talk about taking real action. That was when Adam started to get concerned about him. When the communication stopped, his concern turned to fear.

He found out from the organizers of the charity that

Danny had gotten friendly with a group of men he'd met in one of the local villages. It was only after Danny left the nonprofit that the organizers discovered his new friends were mercenaries.

Adam withdrew the photograph of Danny from his pocket and looked at the familiar face. At the clear, laughing eyes so like his own, but lacking Adam's cynicism and ruthlessness. His fist clenched hard on his thigh.

I must find him. I have to take him home.

The opening of the door interrupted his thoughts and a small, tousled head inserted itself into the room.

Tarek smiled when he saw Adam was awake. "I can put the light on?"

Adam nodded. "Please do."

Tarek's presence was a welcome interruption. The dog he had carried with him on the previous day also seemed to consider himself included in the invitation. After bounding into the room with a shrill bark, the little creature leaped onto the bed and made several enthusiastic attempts to lick Adam's face.

"He likes you." Tarek took the chair at the side of the bed. "He knows you saved us when the Reapers were chasing us."

The dog might have been a terrier, but his unkempt appearance meant his parentage was indeterminate. He was young and friendly, and once his initial exuberance had died down, he curled up on Adam's legs with a contented sigh. Having him there felt curiously comforting.

"What's his name?"

"Leo." Tarek must have been aware of the sudden intensity of Adam's gaze, because he clearly felt the need for further clarification. "I named him after the man who gave him to me."

Leo. It was a long time since he'd heard his brother's

childhood nickname. *Leo the Lyon.* It had been their private joke. Adam felt sharp, unaccustomed tears stinging the back of his eyelids.

"Is this the man who gave you your dog?" He held out Danny's picture.

"Yes." Tarek laughed delightedly as he looked at the picture. "How did you know it was him?"

Although he smiled, his hand reached out for Leo, tangling itself in the wiry fur as though the dog was his comforter.

"Tell me some more about this man, Tarek."

"You sound just like Maja. She wanted to know all about the warriors I have met."

Adam sat up so abruptly it felt like a red-hot wire had been inserted into his shoulder. He also dislodged Leo, who whined a protest. "Maja?"

"The lady with the long gold hair. The one who was dressed like a superhero." Eyeing him with concern, Tarek clearly felt further explanation was necessary. "She brought us here after you were shot."

Adam slumped back on his pillows. The action dislodged something from his hair. A single feather, so pure and white it could only have come from the breast of a swan, drifted down and landed on the worn sheet next to his hand. His fingertips closed over it.

I am not a figment of your imagination. He heard her voice saying the words. Stunned, he remained still for a few minutes, letting Tarek's chatter wash over him.

There were too many questions vying for dominance in Adam's mind. When had Tarek seen Danny, the man who had given him his dog? What did Tarek mean when he said the Reapers had been chasing him? Surely he had just been in the wrong place at the wrong time when Adam rescued him?

Somehow, all the other questions were pushed aside and Adam asked the one that mattered most right now. "Did you see where Maja went?"

Tarek started to answer, but his words were drowned out by the sound of gunfire coming from just outside the building.

Being stranded in the mortal realm without her steed shouldn't feel like a reprieve, but it did. Maja had no doubt that recalling Magtfuld was Brynhild's way of punishing her. Cutting her off from any means of returning to Valhalla would ordinarily feel isolating and frightening. Right now, it felt like she had been handed a lifeline.

This was temporary, Maja told herself, as she did a final check to make sure she really couldn't call Magtfuld from the shadows. Her guess was that Brynhild's plan was to leave her in the mortal realm just long enough to make her suffer. Then her sister was likely to send a rescue party. The message? *Don't step out of line again.* By dismissing her companions, Maja hadn't conformed to the behavior expected of a shield maiden. Brynhild didn't do anger. She did retaliation. Cold, calculated and carefully planned.

This way, Maja might have time to at least salvage part of her reputation. Maybe, just maybe, she could still track down the American Lion. She had an outside chance of succeeding, but she may as well make the attempt. And the key to the whereabouts of the brave warrior she sought was back at the mission. The only brief glimpse she had gotten into his whereabouts had come when Adam had responded when she had mentioned him. His words had suggested that the American Lion was his brother. Although he had refused to discuss the matter, he had not denied it. And Maja had subsequently become somewhat distracted from the topic.

A blush tinged her cheeks. Was she being honest with herself? Was she really seeking the American Lion, or was she looking for an excuse to go back to Adam? She decided the two things were so closely entwined that it would be impossible to separate them. *Tell yourself that. It sounds so much better than the truth...that you cannot stay away from him.*

Unearthing her cloak, helmet and weapons from the space beneath the stairs where she had hidden them, she decided the only way she would know for sure about any connection between Adam and the American Lion would be to ask him outright.

A heavenly dawn light was breaking through the wispy cloud as Maja retraced her steps. She had never had a chance to appreciate the beauty of the mortal realm on previous missions. Although humans had a terrible capacity to cause harm to each other, this world of theirs had the power to move her with its magnificence. The contrast between the destruction that had taken place within the town, and the rolling countryside around it, unveiled now by the emerging light, could not have been starker.

As Maja followed the road out of the village, she picked up the sound of conflict. They were, after all, the sort of noises with which she was most familiar. Angry, raised voices, growled instructions, cries of pain, shocked protests, and gunfire. But it was her job to know when there was hostility in the air, and her finely tuned Valkyrie senses had told that the fighting in Warda was over. Yet this disturbance was coming from the direction of the mission.

Breaking into a run as she used her invisibility as a shield, she dashed into the courtyard in time to see a

group of five men dragging the three male mission workers and Edith Blair out of the old house. They forced the
frightened group to their knees, holding guns to the back
of their heads. One of the attackers paced up and down
in front of them.

He barked a question at them in Arabic. The Valkyries
had a unique understanding of all mortal languages, but
the man repeated the words in English as he paused in
front of Edith. "Where is the boy?"

Maja had to admire the woman's courage as, despite
the gun pressed into the base of her skull, she maintained
eye contact and spoke coolly. "I know a number of boys.
You'll have to be specific."

His lips drew back in a snarl. "Don't play games. We
are looking for the boy called Tarek."

As he spoke, a movement just beyond the edge of the
building caught Maja's eye. Her senses were keener than
those of most mortals and she doubted the leader of the
group who were seeking Tarek would have seen it. The
house was surrounded by a drystone wall. Roughly shoulder height, it dipped in places and had some glaring gaps
in its uneven surface.

It was through one of these gaps that Maja caught sight
of a man's arm. It was the briefest glimpse, but it made
her heart bound. The arm was strong, corded with muscle,
and a white bandage stood out starkly against the tanned
flesh of the shoulder. The man's hand was wrapped protectively around something. Maja could just make out a
mop of dark, curly hair.

She breathed a sigh of relief. Adam would protect
Tarek. Now it was up to her to keep Edith and her mission workers safe. Any thoughts of the Valkyrie Code
were long gone as she strode into the midst of the action.

The Valkyries were not just pretty faces who collected souls for Odin and waited on his soldiers. They were highly trained warriors. Martial arts, street fighting, hand-to-hand combat… Maja was as equally comfortable with her fists and feet as she was with a sword or a gun.

Using her invisibility to give her the element of surprise, she drop-kicked the leader of the attackers in the head. He hit the ground like a fallen statue. As Maja materialized, sword swinging, before his openmouthed followers, she was conscious of a buzz of pure elation. Being the bad Valkyrie was starting to feel very good.

Chapter 4

When the shooting started, the only thing on Adam's mind had been to get Tarek to safety. Since he had only a sketchy idea of the layout of the house, and he guessed the gunmen were on their way inside, he decided the best option was to get outside and try and find a hiding place.

Ignoring the searing pain in his shoulder, he had shielded Tarek with his body as he pulled open the door and glanced left and right. His room opened onto a narrow corridor that, despite the noise, was still empty. Adam judged it was a situation that was unlikely to last long.

"Which way will get us out of here?"

Tarek, still clutching Leo tightly to his chest, didn't hesitate. "Left."

A few feet brought them to a utility area with an industrial-size sink and a washing machine that was in midcycle and seemed to be doing its best to start a small earthquake. Through an open door, Adam could see a small courtyard lined with garbage cans. Beyond that was the familiar undulating countryside.

Keeping hold of Tarek's upper arm with his good hand, he skittered into the morning sunlight at speed, assessing his options the whole time. Making for the hills was no good. They would be too exposed out there in the open. He had no idea what these people wanted. The fact that they were prepared to burst into a charitable mission firing guns didn't make Adam feel inclined to stick around and converse with them. As far as he was concerned, their motives could remain shrouded in mystery.

As they passed the garbage cans, they drew level with the wall that bordered the property. At the same time, the shouting from within the house intensified.

"What are they saying?" Adam asked.

"They are looking for me." Tarek's voice wobbled on a new note of fear.

There wasn't time to ask for clarification about that statement. Instead, the words strengthened Adam's resolve to get the boy out of harm's way. The other side of the wall seemed like a good place to be right now. There were no guarantees the bad guys wouldn't think to look there, but at least they wouldn't be so vulnerable, and they could keep moving while hidden from view.

There was no way Adam's injury would allow him to climb the shoulder-high wall, but its poor state of repair meant there were places where it had deteriorated and become almost a pile of rubble. After scrambling through one of these, he and Tarek clung to the rough rocks on the opposite side of the mission building, making their way along the length of the wall until they were in line with the main entrance.

Hearing Edith's voice, Adam paused, viewing the scene at the front of the mission through a gap in the stones.

What he saw made his blood turn to ice. The kindhearted English doctor and her three assistants were kneeling on the ground with their hands behind their backs, while men with guns stood behind them.

Adam slumped slightly, feeling the rough-hewn rocks pressing into his back. What the hell was he supposed to do? Save the boy or try to help Edith? He almost laughed aloud. *And what exactly are you—a one-armed man— going to do against five gunmen?*

In the end, it came down to one simple fact. He couldn't cower behind a wall while people who had helped him took a bullet to the head. Even if the only thing he could do was walk out there and provide a momentary distraction for the gunmen—*and let's face it, that's likely to be all I can do*—then he would do it.

"Keep going along this wall," he told Tarek, ignoring the boy's look of horror. "Get as far from this place as fast as you can. Don't look back."

Giving Tarek a push to spur him on, Adam moved back in the direction they had just come, finding a broken-down place in the wall. Taking a breath, he clambered over the gap before his resolve faltered. Clenching his jaw to hide his fear, he stepped into the courtyard.

He fully expected the force of five weapons to be turned on him as he walked toward the group of people in front of the mission doors. Instead, no one even glanced his way. That was because their attention was focused entirely on the strange behavior of the leader of the group of militants. Without warning, he stopped screaming at Edith. His head spun so sharply to the right that Adam, still several feet away, heard a crack. It was as if his neck had just broken from an invisible kick to the head. Then the man dropped to the ground.

His followers were still regarding him in surprise,

when the reason for this phenomenon was explained…to Adam, at least. Maja appeared from nowhere, holding her Valkyrie sword in both hands. As she swung the weapon above her head, her eyes met Adam's. The expression in those blue depths reassured and warmed him. She was flesh and blood and she knew what she was doing. He took a moment to feel glad she was on his side.

"Get his gun." She gestured for Adam to go toward the unconscious form of the leader as she approached the other militants. They were briefly stunned into immobility by what had happened, but Adam wasn't hopeful that was going to last.

Sure enough, as Maja drew closer, the man who held his gun at Edith's head raised it and pointed it at the Valkyrie instead. His hand shook wildly as he barked an order at her. Adam could understand the reason for the awestruck expression on his face. With her proud stance and golden hair streaming out behind her, Maja resembled an avenging angel as she bore down on him.

Adam's injury made him feel close to useless, but he was going to do everything he could to help Maja fight these thugs. It looked like he wouldn't get the chance, for the man fired at the precise moment that Adam managed to stoop and snag the leader's discarded gun. As the bullet hit Maja in the abdomen and she doubled over, Adam couldn't believe the force of the emotion that swept through him.

Out of the corner of his eye, he saw Maja go down, and he wanted to roar like a wounded animal in response. He would never have imagined himself capable of anything so primal and raw. Thought took second place to feeling. Acting on nothing but instinct, he raised his arm and fired an answering shot.

Adam's bullet hit the rebel in the throat; the man's

body hitting the red dust shook the mission workers into action. Two of the militants had been taken out, which meant their chances were improving. Seizing the initiative, they turned on their attackers. Although gunshots rang out, Adam didn't see anyone get hit. But that might have been because his attention was on Maja.

After being struck by the bullet, she had dropped to one knee. Now, she was up again and powering forward at a run that would put an Olympic sprinter to shame. Adam shook his head to clear it. He had seen that bullet hit her square in the center of her body. She should be dead or dying, sprawled in the Syrian dust.

She's real, but she's not human.

Right now, he couldn't see a problem with that. As Maja thundered into the fight, sword discarded, Adam was very thankful to have an invincible warrior princess on his side. He watched in admiration as, in one stylish movement, she brought a foot up under the chin of one of the rebels while swinging her elbow full force into the windpipe of another. They would be debilitating blows in any circumstances. He had a feeling, from the way those men crumpled like discarded toys, that from Maja, they were more. She must have a strength over and beyond anything mortal. Those men were never getting up again. The fifth rebel clearly shared his conviction and attempted to run.

"We can't let him get away." Edith sounded almost regretful. "If he goes back to his masters and tells them what happened here, the mission is finished."

Adam helped her to her feet. Edith turned her face away as one of the mission workers fired the final shot at the fifth attacker.

"We need to dispose of these bodies. Fast." Adam's face

was grim. Had he ever envisaged a situation in which he would utter those words?

As he surveyed the scene, Maja moved toward the dry-stone wall. As she neared the gap, Tarek burst through the opening and hurled himself into her arms, twining his small body around her like a monkey climbing a tree. An unusually subdued Leo came to sit at her feet.

"Don't leave me, Maja." The boy's desperate plea reached Adam's ears.

Maja's voice was soft and reassuring as she cradled Tarek to her. "You are safe now. We won't let them hurt you."

Her eyes met Adam's over Tarek's head and there was a silent appeal in those blue depths. When she said "we," she meant the two of them. With an emotion close to shock, he realized he would be the boy's rescuer. He would do whatever it took to keep him safe, and do it happily. For the first time since Danny's disappearance, Adam had someone to care for. He might not like the circumstances, but he didn't dislike the feeling.

Edith was organizing the removal of the bodies. Her men would load them onto the mission truck and drive them out into the desert. Sadly, a pile of anonymous corpses lying in the red sand was not uncommon. Their clothing, with its telltale Reaper insignia, would be burned. No one wanted the Reapers seeking revenge for the deaths of their comrades.

While that activity was taking place outside, Maja carried a terrified Tarek into the building.

"I know you told me to run." He turned his head to look at Adam, who had followed them inside. "But my legs would not work."

"It's okay." Maja could see the lines of pain etched into Adam's face and wondered how he was still standing. "My legs were feeling the same way."

They went into the kitchen and sat at the table that occupied the center of the room. There was a jug of water and Maja poured glasses for Tarek and Adam. They both gulped the lukewarm liquid gratefully.

"Why were those men looking for you, Tarek?" There was a gentle note in Adam's voice that surprised Maja.

Tarek's hand tightened convulsively in Maja's and he turned wide eyes to hers as if seeking reassurance. "You are not in any trouble," she explained. "We can only help you if we know the truth."

Her words seemed to help him reach a decision and he nodded. "It is because I know who he is." He drew a deep breath as though the words were being dragged up from somewhere deep inside him. "The one they call 'the Reaper.'"

Maja was watching Adam's face and she could tell Tarek's admission had a powerful effect on him. His eyes darkened and a frown line pulled his brows together. She sensed he was trying not to express disbelief, and she was glad when he won his internal battle. She might not know much about these things, but if they were going to support Tarek, they had to show him that they believed him unconditionally.

"I don't understand." Maja looked from Tarek to Adam. "Who is this man?"

"The Reaper is a vicious murderer and one of the most feared terrorist masterminds in the world," Adam said. "His network extends across the globe, but his headquarters are thought to be in this part of the world. I'm saying 'thought to be' because no one really knows anything about him. His true identity is carefully concealed. Armed forces have been hunting him for the last two years with no luck."

While his words revealed a disgust for the man who could unleash that sort of terror on the world, they didn't explain the sadness she had seen when he first heard Tarek's words. Sensitivity wasn't Maja's strong point, and patience was not considered a virtue in the Valkyrie, but she decided to wait in case Adam had more to say. After about a minute, during which he appeared lost in thought, he spoke again.

"A bomb was planted in the office of my Boston newspaper headquarters after we published an article condemning the activities of his terrorist group. Luckily, a security guard saw a suspicious package and raised the alarm before it went off, so no one was killed. The building was destroyed."

He smiled, and her heart gave a strange little leap. It was most perplexing, because there was no one she could go to for advice about that. She suspected there was nothing actually wrong with her heart, and that its erratic behavior was an Adam-related occurrence. Until now, she had never envied mortals. Their lives seemed short and drab. Now, she wondered if she might have been wrong. If she had been a mortal woman, she probably would have been able to ask someone about the unnerving effect Adam had on her. She could always ask *him*, of course. Maybe just not right now…

"And the heroic security guard is still alive, so he wasn't picked up by one of your squad mates and transported to Valhalla."

The words heralded a change in approach. They were a definite signal that he no longer viewed her as a figment of his imagination. Which meant he knew what had happened between them had been real. Real and devastating. The thought tipped her world slightly off balance. She had an uncomfortable feeling Adam knew exactly what she was thinking. How had it suddenly gotten so hard to breathe?

Tarek. He was the focus here. The only thing that mattered right now. Yes, she had a whole heap of other problems to deal with, but the child's safety had to come first. She didn't know any other children, but some new instinct, more powerful than anything she had learned in Valkyrie training, told her that. She turned back to the boy. "How do you know this man?"

"I don't know him. I have never met him, but I heard my father talking about him on the phone." Tarek clung to her hand. "I was supposed to be in bed, but I sneaked onto the landing and listened. I was frightened because my father was shouting and he sounded scared. He kept saying 'you have to listen to me.'" He swallowed hard. "I don't think they listened to him."

"Do you know who he was talking to?" Adam asked.

"My father called him 'sir.' Only once, he said his name. Then, he called him 'Shepherd.' I remember everything he said because it scared me so much. He said the Reaper wasn't one man, it was a con-sor-tium." Tarek spoke the word carefully in the manner of one who had rehearsed it many times. Out of the corner of her eye, Maja saw Adam sit up a little straighter. "But he said one man was the brains behind it all. My father said he had two years' worth of evidence on this guy. It was enough to bring him down. The next day—the day after my father made that phone call—they bombed the university where he worked and my father was killed. That was two weeks ago."

Maja wrapped her arms around the trembling boy, holding him close. "Why would they come for you, Tarek? How did those men know you had this information?"

"I don't know." Tears filled his dark eyes. "You are the first people I have told."

"It's possible they were just taking no chances. Getting

rid of any family members just to be sure," Adam said. "But you definitely heard your father say the name of the man behind this corporation?" As Adam asked the question, Maja sensed he was reining in a feeling of urgency.

"It was an easy name to remember. It sounds like a name from a fairy tale," Tarek said. "It was Knight Valentine."

Adam's reaction surprised Maja. Hissing out a breath, he got to his feet. Although it was clear he was still weak and in pain, he paced from one end of the small room to the other for several minutes, clearly lost in thought. That name meant something to him, and whatever the meaning was, she sensed it wasn't good.

Maja, meanwhile, spoke softly to Tarek. Reassuring him that he had done the right thing in telling them everything, she promised they would make sure the Reaper would not be able to find him. Could she carry through that promise? She knew nothing of this world, and she was now an outcast from her own. In an act of rebellion so complete, she had ensured she could never return to Valhalla. That was just the start of her personal problems. Odin was famed for his vindictiveness. He was unlikely to let a rogue Valkyrie live in peace. Scratch that. He was unlikely to let a rogue Valkyrie *live*. And live where? All she knew was her warrior lifestyle, and she wasn't human, so even if she might be able to hide from Odin, there was no place for her here in the mortal realm.

"I will get you out of here." When Adam came back to his seat, his firm voice, together with Maja's encouragement, seemed to boost Tarek's confidence.

Even so, the boy raised troubled eyes to Maja's face. "Will you stay with me?"

She lifted her own eyes to Adam's, seeking confirmation. He nodded. "I'll stay with you. We both will."

Reassured, Tarek went off to find Edith, to organize food for Leo.

"How will we keep our promise?" Maja asked. "How will we get him out of here?"

Adam grinned. "I haven't figured out the finer details. I'll admit that getting a child, a Valkyrie—" the grin turned into a grimace "—and a dog out of a war-torn country is going to stretch my ingenuity. But I'll think of something."

Sitting at the kitchen table in the mission, they planned the operation long into the night. Edith had handed over the keys to her car without blinking. Much the way she had accepted the presence of a corset-clad, sword-wielding Norsewoman in the heart of Syria. Adam suspected that the Englishwoman's life contained many interesting stories. Maja was just one more.

"You can't fly out of Syria without a visa, and we don't have time to obtain one for Tarek," Edith said. She spread a map of the region on the table. Tracing various locations with her finger, she pointed out a route. "One by one, the surrounding countries have closed down their borders. You won't be able to take Tarek across at any official points without the correct documentation, but if you have money, there are places where it can be done."

"I have money." Adam's jacket might be torn and bloodied, but the concealed inner pocket still contained thousands of US dollars and his cell phone. He had a feeling that his best asset in the next few days was sitting at his right-hand side, studying the map in silence. A Valkyrie warrior who could use her invisibility to his advantage was going to be more useful than any amount of money when it came to getting Tarek out of this troubled land.

"The best way out of here will be to drive across the border into Lebanon." Edith tapped the map. "I have a contact near the old port of Batroun. He will take you by boat to Cyprus. From there, you can arrange to travel to the United States."

Those words were the sweetest Adam had ever heard. Even so, it seemed he had a long way to go before he could say he was safely home.

"Does Tarek have a passport?" That was Adam's biggest concern. Maja could take care of herself. Her invisibility would prove to be a handy trick when it came to border control.

Edith nodded. "It was among the possessions that were brought here from his home. It's in my study, along with his other proof of identity."

"So, our biggest problem will be Leo." Adam was thinking ahead. How the hell was he going to get the dog into the United States?

"I'm not going without him." Tarek's expression became stubborn as he wrapped his arms around his pet.

Edith pursed her lips, disappeared briefly and returned with a Leo-sized gym bag.

"He won't like it." Tarek eyed the bag gloomily.

"He'll have to put up with it if he wants to come with us." Adam kept his voice firm. He was in charge, and everyone else—including Leo—had better get used to the idea.

Leo sniffed the gym bag thoughtfully, clearly decided it wasn't too bad, and with a weary sigh, clambered inside it and curled up. Tarek laughed and clapped his hands. "He thinks it's his new bed."

The dog remained asleep as they set off. Three hours later, as dawn broke, Adam figured they must be approaching the point at the border where Edith had thought they would be able to bribe their way across. Following the route she had suggested, their journey had been uneventful, though the roads were poor. Adam had been driving one-handed over the potholes. His whole body was rattled, his shoulder was throbbing and he felt drained of energy.

Maja turned in her seat and studied Tarek as he slumbered in the rear, one arm draped protectively over the gym bag. Even clad in Edith's cast-off clothing, Adam's Valkyrie companion was proving to be a severe test of his ability to remain focused on the journey. Baggy linen pants, battered sneakers and a blouse that might once have been white but was now a faded gray color, made up an uninspiring outfit and covered her figure. Her hair hung in a braid almost to her waist and a baseball cap topped her head. How was it that she still managed to look like the hottest thing he had ever seen? Every time he looked her way, his mind went into overdrive as he pictured the lush curves beneath those drab clothes. At the same time, his body remembered how she had felt in his arms and demanded a replay.

Focus. He was in charge of this bizarre rescue mission. Driving over the border into Lebanon would be difficult enough. Coping with a hard-on at the same time? That really was not going to help matters.

"This is a seat belt." He indicated his own. "It's designed to keep you safe."

He flicked a glance in her direction and encountered her steady blue-eyed stare. "I don't need it."

"I was forgetting. It must be useful to be invincible." He turned his gaze back to the road. "Is there anything that can hurt you?"

"Only Odin's will." Something about the quality of her voice made him look back at her.

The depths of those incredible eyes were suddenly twin pools of fear and sadness. The change was so abrupt, it shook him. During the drive thus far, he had managed to avoid conversation. Tarek had been awake for most of the time, and they had talked of inconsequential things. Big topics such as what would happen once they reached safety, how Adam was going to deal with the information about the identity of the Reaper, and what had happened between him and Maja…well, they could wait for another time. A time when they were safe. But when Maja looked at him as she did now, his defenses were stripped away. He wanted to know everything about her, including why she was hurting.

Just as he was about to ask her to tell him more, they crested a hill and the sight he had been waiting for came into view. A concrete wall, roughly twelve feet high and topped by barbed wire, stretched as far as the eye could see in both directions. The road passed through the wall, but the opening was guarded by a group of men in a variety of military uniforms. They sat around a few trestle tables, eating and playing cards. Adam didn't know whether to be relieved or disappointed at the interruption to the moment of intimacy.

"We're here." He nodded, and Maja shifted in her seat as she followed the direction of his gaze. "This is the border."

Chapter 5

Adam slowed the car as they approached the border. Edith had explained that this was not a recognized checkpoint. The gap in the border wall was not meant to be there, but corrupt officials were turning a blind eye to its existence. The men who were guarding the border were smugglers. They would allow Adam and Tarek to cross for a price. She had stressed that they were ruthless bandits who would not hesitate to kill them if they thought it would be more advantageous. In addition to her car, Edith had given Adam one of the guns they had taken from the Reapers. It rested in the well between the front seats, out of sight, but within reach if he needed it. A constant reminder of the danger they were in.

Adam surveyed the scene. He was used to skirmishes, but prior to his arrival in Syria, they had been of the bloodless variety. He knew his business opponents would describe him as a killer...within the corporate environment. Ruthless and without scruples, Adam had a reputation for doing whatever it took to achieve his goals. He stayed within the law, but it was well known that if there was a way to bend the rules, Adam Lyon would find it.

But this? Facing a group of five armed outlaws, miles from anywhere, with only his wits, a gun and a pocketful of hundred dollar bills? This was outside his experience. Add in the fact that he had taken on responsibility for an eight-year-old child—*and a dog, don't forget the damn dog*—and the whole situation strayed into the realms of the ridiculous.

He turned his head to say as much to Maja, but she had vanished. Although the passenger-side window was fully wound down, Adam hoped she was still with him, poised for a fight. Since they hadn't discussed tactics, he couldn't be sure. That was the problem with invisible companions. They were hell when it came to communication.

The men halted their game of cards as the car approached. One man rose to his feet and, with his machine gun held in an ostentatious pose across his chest, raised a hand for Adam to stop. With a pounding heart, he hit the brakes and wound down his window.

"Do you speak English?" Adam asked. His heart rate spiked further as the man looked in the rear window at Tarek's sleeping figure.

"A little." He came back and leaned on the roof of the car. "You want to cross the border?"

Relieved that he didn't have to embark on a lengthy explanation, Adam nodded. "How much?"

A speculative look crossed the other man's face as he eyed Adam, then the car. "Wait here."

Abruptly, he turned away and strode back to his companions. Adam watched as they talked among themselves for a few minutes. There was much gesturing and pointing in Adam's direction. He wished he could hear what they were saying. Were they discussing how high to set the price? Or deciding whether to kill him and Tarek, take the car and their belongings and dump their bodies in the desert?

Just when the tension was becoming unbearable, Adam's attention was drawn to another man. He had moved slightly to one side of the group and, while the others were talking, he seemed to be distracted. Every now and then, he would raise a hand as though swatting a fly. His movements gradually became more pronounced, until he appeared to be shadow-boxing an invisible opponent.

Adam felt a tiny flicker of hope flare inside him at the thought. *An invisible opponent.* He had been worrying that all he had was his wits and a pistol, when in reality there was a far more powerful weapon on his side all along.

The man reeled back, raising his hands and clawing at his throat. His face darkened and his eyes bulged. As he dropped to his knees, his companions finally became aware that something was wrong, and rushed to his aid. It was too late—the man's head was wrenched around to the right with a sickening twist and he was flung face-down in the dirt. The others halted in their tracks, their expressions stunned.

Immediately, another of the men staggered as his head jerked sharply back, and he cried out in shock. He covered his face with both hands, but blood gushed from between his fingers. Adam's best guess was that someone—that same invisible someone—had kicked him in the face, breaking his nose and probably loosening several teeth.

Panic broke out among the group as a third member dropped like a stone. Clutching his groin, he curled up in the fetal position, a high wail issuing from his lips. Adam allowed himself a brief moment of masculine sympathy.

Maja was clearly fighting hard in every direction. He was just thankful she was on his side. That superhuman strength in the form of a kick in the balls wasn't something he ever wanted to experience.

The remaining two reached for their guns, turning toward Adam as they made the connection between him and the mayhem being unleashed. Adam reached for his own in the same instant that Maja became visible. Stooping to pick up a weapon discarded by one of the fallen men, she shot another bandit in the back as he approached the car.

Four down. At the same time, Adam fired a shot through the car's open window, hitting the fifth man squarely in the chest.

It was the second time he had killed a man in two days. He had known when he came to Syria that he was entering a country where his own life would be in danger. Had he envisaged a situation in which he would be forced to kill? Perhaps it had been at the back of his mind. It didn't make him feel any better. Didn't take away the feelings of nausea and guilt. Telling himself that this man and the terrorist back at the mission would have murdered him without a second thought didn't alter his feelings. Something inside him had changed when he pulled the trigger. That didn't mean he wouldn't do it again.

"Get in." He gestured to Maja as he viewed the scene. They were leaving dead and wounded bandits in their wake. He doubted the authorities would be too concerned, but he didn't want to hang around to find out. He grinned at her as she slid into the seat next to him. "We have a border to cross."

"Thank you."

Adam's eyes were warm on her face as he spoke, and Maja took a moment to enjoy the sensation. After crossing the border into Lebanon, they had traveled for a few more hours until they reached the old coastal city of Batroun. The peaceful blue-and-gold harbor was such a contrast to the strife they had left behind in Warda that it was a shock to her system. Tranquility was outside her experience. When she came to the mortal realm, she entered scenes of bloody battle. This was a new phenomenon.

As she sat on the harbor wall, the warm sea breeze tugged strands of hair loose from her braid and caressed her face. Below them, Tarek threw sticks for Leo to chase along the sand. It was easy to imagine, for a moment, that they were here to enjoy the beach scene.

This mortal capacity to keep going was something that amazed Maja. This land had been ripped apart by war, yet its people continued to find happiness in their daily pursuits. And in each other. The thought brought her back to Adam. Everything brought her back to Adam.

She forced herself to concentrate on what he was saying instead of how he made her feel. Because how he made her feel was dangerous. Exciting, arousing...but forbidden. Was that part of the attraction? If this attraction had been allowed, would it be as powerful? Was this all part of her rebellious streak?

"Why are you thanking me?"

"For saving my life. At the last count, it was three times." He grinned, and it was as if he had just poured boiling water over her. Instantly, her whole body was burning with longing. With an effort, Maja restrained herself from clambering into his lap. "Are you sure you're a Valkyrie and not my guardian angel?"

"No. A guardian angel is assigned to protect and guide an individual. We have no training in that role."

She was about to embark on a more detailed explanation of the differences when Adam caught hold of her hand. Laughing, he raised it to his lips. The action silenced her. Very effectively. It also made her blush all over.

"I was joking." He lowered her hand, but kept it in his, placing it on his leg and holding it there. "Teasing you."

"Oh." Maja was still recovering from the brush of his lips on her hand. Now she had to cope with the sensation of his hard thigh muscles beneath her palm. How many different ways was he going to torture her? "I don't know much about these things."

"Don't tell me... Odin doesn't encourage the Valkyries to have fun?" Adam raised a brow.

"We don't have time for enjoyment."

That made him laugh even more. Maja watched him with mild bewilderment. She didn't know what she'd said to provoke his mirth, but she liked it. Originating deep in his chest, the sound of his laughter washed over her, warm and pleasant. His shoulders shook and she could see the muscles of his abdomen tightening beneath his T-shirt. It was an extension of his smile, a joyful sound that made her want to join in, even though she wasn't sure why.

When he had recovered enough to be able to speak, there was still a suspicion of breathlessness in his voice. "Maja, the last few days haven't given me much to celebrate, but you have been one of the high notes."

She wrinkled her nose. "Is that good?"

"Yes, it's good." Briefly, he squeezed her hand before releasing it. "Now stop making me laugh. It hurts my shoulder."

They had come to the beach in search of the contact Edith had suggested to them, Ali El-Amin.

Having eaten bread, olives and minced lamb at one of the restaurants on the main harbor road, they were waiting now for the last of the fishing boats to return. Ali's wife had described his boat to Tarek. Blue and white, she had said, with a picture of a butterfly on the side.

"There!" Tarek ran up to them, pointing excitedly in the direction of the water. "There is the boat with the butterfly."

Adam raised a hand, shielding his eyes from the still bright sunlight. Maja followed the direction of his gaze. Sure enough, Ali's boat was being dragged ashore. The man who was hauling it was young and stocky. He looked tired and dispirited as he secured his vessel and spoke briefly to some of the other fishermen. His attitude suggested disappointment with the day's catch.

Adam got to his feet and Maja rose with him. "Let's go and see if we can buy ourselves an illegal boat trip to Cyprus."

Ali's expression was suspicious as he listened to Tarek's interpretation of Adam's request. When he spoke, his response was brief and dismissive. Hunching a shoulder, he turned back to his fishing nets.

"He said he is not a smuggler." Tarek's small body drooped with disappointment.

"Ask him how much. Say he can name his price," Adam said.

Tarek spoke again. Although Ali continued with his task, Adam got the feeling he was listening to the boy's words. *Or am I deceiving myself? Having come this far, am I refusing to believe we can't make the final step?*

The problem was it felt too final. He had come here to find Danny and he was going home without him. Coming to Syria had been a long shot. It was a country with a unique set of problems. Communicating, traveling, finding information about his brother...they had all proven every bit as difficult as he had anticipated. Faced with a choice between doing nothing and making an attempt to find Danny, Adam had felt obliged to try. The realist in him told him this was always the likeliest outcome, that he would leave—if he got away at all—without any information. That stubborn streak he had? It was telling him the search wasn't over.

Adam was exhausted, running on adrenaline and determination. The strength of will that got him through the toughest deals was about all that was keeping him upright. He knew what his rivals said of him. Arrogant. Obstinate. Inflexible. Those were among the more generous labels he had heard applied to himself. As long as he got his way, Adam didn't care what they called him.

Now, his shoulder was in agony and the strong, reliable body that he pushed so hard in his day-to-day life was sending him insistent messages that it needed rest. This trip wasn't like the usual demands he made on himself. This wasn't like a fourteen-hour-day at work, followed by a sleepless night. Shock, blood loss, disappointment, and exhaustion had all taken their toll. If he didn't get to safety soon, he would collapse.

But there was something other than his own willpower keeping him going. He cast a sidelong glance at Maja. The evening sunlight lent a golden tint to her skin and the breeze blew tendrils of hair that had escaped from her braid about her face. She raised a hand to brush them away, and even that simple gesture caught him full force. She was stunning and he could watch her forever. Every movement and expression held him spellbound.

Maja's presence was energizing him. Not only because she had come to his rescue so many times during this adventure. He wasn't sure he'd have survived without her, but there was more to it than the way she had rescued him from physical harm. Her allure was keeping his waning strength going. It wasn't macho posturing around an attractive woman. Adam had never succumbed to that sort of display of virility. And without being vain, he knew he didn't need it now. The attraction between them was mutual. He had the memory of the most explosive sex of his life as proof. But he also felt it in the highly charged atmosphere. Maja was too inexperienced to hide her feelings. Even so, he wasn't sure subterfuge was an option for either of them. The magnetism was overpowering. Despite the danger they faced, Maja was uppermost in his mind. Pushing out all other thoughts, she was spurring him on.

"He said you can't afford his price." Tarek's voice intruded into his thoughts.

Reluctantly, Adam withdrew his gaze from Maja. Reaching into the concealed pocket in his jacket, he withdrew the wad of hundred dollar bills. "Tell him this is a deposit."

Adam was prepared to do whatever it took to get them to Cyprus, where his credit card would be good again and his cell phone would work. Somehow, having been to Syria, he felt closer to Danny. He understood Danny's motives. Adam wasn't giving up on his younger brother. He never would. *I should have stopped him.* Even though Adam had tried to talk Danny out of coming to this part of the world, he couldn't shake the feelings of guilt. The sense that he could have done more, then and now. Tried harder to talk Danny out of it. Been more persuasive. Traveled to more of those sorry, ruined towns. Spoken to more sad-eyed people.

Ali's attitude changed dramatically at the sight of the cash. Along with a new enthusiasm came an ability to speak English. Casting a quick glance around, he beckoned Adam closer. "Not here. Meet me at the Masa Bar.

Ten minutes." He gestured to one of the beach bars before turning back to his nets.

The Masa Bar was already filling up, but Adam found a table overlooking the beach. Ordering beer for himself and Ali, and soda for Tarek and Maja, he sank back in the comfortable chair.

"I may never get up again," he sighed. Leo, obviously approving of this plan, curled up on his feet.

It soon became clear why Ali had chosen to meet here. The thumping beat of the music and the constant chatter of the noisy customers meant that, although their conversation had to be conducted in a shout, no one could overhear what they were saying. When Ali joined them, he drained half his beer appreciatively before he spoke.

"I can take you to Cyprus, but it is not easy."

Adam patted his jacket pocket. "I'll pay."

Ali shook his head. "Go to Turkey instead. Much easier."

"No." Adam wasn't budging on this.

Ali sighed and gestured for a waiter to bring him another beer. "You are a US citizen, yes? Why not call your embassy? They will get you out of here."

"The boy is Syrian." It explained everything. Syrian refugees were an international problem. Desperate to escape their own land, they had exhausted all the escape routes into neighboring countries.

"Ah." Ali turned to Maja. "And you?"

She seemed confused, so Adam came to her rescue. "It's complicated."

Ali accepted the explanation without comment, appearing lost in thought as he drained his second beer. "Okay. The weather will be good tonight. We leave at midnight."

In the hours between meeting Ali at the Masa Bar and joining him on the boat, they attempted to get some sleep in the car. Tarek dozed, but Maja stayed awake and worried about Adam. He looked increasingly weary. His face was pale and the fine lines about his eyes appeared more pronounced. Although he closed his eyes and leaned back in the driver's seat, she got the feeling he didn't sleep. When the time came, they abandoned Edith's car in a side street and joined Ali at the harbor.

Maja was surprised when Ali led them to a dinghy instead of to the fishing boat they had seen earlier.

"Faster," he explained as she climbed carefully into the small craft. "I am using my brother's speedboat. We can reach Cyprus in under two hours this way."

Maja didn't like water. It was a fact she had decided not to mention to Adam. He had enough worries to contend with without introducing her phobias into the situation. Besides, they were getting to Cyprus by boat; they weren't swimming.

The sea was mirror-still as the motor-powered dinghy skimmed across the water and Batroun disappeared in the moonlight. Within minutes, the dinghy bumped the side of the speedboat. Ali secured it to the stern of the larger vessel.

Even though there was no light except that thrown out by the full moon, Ali sprang nimbly from the dinghy onto the rear of the speedboat. Holding out a hand, he helped each of them in turn onto the deck. Handing out life jackets, he explained that they should remain seated during the journey. He also gave Tarek a length of rope and instructed him to keep Leo leashed the whole time.

"I am not turning back if your dog goes overboard."

Within minutes the boat had chugged to life and they were gliding over the dark waters. Tarek soon became engrossed in the technicalities of what Ali was doing, and their conversation switched to Arabic. Ali seemed content to answer the questions the boy fired at him, and Maja turned to look at Adam, who was leaning back in one of the cushioned seats that lined the deck.

"You have pushed yourself hard," she said.

"What choice is there?" Adam nodded in Tarek's direction. "What happens to him if I crumble?"

Although she understood what he was saying, she was confused by the depth of his commitment to Tarek, a child he had only just met. Maja shared the same determination to ensure the boy was safe and well, but she had an advantage over Adam. She was invincible, while he was hurting, driving himself to his physical limits.

He hadn't talked much about his brother, but it was clear he had wanted to find him. Maja understood responsibility. But there was more than duty in Adam's eyes when he looked at the man in the photograph. There was an emotion so powerful it tugged at her heart. But there were other feelings as well, ones she couldn't name. They were similar to the ones that made her want to wrap her arms around Tarek and protect him from harm.

"Was there an alternative to this?" she murmured.

Although they were in darkness, he turned toward her and she could see his face in the moonlight. He raised a questioning brow.

"Was there another way to help Tarek without putting yourself at risk?"

He lifted his good shoulder in a one-sided shrug. "You saw those guys who came to the mission. They weren't playing nice. If they'd found Tarek, they would have killed him, because they suspect he knows the name of their leader. He can tell the world who the Reaper is." Adam gave a mirthless laugh. "What they don't realize is the world won't listen to him."

"What does that mean?"

He shifted position slightly, resting his good arm on the seat cushions behind her. "I read an article some months ago that speculated about the very thing that Tarek said. It suggested that the Reaper wasn't driven by religious or political motivation. I wonder now if the anonymous author of that piece could have been Tarek's father. Whoever wrote it believed the Reaper was a large consortium or group of businesses."

"Some of the warriors in the great hall at Valhalla died fighting this thing you mortals call terrorism. They thought they were battling against an ideology. I don't understand how they could have died because of something that was run by a business."

"Exactly. The article I read was widely discredited for that reason. No one was able to believe such a thing could happen. Even though, throughout history, appalling atrocities have been committed for monetary gain, it was impossible to believe that acts as awful as the Reaper's brand of terrorism could be done for profit."

The boat had changed course and Adam's face was shadowed from the moonlight, but she could tell his expression was troubled.

"But Tarek said his father had proof of this man's identity?"

"And he was prepared to go public with his name." Adam lowered his voice as he cast a glance toward where Tarek was still chatting eagerly with Ali. "He died the day after he spoke it out loud."

"You knew that name." Maja studied his profile as he turned to look out over the moonlit water. "When Tarek told it to us, you knew who he meant."

Adam was silent for so long she wondered if he wasn't going to answer her. "Knight Valentine is one of the best-known names in the business world. He is a billionaire property developer. No one in their right mind would believe him capable of something like this."

"So you think Tarek's father was wrong?"

Maja felt there was something more to this. Intuition wasn't necessary to the Valkyries. They needed to be strong. Get in, get the job done, get out. That was what made them effective. More wasn't required. But where Adam was concerned, Maja was developing an extra sense. Now and then, she could tune in to his feelings. She didn't understand why that was, and she wasn't sure she liked it. It was outside her sphere of experience to get so close to another person. But it was there. She was stuck with it. Right now, she sensed his turmoil and something more. She thought it might be anger.

"No, I don't think he was wrong." He turned back to face her. "I know Knight Valentine well—too well for my liking—and I know there is nothing he wouldn't do for money or power."

"How do you know him so well?"

"Knight Valentine is my stepfather."

Chapter 6

"Larnaca."

Adam followed the direction of Ali's pointing finger and saw a line of lights on the horizon. It was the sweetest sight he had ever seen. Ali's next words jolted him out of his happiness.

"Patrol boat. British."

Some distance away, but between them and the welcoming lights of Larnaca, a searchlight was scanning the dark water.

"What can we do?" If Ali said they would have to turn back, Adam might just pull out his gun and use it on him. That was how close to the outer limits of his endurance he was right now.

"There is only one thing we can do." Ali swung the wheel to the right. "I know these waters well. We get in close to the shore and keep out of sight. Play a game like the cat and the mouse." He shook his head. "It could take many hours."

Frustration was a slow-burning fuse inside Adam's head. It bristled outward, brushing over his skin until his whole body was screaming with tension. Relaxation? Neutrality? Going with the flow? Not Adam. He created the flow. He controlled his environment.

Upon leaving college, Adam had taken over a small niche magazine, working day and night to turn it into a thriving business. From there, he had developed his media conglomerate, using the internet to expand until the Lyon logo became instantly recognizable. Now, at age thirty-three, he headed up an empire that comprised over a hundred companies. The name Lyon was an everyday part of the music, media, lifestyle and entertainment industries across the globe. He had always been in charge.

Coming away to Syria had been easy in one sense, because he'd hired the best people and trusted them to take over in his absence. It was difficult in another sense because he had never been out of touch with the deputies of his various companies for such a prolonged period.

He didn't know how to do this. To hand over control to someone else. To wait it out. To be helpless.

"My sister is the Valkyrie leader." Maja's voice intruded on his thoughts and his initial reaction was to shut her out. His nerves were too taut for him to listen to stories about her family tree. But her voice was soothing. A bit like the lulling motion of the boat as Ali weaved in and out along the rocky coastline. "Her name is Brynhild. It is her job to find the bravest warriors and to take them to Valhalla to be part of Odin's great army. But finding those fighters isn't an easy task. She has to rely on the Norns, the Norse goddesses of fate. And sometimes they are not kind."

Despite his gloom, Adam's lips quirked into a smile. "Is this your way of telling me to suck it up?"

"I don't want you to suck anything, Adam." That way she had of taking everything literally should be annoying, but it was part of her. He even found it endearing. "I know how tired you are. This is just a setback. We will be in Larnaca soon."

And suddenly it didn't seem so bad. Frustration wasn't a demon gnawing on his nerve endings. He wasn't happy, but he could live with his impatience. And all it took was a few words from a Valkyrie. Maybe he should employ Maja as some sort of stress relief guru. *Who knows? Maybe one day she might be able to talk me into a decent night's sleep. Even into taking a vacation...*

He forced his muscles to loosen as he eased into a more comfortable position. Inactivity didn't come easily to him. Inactivity under cover of darkness while on the run from a British patrol ship? That was the worst kind of torture for someone used to being in control. As Ali danced the boat in and out of the rocky coves, Adam turned his head and studied Maja's profile. She appeared outwardly serene, yet she had to be worried about what the future held. *By helping you, I may have signed my own death warrant.* That was what she had said to him back at the mission.

"Why did you come back?" He hadn't even been sure what he was going to say until the words left his lips.

She turned her head to look at him, and even though he couldn't see her eyes in the darkness, he felt the weight of her gaze on his face. "I had no choice." For a few moments, it seemed that might be all she was prepared to divulge. Then she sighed. "I returned to the building where I first saw you to find my horse, Magtfuld. He was gone. I had no way of returning to Valhalla."

Adam wasn't sure what to do with that information. Had he wanted to believe she had returned to the mission for him? But what would that mean in reality? For him?

For them? For the future? They had been thrown together by the need to rescue Tarek, but anything longer term would be—he searched for a suitable word—*bizarre*. Because although she had stepped out of his fantasies and into his reality, Maja wasn't mortal.

And I don't do relationships with human women, never mind the nonhuman variety.

Until his father died, Adam's life had been normal. His parents' marriage had been a happy one, and he had known what a normal, loving relationship looked like. His perception changed the day his mother married Knight Valentine. He didn't need anyone else to tell him what he already knew. His view was skewed by what he had seen in his mother's second marriage.

Adam was still that thirteen-year-old boy who had built himself and Danny an imaginary fort in which they could hide away, sneaking only occasional glimpses at the outside world. Now, he flirted, dated, engaged in some steamy and enjoyable sexual encounters, but whenever things got a little too real, when anyone got too close, he pulled up the drawbridge and withdrew.

It had been different for Danny. Too young to be seriously affected by the train wreck of what was happening around them, and protected by Adam, he hadn't established the same defense mechanisms. Adam envied him his light-hearted approach to life. *Normal. It's called normal.*

Maja hadn't come back to the mission because of Adam. She had come back because she had no choice. And now he felt...cheated. Disappointed, because he wanted it to be about him. And that was screwed up, and perverse and everything he didn't want to be...but suddenly was.

"So you are stranded?"

"It looks that way." Maja's voice could sometimes lack emotion. Now she sounded lost.

"Forever?"

"I don't know. I don't understand what this means." She raised a hand to her throat and the simple gesture caught at something inside Adam's chest. She affected him in ways no other woman ever had. This power she had over him had nothing to do with whether she was human or not. "I think it is my sister Brynhild's way of punishing me for defying her." Her smile was rueful. "Valkyries are not supposed to be defiant. But it is worse than that. I have broken the Valkyrie Code. The outcome will not be good."

"You said you feared the death sentence because you helped me," Adam said. "Is it really that bad?"

"I have only known of one other Valkyrie who broke the code recently. Her name was Silja and she was imprisoned for life."

"What did she do?" Adam wasn't sure he wanted to hear the answer.

"She spoke to a mortal man. It is believed she was lost and asked him for directions."

Ah. He could see why Maja might have cause to be alarmed. With that realization came a new feeling. The weight of his responsibility here settled on his shoulders. It was uncomfortable and he didn't like it. What had he wanted? Hot sex—hot, *unprotected* sex; his mind insisted on reminding him of that not so insignificant detail—with a warrior princess and then walk away? *I didn't want anything from this. I didn't know she was real.* After everything that had happened since that night, the thought seemed petulant and he put it aside. She had felt real enough when he was pouring himself into her. She had been real enough when he was calling out her name as he succumbed to the wildest orgasm of his life.

Whether he liked it or not, they were in this together. Not just because of Tarek. Maja was stranded here because she had helped Adam. He didn't know what he might do to help her in return. He didn't even know if there was anything he *could* do. But telling himself he wasn't involved didn't work. He had no idea what his involvement looked like, and right now his tired brain was incapable of trying to work it out. All he knew was that as well as a Syrian orphan and his dog to care for, he also had an abandoned Valkyrie. He wasn't sure his luxury New York penthouse was going to be the ideal home for this unique group of visitors.

Ali had been right. It was several hours before the patrol boat left the waters around Larnaca. Although they were in danger, those hours were mind-numbingly boring. Even Tarek fell silent and was reduced to sighing wearily now and then. Maja found the time passed in a strange manner. It would seem to slow to a standstill and then speed to a gallop. It alternated this way as Ali skillfully maneuvered the speedboat in and out of the rocky coves along the shoreline, using them to keep out of sight of the patrol boat's powerful searchlight.

Eventually, he was happy that the boat was gone. "We can go ashore now." He pointed his vessel in the direction of the lights of Larnaca. "Not into the town center. We will take the dinghy to a nearby beach and walk the rest of the way."

By the time they finally felt the sand crunching beneath their feet, they were a bedraggled and weary group. It seemed to Maja that they were embarking on another journey. Although they had left behind them the strife of Syria, this was not their final destination.

Ali explained that Larnaca was popular with tourists. "Even at this time of the morning, the town will be busy."

"Good." As they entered the town, Maja could see the grayish tinge to Adam's face in the light cast by the overhead streetlamps.

"Before we check into a hotel, I need to find an ATM and a pharmacy," he announced.

Maja raised her brows in a question. She had no idea what he was talking about.

"An ATM is a machine that dispenses cash. I have to give Ali the rest of his money. A pharmacy sells medical items. I want to change the dressing on this wound." He grimaced. "And I need painkillers."

Ali led them to the main street, pointing out the places Adam sought. While Adam inserted a card into a machine in the wall and withdrew the money he needed, Maja looked around with interest. This town was different from both Warda and Batroun. Although it was now early morning, there was an atmosphere that was tangible. There were still a few people on the streets and they seemed to be determinedly enjoying themselves.

Ali, following the direction of her gaze, seemed to feel some explanation was needed. "Tourists. People come here on vacation."

It was difficult to process that information. In such a short space of time, and not far away, they had left behind them so much pain and suffering. Yet here, people were partying as if this was all there was. Maybe the human capacity to do that, to make the best of here and now, was a good thing. Maybe she should try it before she left the mortal realm.

Adam handed over the rest of Ali's money. "I wish you good luck," he told him. "And thank you."

Ali shook hands with each of them in turn. He ruffled Tarek's hair. "Keep practicing your Arabic. It is your heritage."

As they watched him walk away, Tarek slid his hand into Maja's. "How could I forget my Arabic? I know it better than English."

"Perhaps it is easy to forget one language if all you hear is another."

"I won't forget." His little face was serious and his voice was determined.

They found a twenty-four-hour pharmacy and Maja waited outside with Tarek and Leo while Adam purchased the items he needed.

When he emerged, he looked even more exhausted. "Now we find a hotel."

"How will we know which one to choose?" Maja asked. The seafront was lined with imposing, brightly lit buildings. All of them had the word *hotel* in their name.

"Easy. We find the one that looks the most expensive." He nodded to Tarek. "Time for Leo to go into hiding."

The little dog seemed happy to clamber into the gym bag and curl up inside. Maja zipped it up and carried it as they walked along, inspecting the hotels until they found one with which Adam was happy.

"This one." He paused at the entrance of the largest and most elegant.

Set slightly back from the promenade in its own gardens, the Cyprus Sands Hotel didn't look like the sort of place that would welcome three tired, dirty travelers with no luggage except a suspicious-looking gym bag. As Adam strode purposefully inside and up to the reception desk, Maja kept that thought to herself. Holding Tarek's hand, she followed him.

"I need a suite."

How had she not noticed that air of authority about

Adam until now? Even though he was almost dropping to his knees with exhaustion—his clothes dusty, his jacket torn and bloodied—he exuded the calm confidence of a man used to getting what he wanted.

"We only have our premier suite available, sir. It's our most expensive." The desk clerk was polite, but slightly wary.

"I'll take it." Adam handed over his passport and credit card with a mixture of boredom and impatience. His manner brought about a remarkable change in approach from the clerk, who was suddenly very eager to please.

Within minutes they were in the elevator, another new experience for Maja, and Tarek was eyeing Adam with respect. "Do people always look at you like that?"

"Like what?" Adam regarded him with a trace of amusement.

"I don't know." Tarek's English was usually good, but now he struggled to find the words. "Like you are the king."

Adam laughed as the elevator reached their floor. "I hope so, because right now I want king-size room service."

That suggestion found favor with Tarek, and after he had bounded around the suite, exclaiming at the size and luxury of the rooms, the view from the balcony, and the mini-bar, he returned to study the room service menu.

"Burger and fries for breakfast?" Adam wrinkled his nose. "Tarek, your stomach must be made of iron. Is it okay for you to eat these things?"

"It says here the meat is halal." Tarek pointed to the menu.

"How about you?" Adam held the menu out to Maja.

"I don't know what half these meals are." She seemed

to be spending all her time confessing her ignorance of all things mortal. "What are you having?"

"Toast, eggs and a gallon of coffee. Shall I order the same for you?" She nodded and he picked up the phone. Having place their order, he sank back in chair. "After I've eaten, I'm going to sleep…for about a week. I suggest the two of you do the same. Then we can take care of the practicalities, like getting some clean clothes and getting out of here."

Tarek had fallen asleep as soon as he and Leo had shared his burger and fries. The little dog was now curled up protectively beneath the boy's bed. Maja closed the door on them with a smile.

"Maybe I should have made him bathe first, but he was exhausted."

"We all are. I think sleep comes first today." Adam rose from his chair. Every movement felt like an effort as he picked up the bag of items he had purchased at the pharmacy. "Can you help me with this dressing? I can't reach it on my own."

"Of course." She followed him into the bathroom.

Before he did anything else, Adam swallowed two extra-strength painkillers with a glass of water. When he tried to slide his jacket off, he found to his dismay that he couldn't get his left arm working properly. Without saying anything, Maja came to his aid. After easing the jacket carefully off his right shoulder and arm first, she repeated the action on the left. Although the stiff material rasped against his injury, Adam bore it. Anything was better than trying to pull the garment off by himself.

His T-shirt was more troublesome. Maja had to hook her hands into the hem and pull it up inch by inch. Adam was able to raise his right arm above his head to assist her, but his left arm was useless. She managed to get the garment over his head and gently drew it down his injured shoulder. It hurt like hell, and he had no idea how he was ever going to get it back on again, but it was done.

The dressings Edith had put in place were neat and efficient. Blood had seeped through, staining the white bandages dark red, and Adam wondered what that meant about the state of his wound.

"Can you remove these dressings?"

Maja bit her lip. "I am not used to living people."

"That's not exactly reassuring, but I need your help anyway."

A smile trembled on her lips. "You don't understand. I'm scared of hurting you."

"Maja, it's probably going to hurt like hell whichever one of us does this. But you have the advantage over me. I can only use one hand."

She nodded determinedly. "I'll do my best."

Adam sat on the edge of the bathtub and Maja came to stand over him. Her fingers were hesitant at first as she got to work removing the adhesive bandages that Edith had used to hold the sterile dressings in place. Gradually, as he sat very still and didn't make a sound, she gained confidence. Once the dressing was stripped away, Adam rose and went to look in the mirror. The wound at the front of his shoulder was large and ragged, although Edith's stitching had carefully pulled the edges together. It was this injury, where the bullet had exited and ripped through his muscles, that was causing him the most pain. There was some dried blood around the stitches, but he couldn't see any signs of infection. Turning to get a look at his back, he saw a smaller, neater wound where the bullet had entered. Again, it didn't appear to be infected, and he said another silent thank-you to Edith for her medical skills.

Withdrawing a pack of antiseptic wipes and a pair of disposable gloves from the bag, he handed them to Maja. "You need to use these to clean the wound thoroughly."

He returned to his seat on the edge of the tub. Maja bent her head to her task. At the first tentative touch of the antiseptic wipe, Adam hissed in a breath and she looked up at him.

"I'm sorry."

"Not your fault. And it has to be done." Clenching his jaw so hard he thought it might shatter, he nodded for her to continue.

She worked efficiently then, seeming to sense that hesitation would only prolong his agony. Meticulously, she cleaned around and between each stitch until every trace of dried blood was gone. When she had finished cleaning the wound at the front, Adam shifted position and she repeated the process with the injury to the back of his shoulder.

"You are good at this."

"I'm a Valkyrie. I know how to follow instructions." Her breath tickled his neck, momentarily distracting him from the pain.

Finally, she was finished, and all that was left for her to do was cover his injuries with clean dressings. The back one was quick and easy. The wound at the front of his shoulder took longer. Maja had to use the scissors in the hotel sewing kit to cut two sterile dressings to fit lengthwise over the stitches, then secure them in place with adhesive bandages.

When she had finished, she studied her handiwork with her head tipped to one side. "It's not very neat, but I don't think it will come off."

Her hand was resting on his abdomen and her face was inches from his. It was incredible how quickly exhaustion could disappear in the right circumstances. And these circumstances felt very right. As he looked up at her, Maja's lips parted as if she was about to say something else. Then, as if she sensed the change in his mood, a faint blush stained her cheeks.

Adam leaned forward, ignoring the protest from his shoulder, and caught hold of her braid, drawing her closer. His lips brushed hers and that feeling thrummed through him again. The same one he had felt back at the mission. Kissing a Valkyrie was like an out-of-body experience. Sweet, heady and darkly delicious. Maja's mouth opened eagerly beneath his and he held her head while he kissed her gently. Slow and easy. It wasn't because she was a Valkyrie. She could be a royal princess, an A-list celebrity, a wicked witch or a faerie queen. How she made him feel had nothing to do with the label she wore and everything to do with who she was on the inside. It was because she was Maja.

This wasn't going anywhere. Not because the heat between them was gone. It was there in the background, waiting to ignite anytime they wanted it. But right now, they needed this and nothing more.

Cradling her face between his hands, Adam ran his thumb over her lower lip. "Let's get some sleep."

And, wrapping his good arm around Maja as they lay in the huge bed, Adam was surprised to find slumber enveloping him almost immediately.

Chapter 7

When Maja woke from a deep sleep, she experienced a curious feeling of panic. Until now, she had never been roused from slumber in a strange place. Throughout her life, it had always been the same. When she opened her eyes, she was always in her room at the palace in Asgard.

Now, she was in a room she didn't recognize. She fought off the mists of repose as she briefly struggled to piece together the events that had brought her here. There was one very obvious clue. Her back was pressed up against a warm, hard body and a possessive arm was tight around her waist. She studied that arm for a moment or two. Strong and sinewy. Corded with muscle and lightly covered with dark, masculine hair. The hand was big and capable, with neatly trimmed nails. A memory of what that hand could do to her body came flooding back and she squirmed slightly.

The movement made Adam murmur in his sleep and

she subsided back into immobility. The last few days had been a whirlwind in which every second had been taken up with Tarek's safety. She had no brothers and she didn't know any children, but her protective feelings toward Tarek were strong and unswerving. She guessed these must be the maternal instincts she wasn't meant to possess. Since she would never have a child of her own, she decided she liked caring for Tarek. In doing so, she had barely had a moment to consider her own situation, but it was time to reflect on it now.

She was a runaway Valkyrie. It was no good telling herself that this was all Brynhild's fault for leaving her stranded. The right thing to do—the *only* thing to do— would have been to wait patiently until Brynhild sent Magtfuld or came herself to take her back to Valhalla.

But I would have been returning to face a death sentence.

It didn't matter. Obedience was the Valkyrie watchword. Questioning the will of Odin, or Brynhild as his representative, should not have entered Maja's head.

But it did. So what does that make me? A damaged Valkyrie. Not the first in the history of time to dare to think differently, but the first to do it so spectacularly.

It seemed she had a faulty gene. She was a shield maiden who didn't follow the rules. Having broken them once, she had continued further down the route of disobedience, flouting the Valkyrie Code wildly at every opportunity.

And I'm not sorry. Wherever this adventure led her, and it was likely to lead her straight to Odin's court of law, she would not have missed it. This time in the mortal realm had made her see her own life in a new light. She touched a finger to her lips, recalling that brief, tender kiss in the bathroom. Adam had made her feel alive in a way she had not imagined possible. She had never been

Odin's puppet, mindlessly following instructions. She had a will of her own. She had emotions, strong ones. And she had choices. Having broken free of her bonds, she found that, despite the fear and uncertainty, she liked this new and unexpected freedom.

Going on the run in the mortal realm was the ultimate act of defiance. Even if Odin might be inclined to show her mercy for her previous misdeeds—with difficulty, she stifled a laugh at the thought—this would be the crowning sin. But Maja didn't fool herself that she would be able to hide forever. If Brynhild could use the Norns to track down the bravest warriors, surely she could use the same method to find her errant younger sister? Or did her tracking system work only for mortals? It was a question Maja had never needed to ask. Until now…

There was a knock on the door and Tarek called her name. Maja eased carefully away from Adam and slipped quietly into the next room.

"I need to take Leo for a walk."

Maja looked at the clock on the wall. Mortal time wasn't an easy concept for her, but she calculated that they had been asleep for several hours and it was now afternoon. Although this felt like a safe place, she didn't want to let Tarek go out alone.

"I'll come with you. We are not supposed to have Leo with us, remember? We need to take him downstairs in the gym bag."

Tarek rolled his eyes, but complied. Leo, who seemed to have accepted the bag as his fate, hopped in and settled down.

"Should we leave a note for Adam?" Tarek asked.

Maja nodded and snatched up a piece of paper from a pad in the sitting room, scribbling a few words on it before leaving it on the table. They made their way down in the elevator and exited the hotel into brilliant sunlight. Once outside, Maja, for the first time in her life, became aware of what she was wearing. All around them people had the maximum amount of flesh on display. As they walked through the hotel gardens, past a vast swimming pool and onto the promenade that ran the length of the beach, Maja was conscious of women with beautiful, bikini-clad bodies. In contrast, she wore Edith's travel-dusted, all-concealing baggy blouse and pants. A few strange glances were cast in their direction. She supposed a grungy woman and boy who withdrew a scruffy dog from the bag they were carrying before tying a piece of rope around his neck and walking him along the promenade did look out of place.

While her appearance should probably be the last thing on her mind in the circumstances, she was acutely aware of the contrast. She was also conscious that she didn't want Adam to start making the same comparisons she was. If he saw all this golden flesh and glossy hair, she was fairly sure that the warm light she had seen in his eyes last night would quickly disappear. The problem was, she had no idea what she could do about it.

She was still pondering the problem by the time they had walked the length of the promenade and returned to the hotel. When they got back to their suite, Adam had showered and was in the sitting room talking on his cell phone. He was wrapped in a towel and the sight of his bare chest and abdomen did something primal to Maja's midsection. It was as if her heart and her stomach were fighting to change places.

He looked up as they walked in and the smile in his eyes only intensified the feeling. *I could have stayed in Valhalla, continued in my safe life and not risked Odin's wrath. But if I had, I would never have known this feel-*

ing. There was no contest. She would make the same choice every time.

She pointed Tarek in the direction of the bathroom. "Your turn."

A few minutes later, she heard the sound of the shower.

Adam ended his call and indicated his shoulder. "Your dressing survived." He flexed his arm warily. "And it feels easier. Probably a combination of sleep and painkillers."

She was achingly aware of his nearness. Of the fresh, clean smell of his body and the delicious sight of his muscular torso. After her walk on the promenade, she was also conscious of the shortcomings in her own appearance. "What happens next?"

"I've been making arrangements to get us out of here. If I was alone, I'd simply book a seat on the next flight to England. From there I'd get a transatlantic flight to New York."

Maja stared blankly at him. Every conversation they had seemed to reach a point at which she confessed to not understanding what he was saying, but this one had gotten there superfast.

He grinned, appreciating her confusion. "A lot of British tourists visit Cyprus, so there are several flights every day to England. It is a useful place for Americans to fly to because there are international flights across the Atlantic Ocean to my hometown, New York. Does that make more sense?"

"A little. But you can't do that this time because you are not alone?"

"No. Tarek really needs a document called a visa to get into America." Adam frowned. "But it would take a long time to arrange that. So I'm hoping to pull some strings."

Maja's brow wrinkled in an effort to concentrate. "What sort of strings are these?"

Adam laughed. "I keep forgetting I'm talking to a Valkyrie. It's an expression. It means I'm going to try and manipulate the system. I was just on the phone to my attorney. He is the person who deals with legal matters for me. And I was making arrangements to get us a private plane. It will be expensive, but it's the only way I can see this working."

"Expensive? That means it costs a lot of money, is that right?" Adam nodded his confirmation. "And money is very important in your world?" He nodded again. "And you have a lot of money?"

"I do."

"Then you must be a very happy man, Adam."

The laughter faded, and in its place she saw a flash of something darker. It might have been pain.

"I should be, shouldn't I?"

No matter how hard he tried, Adam was unable to arrange a private plane for the same day. They would have to stay in Larnaca for another twenty-four hours. In one sense, he was relieved. He hadn't completely recovered from that grueling journey, but he was starting to feel more human again.

After they had all showered and eaten, his next task had been to take his companions shopping. Trying to persuade Tarek that he needed only a basic wardrobe was hard enough, but Maja's sudden, inexplicable desire to own a bikini came like a bolt from the blue.

"We are only here for a day. How much swimming and sunbathing are you planning to do?" At the same time as he was saying words, Adam was wondering why he was trying to talk her out of it. The image of Maja in a bikini was, after all, a very appealing one.

"We could all go swimming." Tarek joined in the conversation. "You, too, Adam."

"I was thinking more of sunbathing than swimming," Maja said.

They left the store, having purchased new swimwear for all of them. Adam had the strangest feeling he had just lost control of part of his life. If that was the case, he wondered why he should be in such high spirits as they returned to the hotel. It was a mood that infected them all, even Leo, who dashed around the suite excitedly as they unpacked their new purchases, which included a collar and lead.

At Tarek's request, they ordered pizza and watched a film. It wasn't long before Tarek's eyelids were drooping, and Maja tucked him up in his bed before heading for the bathroom with bottle of bath oil she had purchased earlier.

Adam snagged a beer from the mini-bar and went out onto the balcony. The night air was warm and he savored the crisp, cold taste and the salt tang of the sea breeze. It was some time later when Maja emerged from the bathroom. Wrapped in a white bathrobe, with her hair fluffed up from the dryer, she looked impossibly desirable... which reminded him of something he needed to say to her.

"Do you want a drink?" He tilted his beer bottle toward her.

She wrinkled her nose at the smell. "Is there anything else?"

"There's wine in the fridge. Or there's a coffeemaker."

"I'll get some water in a minute." She came to stand next to him, leaning over the balcony rail. "I have only ever come into your world when there is conflict." She gestured to the beach scene below them. Although it was quiet, there were people wandering back from restaurants and bars. "I've never seen this side of it. It's very beautiful."

"It can be." He took a slug of his beer. "Maja, I need to talk to you about what happened between us back at the mission."

She kept her eyes on the beach, but he sensed the tension in her. Although the light over the balcony door was dim, he could see the blush staining her cheeks. "Oh."

It wasn't exactly encouraging, but this needed to be done. "We didn't use any protection."

Maja hung her head. "I don't know what that means." Her voice was barely audible.

Adam took pity on her then. She was clearly eaten up with embarrassment, and he wasn't helping the situation by treating her as if she was experienced at this sort of thing.

"Maja—" he set his beer down on the table and caught hold of her upper arms, turning her to face him "—look at me." Obediently, she lifted her head. "I just want to know if this is something we should worry about. I don't suppose you use any birth control?"

It was a long shot. She had told him that she hadn't been taught anything about her body because sex was something that would never happen to her. It seemed unlikely, in those circumstances, that she would have any need of contraception.

Her confused expression told him she still didn't understand. Of all the ways Adam had anticipated this conversation going, a basic explanation of human anatomy had not been one of them. "Maja, when we had sex, I ejaculated inside you. That means there is a chance that you could be pregnant. Unless your body is different from that of a mortal woman?"

She shook her head. "My body is mortal. I just have

extra powers." Her lip wobbled. "And there is nothing we can do about this?"

"Hey." He drew her closer, running a hand down the shining mass of her hair in a soothing gesture. She smelled delicious. Fresh from the bathtub, clean, with her own sweet undertones. "Let's not worry until there is something to worry about."

"You don't understand. I have already broken the Valkyrie Code in so many ways. I may as well have ripped it up and thrown the pieces into Odin's face. He is likely to hunt me down and have me killed for my crimes. But a child? Living proof of my shame? That is something he would never permit."

There were so many things wrong with that statement Adam hardly knew where to begin. He settled on the basics. "Shame? Sex isn't shameful."

"Maybe not in your world, but to a Valkyrie it is the worst thing imaginable."

"Is that how it felt to you? Like the worst thing imaginable?" Adam ducked his head to get a better look at her face. He wondered where he was going with this. Was it about his ego? Had he become so insecure he needed reassurance about his performance? But he knew it wasn't that. That night had been magical. He needed to know Maja had felt it, too. He needed to hear her say the words.

"You know it didn't." Her voice was a husky whisper.

"Tell me how it felt." *Shit.* He didn't know how it had happened, but the atmosphere had gone from serious to searing in seconds. What had happened to his promise that, from now on, he would keep his distance? To hell with promises. What did promises matter when, right now, he couldn't concentrate on his own breathing because he wanted her so much?

She tilted her head back to look at him. "Like the most wonderful thing in the world."

And he was lost. Utterly. His hands loosened the tie of her robe and slid inside as his lips plundered the soft flesh of her neck. Maja quivered in his arms as he held her, chest to chest. It was hard to tell where her trembling ended and his began. Impossible to tell whose heartbeat he felt pounding through him. She was like a fever in his blood, storming through him and wiping out the last remnants of his control. Ignoring the pain in his shoulder as he scooped her up into his arms, he carried her through to the bedroom and placed her on the bed.

Maja's eyes were the color of violets as he lay next to her. "I don't understand. We still don't have this protection you spoke of."

"No, we don't." He slid the robe from her shoulders, kissing his way down her body. "But there are other things we can do."

It didn't matter how many times she told herself this was wrong, that she had enough trouble, that getting in deeper was not the way to go. Where Adam was concerned, she was long past the point of no return, fighting what she felt was trying to hold back the inevitable. She was drawn to him like a moth to a flame. Her feelings were just as heated, and they had already proved just as destructive.

Adam's lips reached her breasts and he paused, raising his head to stare at her. Through half-closed eyes, Maja drank in his expression and shivered. He looked worshipful, intent…almost savage. He looked like he was about to devour her. Her chest rose and fell in time with her hurried breathing, and her dark pink nipples were already rock hard. Lowering his head, Adam swiped his tongue over one delicate bud and her head fell back as her hips jerked upward sharply.

Hungrily, he covered her nipple with his mouth as he worked her robe out from under her and threw it on the floor. Maja arched upward, her hands locking in his hair as he sucked on her sensitized flesh. Heat tore through her and she gave herself up to the sensation.

Licking and kissing his way lower, he moved down her body, sending electric currents of arousal pulsing through her. His hands spread her thighs wide and he moved his head between them. Maja jerked in shock as his tongue flicked her clit.

His hands drew her closer as his mouth closed over her slick entrance. Maja cried out, her fingers clenching in the sheets as he sucked and licked her. His tongue pushed inside her with slow, even strokes, and she bucked wildly against him until he had to hold her down with his hands on her hips.

Her body was wild with arousal now, tightening, higher and harder, until she was stretched out of control. She shuddered, gasped, pleaded, but that delicious mouth continued to torment her. His tongue commenced a relentless, magical rhythm. Licking, circling and caressing, before driving deep inside. Then his lips returned to her throbbing clit, sucking hard as he pushed two fingers into her. She arched up to him, her muscles quivering as he drove into her, and her control broke. Waves of pleasure broke over her and she gasped his name as she was pulled under. Adam continued to lap at her as she shuddered wildly.

Finally, he shifted position and came to lie beside her, pressing a kiss to her lips. Maja could taste herself on him and the feeling made her squirm with pleasure. She slid her hand down his body to the front of his pants, to where his erection was rock hard and straining at the cloth. Fumbling slightly, she undid his zipper to free his cock and stroke his length. His breath was an indrawn hiss.

"I want to please you now." Lightly, she drew her finger around his tip, and Adam shuddered.

"That feels so good." His voice was hoarse.

"I want to make it feel even better." She wrapped her hand around his erection, then, leaning over him, took the head of his cock between her lips. Pausing, she looked up. "Is this okay?"

His reply was a tortured groan as he tangled his fingers in her hair and guided her, pushing her mouth back down to his erection. Experimentally, Maja ran her tongue along the length of his shaft, flicking it lightly on the underside. Adam's whole body jerked, and she took that to be a sign of approval. He held her in place with a hand at the back of her neck while she moved her mouth up and down. Although her movements were hesitant at first, the sounds of his ragged breathing increased her confidence and she grew bolder, taking him deeper. The suction of her mouth on his hardness added to her arousal, and her moans vibrated against his shaft. She decided she liked this new sensation of being in control.

Adam thrust his hips upward rhythmically in time with her sucking. Gaining in boldness, Maja moved her hand inside his pants to cup the tight sac between his legs. The action tipped him over the edge and his hot release filled her mouth. His fingers tightened in her hair as he called out her name.

Adam drew her up and into his arms, holding her close against his uninjured side. Lying in his arms felt right and Maja curled into his body, listening to his breathing as he dozed. It was tempting to imagine this could last. That she could find a place here in the mortal realm. She slid an experimental hand over her flat stomach. What if there was a child? A tremor of fear ran through her. Odin's grandchild? Proof of an impure Valkyrie? She couldn't imagine the storm of wrath such a situation would provoke. As she stirred restlessly, Adam flung out his good arm to draw her closer.

For now, she would focus on him and on Tarek. Their safety was what mattered. This Reaper was threatening them, and she would help Adam any way she could. After that, she would return to the subject of her own problems. *I will take care of myself...and anyone else who comes along.*

With that thought, she closed her eyes and enjoyed the warmth of Adam's body against hers.

Chapter 8

Adam had called it pulling strings. Whatever those strings were made of, Maja decided they must have a powerful effect. Two days after leaving Cyprus, they were finally approaching his hometown.

Tarek was beside himself with excitement as he gazed wide-eyed out the airplane window. "New York City." His voice was breathless with wonder.

"He has only just recovered from the luxury of this airplane," Maja said. "Now you are taking him to a place that he thinks of as a wonderland."

Adam had just finished another lengthy phone call. "My attorney is meeting us when we land to go through the immigration formalities."

Their story was straightforward. Edith had given Adam Tarek's documents and a letter confirming that he had no living relatives. Since Adam was one of the wealthiest men in the country, his attorney couldn't see any reason why there should be any problem with his proposed adoption of a Syrian orphan, and therefore Tarek's immediate entry into the country. It would be an emergency family-based immigration.

"And you will do this for him?" Maja turned away from Tarek's enjoyment of the view to look at Adam. "You will make him your son?"

He seemed surprised at the question. "I have already begun the process."

She moved closer to him, placing a hand on his shoulder. "I have known many men who call themselves brave."

Every mortal man she had ever known had earned that title. That was why they had been at Valhalla.

"But what you are doing, Adam Lyon, is the finest thing I have ever known." Swiftly, she pressed her lips to his cheek.

A strange sensation came over her. Something sharp stung the back of her eyelids and her throat felt tight and raw. Her lip trembled and, as she blinked in surprise, water spilled from her eyes and trickled down her cheeks. She had never felt so vulnerable. When Adam looked at her in concern and she tried to explain what was happening, the only sound she could make was a muffled whimper.

"Maja, are you crying?"

"I don't know. I've never cried before." When he caught hold of her and tried to draw her into his arms, she found to her horror that the symptoms became worse. Tears poured down her face like water from a dam, and she made a noise like an injured child.

"Crying is a demonstration of sorrow or pain. I have seen warriors in the hall at Valhalla who shed tears when a comrade dies in battle or the pain of an injury is too great to bear." That was her only experience of tears. "I can't be crying now. I feel good about what you're doing for Tarek."

The plane had every luxury and convenience, and Adam reached for a tissue from the dispenser on the table and handed it to her. Placing his right arm around her shoulders, he drew her against his side. "Crying can be a response to any strong emotion, whether positive or negative. It's a way of releasing your feelings."

"But I don't have feelings." The words made her cry even more. She pressed her forehead against Adam's chest. Somehow, having him there to lean against while she was buffeted by sobs made the storm of sensation easier to bear.

Adam gripped her chin between his thumb and forefinger, tilting her face up to his. "Who told you that?"

"The Valkyries are not allowed emotions." It was what she had been told throughout her life. Moods, sentiment, passion...they were for mortals. Such mundane things were beneath the daughters and stepdaughters of Odin. Purity, duty and loyalty: They were the only things that mattered to the shield maidens.

"Bullshit." Adam didn't mince his words. "You said yourself you have the body of a mortal woman." He drew her out of earshot of Tarek. "And when I hold you in my arms, Maja, I know you have the same emotions as a human. Whoever fed you that line was trying to destroy the real you, turning you into a robot instead of a woman."

"But we were taught that feelings are destructive."

"They can be. Anger, hatred, greed, grief. They can all bring about terrible damage. But feelings can be wonderful too. Love, happiness, empathy, excitement. Feelings are dark and light." His face seemed to tell its own story about that. "You can't have the good ones without the bad.

And existing in some neutral place where you don't have either? That world would be a very dull place."

What he was saying struck a chord within her. Her world *was* a dull place. A place of drudgery and servitude. But it was all she knew...and now she no longer had even that. She had lost her place in the only life she had ever known.

Was Adam right about her? That she was able to feel, but had been conditioned to believe otherwise? It was a scary thought. After all these years, she wasn't sure she was ready to deal with this sudden revelation. Being shaken out of her certainty was not something she wanted to confront on top of everything else that was happening. And crying was definitely not an experience she wanted to repeat.

Fortunately, the tears seemed to have stopped. After using more tissues to remove the traces of wetness from her cheeks, she blew her nose—another unpleasant side effect—and gave a determined nod. She wasn't sure whether her intention was to show Adam or herself that she had recovered from her unseemly display.

Further conversation on the subject was suspended when the pilot announced that they were beginning their descent, and requested that they take their seats.

"What do you need me to do next?" Maja asked as she buckled her seat belt.

"Well, your presence would take some explaining." Adam smiled. "Getting Tarek into the country is going to take some legal haggling. But you? Not only do you have no documents, you have no identity. Not as far as the mortal realm is concerned."

I have no identity. It was true. So why should it matter? *Would* it matter if anyone other than Adam had said it?

"So I need to be invisible?"

"Yes. And you have a very important job to do." Adam jerked his chin in the direction of the plane's luxurious bedroom. "Make sure the damn dog stays quiet."

"This is your home?" Later that day, Maja's voice contained a note of awe similar to that of Tarek's as they stood together at the full-length windows and studied the view of Central Park.

The question shouldn't have required any thought. He had occupied the penthouse apartment in this prestigious building for two years. But it didn't feel like home. He clearly remembered the last time anywhere had felt like home. He had been thirteen, Danny had been three and their father had still been alive.

"This is where I live."

"Alone?" She turned full circle, surveying the luxurious space.

"Yes, alone. Well, most of the time." Aware of how that sounded, he decided the statement needed clarification. "My brother used to stay with me regularly."

Why had he done that? He had never before felt the need to discuss his private life with a woman. Why change those boundaries now? Maja may have come into his life in a bizarre way, but that didn't confer rights upon her. He had no idea where this unusual relationship was going, but it wasn't forever. How could it be? She lived in another world, and she would go back there. Adam didn't do any sort of relationship, and even if he had, that was taking long distance to extremes.

"And I'm not alone right now," he added. Maja still looked slightly stunned at she turned back to face him. "You, Tarek and Leo are here."

"But this…" She swept her arm around the room.

"It's—" he could see her struggling to find the right word "—frightening."

"Frightening?"

Adam watched her as she moved closer to the window. She was wearing the jeans, sweatshirt and sneakers they had purchased in Larnaca, and her hair was tied back in a loose ponytail. It was hardly the most alluring outfit, but he was captivated all over again by her. Every time he looked at her, he burned with desire. And something more. Something that scared and intrigued him at the same time.

When Maja turned back to face him, her eyes were troubled. "This life of yours is not going to be easy to learn. I want to help Tarek, but I have no idea how to do that. This is as strange to me as it is to him."

"He wants you here. That's what matters." I *want you here.* The thought startled him.

She nodded. "And I will keep my promise. I will be here to help him settle in his new home." Her brow furrowed. "As long as you don't mind?"

Mind? He wanted her here. If he told her that, he would make himself vulnerable. And this fascination she held for him would pass. He was sure of that.

"Maja, this is what we agreed. Now stop worrying and come and see the rest of the apartment."

"There's more?" Her face was serious, but her eyes were teasing. Maja had just made her first joke.

Tarek had overcome his initial shock and was now running in and out of the four spare bedrooms, trying to decide which he wanted. Leo, entering into the spirit of the chase, was barking wildly as he skittered at his heels.

"You can stop that." Adam spoke sternly to the dog. Leo obediently subsided into silence, flattening his ears and wagging his tail. "We have downstairs neighbors."

As Tarek and Leo disappeared into one of the rooms,

Adam turned to Maja. "I'm not fooling myself that the adjustment is going to be as easy as it looks right now. He appears to be resilient, but he's been through so much."

"I think finding friends his own age will help," Maja said. "And he was very determined not to forget his Syrian heritage."

"You're right." Adam had almost forgotten Tarek's words when they had parted from Ali in Larnaca. "I'll see if there are Arabic classes he can attend."

As he showed Maja around, he stretched his injured shoulder, grimacing at the continuing tightness of the muscles. He had a feeling it was going to take some intensive physiotherapy—and probably a lot more pain—before he had a normal range of movement in that arm.

The second floor of the apartment contained Adam's bedroom, bathroom and closet. Maja surveyed the huge bed in the center of the bedroom without comment. Only a slight blush revealed that she could have been speculating about their sleeping arrangements.

"What is your daily routine?"

Her question took his thoughts away from the pleasurable image of her in his bed. Although he wasn't happy at the interruption, Adam forced himself to think about a return to normality. He could hardly say his life was back on track, but he was here. He would have to face his responsibilities again, along with some new challenges.

And Danny was still missing. Normality would never be quite the same without him. Until he knew where his brother was, there would always be that nagging worry at the back of his mind, that need to keep sending out inquiries, to keep trying to find him.

"Work." When Maja raised an inquiring brow, he elaborated. "That's my daily routine. Dawn till late. I work."

"Do you do any other things?"

"Sometimes. But not often." He couldn't tell her the only other thing he did with any regularity. *Does that make me a workaholic sex addict?* It sounded scarily accurate.

"And now you have returned? Now you have Tarek to care for?"

"That changes things." He sat on the bed, patting the space next to him. Maja joined him. "I didn't expect to return from Syria with an adopted son." He saw her look of concern and shook his head. "Don't get me wrong. I'm not sorry we did this. But I went there to find my brother and I still intend to do that. And there is something else I have to do."

Her eyes were troubled. "You are talking about the Reaper."

"I can't keep the information I have about the Reaper to myself, Maja. People have died—are dying—because of this evil consortium. And if Tarek is right—" he drew a breath, fighting the emotions and the memories "—if Knight Valentine if behind this, then I don't just have a duty to do something, I *want* to do it."

He couldn't begin to explain what those words meant. Their father had still been alive when Knight first featured in Adam's life. A handsome, smiling figure, he was a friend to both his parents. Once Robert Lyon had died, Knight was almost permanently at his widow's side. To the outside world, he was the support grieving Belinda Lyon needed. Always attentive, always careful not to do anything that would upset her sons. *He upset me just by breathing.*

From the first moment he saw him, Adam had disliked his stepfather. He couldn't explain why, then. Later, of course, he knew. And despite Knight's smiles and reassurance, Adam knew the feeling was mutual. Now his mother was dead, and the two men rarely saw each other. The occasional party, an unavoidable meeting now and then. If he saw that cold smile once every six months it was too often for Adam.

"But you could get hurt." Maja reached for his hand, lifting it to her cheek. The more time they spent together, the more he was noticing these small gestures of affection from her. It was fine with him. "What will I... What will Tarek do then?"

"I'm a survivor."

A grim smile twisted his lips. How many times had he said that to Danny? *"I'm a survivor."*

And Danny would reply the same way every time: *"I'm a thriver. We have more fun."*

"You are going to see him." Maja had a knack for stating his next move.

"I have to." Not by choice. Adam would never willingly look into Knight Valentine's eyes. Blank and dark, they were the eyes of a shark. Although they seemed to look right through him, Adam knew the truth. Those eyes viewed the whole world as prey. "Oh, don't worry. I won't tell him about Tarek. But I want to see if I can shake him up."

Adam almost laughed at his own foolishness. Nothing rattled Knight Valentine. He was the one who did the shaking. Known for his dirty dealing and dodgy connections, he had managed to claw his way to the top by kicking everyone else out of his way. He had billions. Now it looked like he wanted to rule the world.

Maja nodded decisively. "In that case, you are not going alone."

Adam regarded her in surprise. "I thought you were in enough trouble. What would Odin say?"

"Odin can add this to the list of my crimes." She smiled, and he decided he liked this new, mischievous side that was emerging. "If he can find me."

Nothing was going to stop Tarek from seeing the sights on his first evening in the most famous city in the world. Adam was surprised to find himself enjoying the experience of his hometown through the eyes of an eight-year-old...and a shield maiden from Valhalla.

Instead of his usual annoyance at the crowds, noise and dirt of Times Square, he relaxed and joined in with their enjoyment. Felt the thrill of the buildings looming overhead. Smelled the mingling aromas from the wares of the street vendors at the busy intersections. Listened to the sound of music in the distance. Watched cabs racing by or screeching to a halt when hailed by a customer. Looked up at the theater marquees and wondered which show would bring the brightest sparkle to Maja's eyes. Took her hand as she held Tarek's and they zigzagged between the seething crowds. Waited with the crowds for the crossing light to change. Joined in the dash to the other sidewalk as horns honked and tourists chattered.

His doctor had called at the apartment and Adam's left arm was now in a sling. Stronger painkillers had taken away that residual scream in his muscles every time he moved. Follow-up medical appointments had been organized. The fear that he would be left with permanent damage was receding.

I'm having fun.

When had he had been able to say that? Had he *ever* said it? Maybe now and then when Danny was small and he'd taken him out for the day. Just the two of them. It had been their way of escaping from the rigid formality that prevailed in their stepfather's home. Later, when Danny had lived with Adam, they'd had more opportunities to enjoy each other's company, but Adam had been building up the business. They had become missed opportunities.

So this was what happiness felt like. Who'd have known all it took was pizza, soda, a child's laughter and the thought of going home with a sexy Valkyrie on his arm? Even the prospect of a visit to Valentine Tower the following day couldn't quite take the edge off his pleasure. He was happy to sit back and watch Maja as she chatted to Tarek about the sights they had seen. The light in her blue eyes loosened something in his chest he didn't even know had been tight. The slender length of her thigh pressed against his in the restaurant booth felt like it was meant to be there. And when she shifted in her seat to talk to him, her smile tilted him off balance ever so slightly. Just the way he liked it.

Although Tarek said he was looking forward to starting school in a few days, there was a worried look in his eyes. Adam had seen that expression before. In Danny's eyes. His brother had hidden his fears from the world beneath a cheerful exterior. Only Adam knew how hard he fought to overcome his problems. There was no denying the twin issues ahead for Tarek. Not only would he be studying in his second language, he also had learning difficulties. They didn't have his records from his teachers in Syria, so they would need a diagnosis from his new school. It would feel like he had two mountains to climb every day.

"The teachers at the school I have in mind understand each student's needs and adapt their methods to focus on special education." Adam did his best to reassure him. "It's the school my brother transferred to when he was eleven, and it made a huge difference to him. Believe me, no one is going to force you to do something that is too much for you."

Tarek seemed reassured by what he was saying. They finished their meal with ice cream and planned a shopping expedition for the following day to buy more clothes.

"We bought new clothes in Larnaca," Maja pointed out. "Why do we need more?"

Adam laughed. "You must be the only woman in the world to think two pairs of jeans and two sweatshirts is enough."

She looked bemused. "It's your money."

He was about to tell her how much he was going to enjoy spending it on her when he got the strangest feeling that they were being watched. It wasn't anything he could pinpoint. Just a slight crawling sensation up his spine, making the hairs on the back of his neck prickle. When he looked around, he couldn't identify the source of his unease. The restaurant was busy, crowded mostly with families. They blended in, looking like two parents with their child. No one seemed remotely interested in their table.

Syria has gotten to you. And the thought of tomorrow's meeting is unnerving you. Get over it.

It didn't matter what he told himself, the feeling persisted. As he asked for the check and they got ready to leave, he had to resist the impulse to keep looking over his shoulder. When they got outside onto the busy sidewalk, the sensation grew stronger. It felt like invisible eyes were boring into his skull. What *was* this?

Annoyed at the way his mood had plummeted for no good reason, he hailed a cab. As he was holding the door open to allow Maja and Tarek to get in, Adam took a final look around. People. Lights. Movement. And there. Over to his left. One man, standing totally still, allowing the crowds to flow around him like a river. That guy was the source of his unease. Without knowing why, Adam knew.

He was tall and muscular, clad all in black, with a shaved head. Adam was fairly sure he hadn't seen him before, but while there was nothing threatening in his stance, the sense of menace he emanated was tangible, eating up the distance between them.

As he joined his companions in the cab, Adam slewed his body around to keep his gaze fixed on the sidewalk. The man watching him didn't move, didn't flinch. As the car pulled away, he maintained eye contact, letting Adam feel that silent gaze.

Even after Adam could no longer see him.

Chapter 9

Tarek had selected the best room. With full-length windows dominating two walls, it was far too grown-up for a child his age, with every possible luxury to distract him. Maja gently pried the TV remote control from him as she explained the need to get into a routine.

"When you start school, you will have to be rested each morning so you are ready to learn."

"When I'm at school, will you be here to look after Leo?" He looked very small as he snuggled down in the huge bed. "He'll be lonely on his own."

She knew it was his way of checking that she wasn't going away. While she didn't want to make promises she couldn't keep, she also didn't want to cause him any anxiety. When the time came for her to leave, they would deal with the best way to tell him. For now, she was here.

As much as it hurt her to think about leaving, she knew it would have to happen. It frightened her to think how much this already felt comfortable. How much she enjoyed being here with Adam and Tarek. How hard it was to think of their lives going on without her.

Against all the odds, she was enjoying being a mom to Tarek, slipping into the role naturally without even knowing how it was done. Her own mother, the goddess Freyja, was hardly a warm and caring role model. Yet somehow, Maja was finding her way and Tarek seemed to appreciate her efforts.

"Leo will be fine." She bent and kissed his cheek. "Go to sleep."

When she went back into the sitting room, Adam was standing by one of the windows. The room was lit only by the lights of the city below them and the moon. Maja felt unaccountably nervous as she approached him, as though she was meeting him for the first time. As though, without the drama and fury of Syria and their escape, without Tarek to focus on, they had nothing. They didn't know each other...

Before she could speak, Adam caught hold of her wrist with his right hand, pulling her to him. He bent his head until his lips were inches from hers. Her nervousness evaporated, and was replaced by a delicious anticipation.

"I thought you'd decided to spend the night in there."

"Tarek wanted to talk." Her heart had begun a disturbing, uneven rhythm.

"What about what I want?" He brushed his lips across hers. Soft and warm and teasing.

"What do you want, Adam?" The words came out with a gasp.

"You, Maja. All of you."

He backed her up against one of the pillars, pinning her in place with his body. There was nothing soft and teasing about the way he kissed her this time. His tongue was velvet fire invading her mouth; his hips ground hard against her, illustrating exactly what he wanted. If the pillar hadn't been there, Maja would have melted in a hopeless puddle of desire at his feet.

"I guess this means we don't have to discuss our sleeping arrangements?"

He rested his forehead on hers. "I don't plan on letting you get much sleep."

Taking her hand, he led her up the stairs to his bedroom. He flicked a switch and the room was immersed in low-level lighting.

"I'm going to need some help with the clothes. Let's start with yours."

His gaze warmed her as she removed her clothing, and Maja resisted the desire to hide herself from his gaze. The half-light showed her the appreciation in his eyes as they roamed over her body. That look was as powerful as a touch. By the time she stood naked before him, she was shivering with need.

"Maja. You are incredible." There was a new note in his voice. Hoarse and demanding, it conjured up images that made her want to get on her knees and beg. "Now my clothes."

He was so virile and commanding. So masculine. It was this that appealed to her, made her feel so alive with longing. The knowledge that she could touch and stroke this big, beautiful male body made her shiver with pleasure.

He had already removed his shoes and socks. Standing on tiptoe, she undid the sling, which was fastened at the back of his neck, and placed it to one side. With fingers that weren't quite steady, Maja undid the buttons on his shirt and pushed it down his right shoulder.

Her fingers skimmed the hard muscle of his abdomen

as she reached for his belt buckle, and he sucked in a breath. She liked the idea that her touch provoked such an extreme reaction from him. He affected her so profoundly, it felt good to have proof that the feelings were mutual. There were other clues. Each time he kissed her, she could feel his heartbeat. Now, as she unbuckled his belt and reached lower, she could feel his erection straining against his zipper.

When his pants fell to the floor, Adam kicked them aside. Maja's eyes widened as he moved toward her, walking her backward until her knees hit the bed. For an instant, as she sank into a sitting position, her eyes were level with his cock and she experienced a powerful desire. She wanted to taste him. Before she could do anything about it, Adam was beside her, drawing her down next to him. His lips found hers and she was lost in him.

She tingled with desire… Every part of her actually burned. He was seducing her with his touch and she loved every wicked caress. She wanted all the things she had been brought up to believe were wrong. Welcomed them along with the intimate pleasure of his fingertips on her flesh.

"This protection you talked about…?"

"Taken care of."

Moving his hand between her legs, he found the exact spot that craved his touch, and Maja's whole body combusted. She writhed against him, returning his kisses frantically as he rubbed her sensitized nub exactly the way she needed. Helplessly, she spread her legs wider and rocked her pelvis against his hand, straining to get nearer to him. To close every gap, so there was nothing between them, not even air. Every stroke of his fingers, every tiny movement, the friction against her slippery flesh, was exquisite torture. His lips against her mouth, the rich texture of his tongue, the longed-for, forbidden taste of him. *This is what my body was made for. I was made for Adam.*

His mouth moved lower, finding her nipple, tugging on the hardened tip. Maja cried out. It was too much. Not enough. She needed more. But more would drive away the last remnants of her sanity. Her body started to tremble and she threw her head back.

"Please…"

"Please what?" Adam's eyes were hooded, a wicked gleam in their depths as he watched her face. "Tell me what you want, Maja."

"More." She licked her lips, her head thrashing from side to side. "I want you…"

"And you'll get me. Every part of me. But not yet." His teeth shone white as he smiled. "I told you we were going to do better than nice this time."

Ignoring her little cry of frustration, he moved lower, burying his face between her legs. Maja squirmed as he licked her from her entrance to her clit, sucking hard before going back to penetrate her with his tongue. Her back arched off the bed. Need powered through her like a firestorm scorching her flesh. Her whole body thrummed, her breathing came in ragged bursts and her heart pounded in time with the rhythm of Adam's demands.

She took her weight on her elbows, wanting to see him, watching his dark head as he devoured her. Adam locked his eyes on hers, his intense stare searing soul-deep into her.

Although Adam's eyes on her body could draw out desires she never knew existed, the look in them now triggered a different exchange. Maja was transfixed by the emotion in their dark depths. They told her he was hers, to do with as she wished. In that instant and beyond. It was a connection that transcended the physical bond between them, taking her feelings to new heights.

Her legs began to shake, and her eyes shuttered closed. She was hanging on to a precipice, and as Adam sucked harder, she let go. Falling into an abyss that was both terrifying and exhilarating, she tensed in response to the mindless sensations ripping through her body.

"Relax. Just let it happen." How did he know she found trust hard? Even with him, it was hard to let go of the prohibitions that had been so much a part of her life.

But this was Adam. She did trust him. She let go so completely, she thought she might pass out. Just at the point where the darkness took over, pure hot light rippled through her, tipping her over the edge of infinite pleasure. Moaning and gasping, she tumbled headlong into it as a thousand stars exploded inside her head.

Adam held her close as she trembled wildly, kissing her and stroking her hair. She heard him reaching for something before he muttered a curse.

"I'm going to need your help."

She opened her eyes, allowing the room to stop spinning. Adam was holding a small foil packet.

"This is a condom. It's the protection we need. Can you help me by opening this?"

She took the packet from him and tore it open. "Tell me what else to do."

Adam took the small rubber object from her and placed it over the head of his cock. "You need to roll it all the way down."

Maja moved her hands to replace his. "Like this?" Slowly, she guided the condom down his shaft, watching his face the whole time.

His eyelids fluttered. "Exactly like that."

When she had finished, he caught her to him with his

good arm. "Getting a condom on has never been so enjoyable."

His tongue tangled with hers, and he shifted his weight onto his right elbow as he moved over her. Spreading her legs apart, he pressed against her opening. Maja lifted her hips, urging him on.

"Yes, Adam. Now, please." Getting the condom on had fired her desire up to peak levels again and she couldn't wait any longer.

Slowly, he eased the tip of his cock into her. And it was perfect. Nothing could compare to this moment. To the swirl of sensations provoked by Adam pushing into her inch by inch, allowing her to adjust to his size.

"You feel so good around me." The words were a husky murmur against her lips when he was all the way inside her. "So hot and tight."

Maja wanted to grip his shoulders, to hold him tighter. She clasped her arms around his back, holding him as close to her as she could, wanting every inch of his skin on hers, feeling his muscles flex as he moved.

His right hand reached around her to cup her buttock, angling her hips to take every last inch of him, and she gasped at the fullness of him stretching her, of his body opening her to him. When he began to thrust, it was slow and consuming, accompanied by heady kisses. And heat, nothing but scorching heat. It radiated from them, so powerful that Maja felt she was absorbing him through her skin. He was imprinting himself into her. She could feel his passion everywhere. In the touch of his lips, the glide of his tongue, in the fingers that gripped her ass cheek, in every ridge and vein of his cock, in every beat of his heart.

She took him. Met his movements with a matching fever of her own, her body revealing the emotions she had believed she couldn't feel. There was no hiding place. No pretense. She gave him everything. *All of you.* That was what he had said he wanted. And Maja didn't hold back.

From a life of near sensory deprivation, she was flung into a world of color and light, taste and scent, touch and texture. And Adam was at its center, the intimacy between them the source of this swooping emotional high. So many feelings were crowding in on her at once, it was overwhelming. She didn't know their names, but she guessed there was joy alongside the passion. And a sense of wonder that something so incredible could happen to her body. That Adam could make her feel this way and she could give him pleasure in return. And it was perfect...

"Please." She was coming apart, her hands clawing at his lower back, her hips lifting in time with his thrusts. Arching. Panting. Moaning. "More."

In response, he began to thrust harder and faster. Maja's back arched off the bed in a frenzy of pleasure as she matched his rhythm, grinding her pelvis against his. Deeper. Rougher. Frenzied and frantic, she could feel Adam losing control in the same instant that she began to climax.

"Maja." Her name was a hoarse groan on his lips as, shaking, he kissed her passionately.

That kiss heightened the sensations in Maja's body. She was conscious of her muscles tightening and releasing around his cock. Her whole body was stretched taut, while her mind was empty of everything except *this*. There was a building of pressure, of her nerve endings vibrating wildly, the feeling moving out from her core to her lower belly and her thighs. Spreading fast, like wildfire, setting her whole body alight, holding it in a grip of rapture so tight and fierce that even breathing was painful.

Nothing could compare to this feeling. Maja almost laughed when she thought back to the person she had been before she had her first orgasm. Back then, she'd have listed life's most amazing physical experiences as a hot bath after braving the snows of Asgard, an intense workout or slipping between fresh, clean sheets. This? It was pure pleasure fizzing through her bloodstream, totally connecting with every part of herself.

Even when the initial storm had subsided, she was left trembling in its wake, forcing herself to remember to breathe. Her head was still spinning, her body tense, her limbs heavy. She became aware of her curled toes, her fingers digging deep into Adam's flesh, her heart hammering in an attempt to restore its normal beat.

Her internal muscles were still shuddering, giving fluttering echoes of the powerful surges of moments earlier. Like the aftershocks that followed a violent earthquake. She could feel Adam's cock jerking in time with the movements, and she squirmed with pleasure.

Adam kissed her again, softer this time. Easing out of her, he moved to one side.

"Tell me that was better than nice."

"It was wonderful." If she searched forever, she wouldn't find the words to describe how perfect it had been.

He went to the bathroom and she guessed he was disposing of the condom. When he returned, he drew her to him, holding her tightly against his chest. Maja pressed even closer, loving the feel of his skin on hers. Slowly, he kissed her lips, then down to her neck, before returning to her mouth again.

"Get some sleep. We have an important meeting tomorrow."

Maja slowly lifted her head to look into his face. Rolling onto his side, Adam threw his leg over her thigh to pin her to the bed, as though keeping her where he wanted her. It felt right. Maja's chest fluttered with something that was more than desire. The connection between them went so much deeper than that. It felt like he was in her heart and mind as well as her body. She couldn't wish him away and she didn't want to. Whatever happened in the coming days and weeks, she would be content with this. She had made a promise to Tarek, but it went deeper. She would be here when Adam needed her.

Adam watched Maja as she slept. He had switched off the light, but the drapes were open, allowing the moonlight to highlight her face. In a way, things had been easier when he thought she was a fantasy. Now he could touch her, talk to her, hold her in his arms and have mindblowing sex with her. But she would never be part of his life. Some crazy quirk of fate had brought her to him at just the right moment. He had jokingly asked her if she might be his guardian angel instead of a Valkyrie, and in typical Maja style, she had started to lecture him about how the cosmos didn't work that way.

Maja might as well have been a protecting spirit. She had appeared in his life when he was at the point of death, and had watched over him ever since, hauling him out of one dangerous situation after another. And her genuine care for Tarek shone through everything else, demonstrating that she wasn't the unfeeling warrior she liked to portray herself as. She also happened to be the most perfect woman he had ever met. Setting aside her looks, she was smart, compassionate and—even though she appeared not to know it—she had a killer sense of humor.

Just my luck. I find there might actually be a woman of my dreams. The catch is, she comes from another world.

They had so many other things going on that maybe they should have resisted this incredible attraction between them. Adam almost laughed out loud. He may as well try to resist the impulse to keep breathing. It would be easy to say Maja was an addiction. She was more. She was a need. While she was here with him, he had to have her. He had experienced intense cravings in his business life: the need to complete a takeover, to see an acquisition through, to beat a competitor. Those things faded into insignificance beside his hunger for Maja.

But the issues facing them were enormous and growing. They might have escaped the immediate dangers of Syria, but that didn't mean they were safe. They kept a huge secret. If Tarek was right about what he had overheard, then the task ahead of them was enormous. Knight Valentine was one of the most well-known men on the planet. Though he was not universally liked, he was well-respected. He was a business leader, charitable donor, friend to presidents and princes, a man whose clever, sharp-featured face had dominated the world's media for three decades.

If Adam took his story to the press, the first question— after the reporter he approached got up off the floor and stopped laughing at the absurdity of the story—would be "why?" Why would Knight Valentine, the man who had everything, risk it all to become the brains behind the Reapers?

Only Adam, and possibly Danny, could answer that question. Only someone who had lived with Knight, and seen that the man had no soul, could truly understand what he was capable of.

Going to the press with the Reaper story wasn't their only option, of course. Adam didn't expect great things from his meeting in the morning. Knight wasn't going to crumble, confess all, express remorse and give himself up. The best Adam could hope for was to look Knight in the eye and see his suspicions confirmed, or try and get evidence that he was the Reaper. The trick would be to do that without giving Knight any clue as to what he was doing. Adam had no problem about placing himself in the firing line of his stepfather's rage, but he had Tarek to think of now. And Maja, of course...but somehow he sensed his feisty Valkyrie might enjoy using her skills against the man who had chosen to use terrorism as a means of making money.

How did that work? It was such a cynical concept, Adam found it hard to grasp the thinking behind it. Last night, while Maja had been settling Tarek into his new room, he had found that article on his laptop, the one he suspected could have been written by Tarek's father, and reread it. The author of the article explained his or her beliefs in simple terms. The Reaper's targets were not random. There had been a map illustrating the point. Although the human toll was high—loss of life and injury were devastating features of a Reaper attack—the strikes took place inside high-profile office buildings, shopping malls, hotels and restaurants. Each time, the targeted organization suffered crippling aftereffects. Knight's businesses had never been attacked, but the writer didn't mention that, and it wasn't conclusive proof of his guilt. The article argued that rival organizations would benefit hugely from such a situation. Adam recalled the outcry that had followed the publication of the article. It had been denounced as the worst kind of alarmist journalism. What kind of monster would set out to profit from global terror?

Adam conjured up an image of his stepfather's face and knew exactly what kind. He knew exactly how evil his stepfather could be.

His thoughts moved on to another aspect of the problems facing them. When he'd told them about his father's conversation, Tarek had mention another name. He'd said his father was speaking to a man called Shepherd. That was an interesting snippet of information that Adam needed to explore. If Shepherd was the high profile person Adam suspected he might be, they would have to tread carefully, particularly as Tarek's father had been killed the day after that call.

But the Reaper was not their only problem. The man watching them last night had not been a figment of Adam's imagination. He had no idea who the figure was, but he had been very real and very menacing. Could they have been followed from Syria? Could the Reaper already know Tarek was here in New York? Or did their mystery watcher have something to do with Maja? Had Odin sent him to let her know he was coming for his rebel Valkyrie? There was always the possibility that he could have been paparazzi. Adam was well-known. A picture of him with a mystery woman and kid would be worth something. Although Adam hadn't seen any sign of a camera, it was a possibility. The least worrying one. Because the guy had looked like trouble. More trouble.

For Adam personally, there was also the issue that he'd returned from Syria without finding Danny. The feelings of guilt and despair that had driven him to go to such desperate measures to find his brother hadn't gone away. If anything, having been to Syria and seen the suffering there for himself, they had intensified. The problem was his inquiries had reached a dead end. He had no idea where to go next. The only person he could think of to ask for help was Edith Blair. Although she hadn't recognized Danny's picture, she might be able to ask some questions among her network in Syria. Adam was intending to send some money to the mission, so he needed to speak to her, anyway.

Also on the list of problems facing them was the question that had been gnawing at the back of his mind since he had realized Maja wasn't a figment of his imagination. They had spoken of it only once, but there was still the lingering unprotected-sex issue hanging over them. What if she *was* pregnant? It was all very well to keep telling himself she would be gone soon. But what if that meant she would be leaving and taking their child with her? It wasn't like she would be moving to another town, another state or even another country. Maja belonged to another *world*. One that didn't allow visitation rights.

It was all very well to tell himself he would worry about this if and when it happened. His mind persisted in returning to the issue. And he had a worrying feeling about why that was. It would be a link between them, a deeper connection.

It would be a complication. An insurmountable one. Another *one*.

For some reason, every time Adam told himself that, his imagination veered off at a tangent, picturing their child. His and Maja's. A family of four. Five, if you included Leo. Six, if, as hoped, Danny returned... And what the hell was wrong with him?

Not only was he attracted to a Valkyrie, but now he was picturing a future with her? Because that could happen? Ever since he had met Maja, he had been unable to think straight where she was concerned. He had to sort that problem out fast, because he needed a clear head for the challenges ahead.

And right now, he needed to stop staring at her like a lovesick schoolboy and get some sleep. With that determined thought, Adam drew her into the crook of his good arm, settled her delicious weight close against his body and closed his eyes.

Chapter 10

Although Maja had initially been wary about the arrangement, they left Tarek in the care of Adam's housekeeper, a pleasant young woman named Sophie.

"He has so many new things going on in his life. Another new person may not be a good thing."

Sophie arrived as they were eating breakfast, and Leo greeted her with a volley of warning barks. This was his new home and she was an intruder. Clearly, he felt she should be evicted immediately.

Sophie knelt and, unfazed by the noisy welcome, stroked Leo's head. "Oh, isn't he sweet? I didn't know you were getting a dog, Mr. Lyon."

The brave guard dog instantly rolled over and invited her to tickle his belly. When she obliged, Leo became her devoted servant. Since she also turned out to be a fan of gaming, it wasn't long before she had captured Tarek's heart, as well.

"I think we can leave him without worrying to much about his well-being, don't you?" Adam had quirked a brow in Maja's direction.

Although this meeting was so important, she was having a hard time gathering her thoughts. Her mind insisted on returning to the events of the previous night. How could it be possible that sex with Adam kept getting better? That first time he had captured her body in a magical spell, but since then he had woven an enchantment that released new emotions, feelings she hadn't known existed. She was becoming more and more enraptured with him, the invisible threads that bound her to him growing stronger by the minute. Which meant that, when the time came, they would be harder to break.

Her only interactions with mortals had been on the battlefield, so she didn't know if this was normal. Some of the movies she watched with Tarek showed kissing and mild love scenes, but they didn't explain what the characters were feeling. It was frustrating not to know if she was the only person to ever feel this way. And to not know *what* she was feeling.

She was intensely aware of her every action in relation to his. Although she was comfortable around Adam now, that mindfulness extended to an appreciation of her body in relation to his. Of how he stood when he was close to her, his shoulder just brushing hers, his right hand occasionally touching her forearm.

While Adam treated such innocent interactions casually, Maja couldn't. She watched him in fascination, her eyes following the movements of his hands. Was she forever condemned to a state of aching arousal at the thought of those hands? Her lips felt bruised and swollen when she looked at his heartbreakingly sensual mouth. The memory of those lips anointing her skin, the scratch of his stubble on her tender flesh, his tongue tracing its determined, downward pathway made her quiver. Her nipples tightened painfully whenever she thought of that tongue probing the secret recesses of her flesh.

Now and then, when he spoke, she didn't hear the words he said because she was so lost in the erotic memory of his touch. And when that happened, Adam would give her a wicked smile to let her know he knew exactly where her thoughts were going.

Right now, she forced her thoughts in the direction of the coming meeting with Knight Valentine.

"Visible, or not?" she asked as they descended from the penthouse in Adam's private elevator.

"No matter how many times you ask me that question, I'm never going to tire of hearing it." He gave it some thought. "I think invisible will be a good way to do this. That way you can get a good look at Knight without having to interact with him. You can tell me what you really think of him after the meeting."

"Does he know you're coming?" They stepped out into the expensive marble lobby.

"No, I thought it would be a nice surprise if I just turned up."

Maja was getting better at interpreting Adam's moods. She knew this was one of those occasions when he meant the opposite of what he said. What was the human word for it? *"Sarcasm."*

Adam glanced down at her in surprise. "Pardon?"

"That was what you just did, wasn't it? You used sarcasm. You don't really think it will be a nice surprise for Knight if you turn up unannounced."

"You are getting better at this, Maja." He smiled at her as he held the door open so she could pass through. "We'll make a mortal of you yet."

The words jolted her, but she wasn't sure why. It was the fault of these strange new feelings. This one was like a tight little wire being twisted inside her chest. She wondered if it might be sorrow. But it would be foolish to feel regret that she couldn't be mortal. It would be mourning the loss of something she knew she could never have. Like a mortal wishing for a million dollars and then crying when it didn't materialize. Why would she waste her time on that? Surely she had enough problems?

They took a cab to the soaring black-windowed edifice called Valentine Tower. When they stepped out onto the busy sidewalk, Maja used the cloak of the crowds to use her powers and become invisible, although she remained at Adam's side. As she followed him through the revolving doors into a magnificent lobby, she became aware of a figure on the periphery of her vision. They were being followed.

She turned to look at the man who had walked into the building at the same time as them. Dressed all in black, he was tall and muscular. His shaved head gleamed in the overhead lights of the foyer. He made no move toward Adam, and she didn't know why she had gained the impression that he was following them. Except...

As she looked at him, he stared directly back at her and grinned.

He can see me!

As soon as the thought hit her, the man ducked his head, as if in acknowledgment of its truth, before walking away. It seemed his only reason for entering the building had been to let her know he was tailing them. Since Adam was already striding toward the reception desk, Maja had no time to do anything about the encounter except store it away to be dealt with later.

"Please let Knight Valentine know Adam Lyon is here to see him."

The polished young woman behind the counter gave him a smile that reminded Maja of a cat eyeing a bowl of cream. Maja got the impression she knew exactly who Adam was, even though he had said this was his first visit to Valentine Tower. Another new emotion assailed her. One that made her want to materialize and tell the woman to stop looking at Adam that way.

"Is Mr. Valentine expecting you?"

"No, but I'm sure he'll see me." Adam's smile provoked an even more annoying response, both from the woman and deep within Maja's chest. It was uncomfortable and she didn't like it. Adam had a devastating smile. How could she, who felt it rock her to the depths of her soul, blame anyone for being affected by it? Could this new feeling be *jealousy*? She must be wrong. Jealousy implied she had a claim on Adam, a right to this feeling of annoyance. She sighed. Life had been so much simpler before feelings.

"I'll call his secretary and see if he's available."

While Adam waited, Maja looked around the lobby. It had been designed to impress. The color scheme was black and silver, with concentric circles on the floor and walls. Three huge chandeliers of silver teardrops were suspended from the ceiling and one wall was a bank of screens, each showing a film highlighting the achievements of the Valentine Organization. Hotels, luxury apartment blocks, office buildings, leisure complexes, and sports arenas flashed onto the screen. Knight Valentine liked to advertise his successes to the world.

"Mr. Valentine will see you. Please take the elevator to the twenty-seventh floor. His secretary will meet you there."

Maja joined Adam in the elevator. Until now, she had never stopped to consider the mechanics of her invisibility. Once she had assumed her cover of concealment, she could interact with mortals if she chose. If she tried to touch Adam, he would be able to feel her. If she spoke, he would hear her voice. Since there were other people in the elevator, she decided against doing either of those things.

Odin had granted the Valkyries invisibility along with their great strength. It was a useful skill. It enabled the Valkyries to move around the mortal realm in search of the warrior souls they needed. On this occasion, it would allow Maja to observe the man Adam suspected of being responsible for these evil crimes.

Maja followed close behind as Knight's secretary escorted Adam down a long, featureless corridor and knocked before showing him into a large office. The man seated at the desk had been contemplating the view, but he swiveled his chair when Adam entered, turning to face his visitor.

As he smiled, Maja, entering the room just behind Adam, recoiled in shock. She had never felt such undiluted evil. It was coming off him in thick, oily waves.

Knight was of average height and slim build. His slicked back hair was dark and graying at the temples. Maja supposed his sharp, clever features were handsome, but she barely noticed them. Not when her attention was drawn to his eyes. Black as midnight, they seemed to draw every speck of light from the room into their depths. There was something very wrong about those eyes.

"It's been a long time." Knight gestured for Adam to take a seat on the opposite side of the desk.

Although Adam complied, Maja wanted to grab his arm and propel him away from this man. To yell at him to run away. The sense of malice in this room was so overwhelming, it made her feel nauseous. She was a Valkyrie; how could he, a mere mortal, stand it?

"Never long enough for me, Knight." Although the words were hostile, Adam's smile was pleasant. Yet she knew there was a world of painful memories behind his expression.

Maja searched her knowledge of the many beings who dwelled in Otherworld, wondering if Knight Valentine might not be mortal. Was he a demon determined to destroy mankind? A rogue vampire breaking free of the restraints of his leader? A phantom, lingering after his death to settle an old score? But no, he was a man. She was certain of it. Although he was human, he was more than that. Just as Maja herself had the body of a woman and superpowers, Knight, too, had something extra. She didn't know what it was, but she knew it was bad.

Knight displayed no anger at Adam's words. He had a curiously flat way of speaking, with very little rise and fall to his speech. It should have made him dull to listen to. Instead, because Maja sensed so much darkness in him, she wanted to hear every word. "And yet you are here. Why is that?"

"I've just returned from Syria." Adam indicated his sling. "Had myself quite an adventure. I was shot by some of the Reaper's men."

Maja could see Adam watching Knight closely, looking for a reaction. There was none. "If that is the result of an encounter with the Reaper, you were lucky to get out alive. Why did you go there?"

"I was looking for Danny. He's gone missing out there," Adam said. "That's why I'm here. I was hoping you could use your contacts in Syria to help me find him."

Maja thought she saw something then. Like a ripple on the surface of a pond, just the faintest flicker disturbed

Knight's practiced smile. It settled back into place almost immediately. "What makes you think I have contacts in Syria?"

"Don't you?" Adam fired the words back at him like a gunshot.

Knight laughed. It wasn't a pleasant sound. It sounded like someone had once described laughter to him and, never having heard it, he'd tried it out a few times while alone. Rough and crackly, it had a hoarse note to it that set her teeth on edge.

"I have contacts all over the world. Email me the details of where and when he went missing and I'll see what I can do."

Maja was growing tired of this. Knight wasn't going to give anything away, but she wanted to see that composure crack. Just a little. Adam had brought her along to observe, and she had done that. She had formed an opinion. This man was capable of any evil.

Now she stepped behind Knight and very gently blew in his ear.

Adam could feel all the old antagonism and frustration bubbling up inside him as he faced Knight across the shiny expanse of the other man's empty desk. Why had he ever thought this would work? He had been thirteen when his mother married Knight and he had never managed to get the better of his stepfather in an argument. Knight didn't do argument. Didn't do emotion. He just did *this*. Sat there calmly and didn't engage.

When Knight married his mother, he had systematically ruined Adam's life. The man sitting opposite him now was a sadist who had thought nothing of torturing a thirteen-year-old boy.

We both know it, yet you think you can look me in the eye and pretend it never happened.

There had been that brief glimmer when Adam had mentioned Knight's contacts in Syria. Like a snake's forked tongue flickering out, it had vanished as quickly as it had appeared. For the first time ever, Adam felt he had gotten to Knight. He had touched a nerve. But the other man had recovered now, and Adam didn't know how to press his advantage.

Because you don't have an advantage. This is Knight Valentine. He always has the upper hand.

Having asked Adam to email him the details of Danny's disappearance, Knight seemed to be signaling that the meeting was at an end. Until he momentarily closed his eyes and shivered.

Adam stared at him in surprise. It was the first time he had ever seen that facade slip. Okay, he hadn't been up close to Knight in the seven years since his mother's death. Maybe the man had developed a tic...

Just as Knight appeared to regain his composure, he suddenly raised a hand to his cheek, his eyes widening.

"Is everything okay?" Adam asked, the realization of what was going on beginning to dawn on him. He suspected Maja may have just caressed Knight's cheek.

"Yes." Although Knight answered with his usual composure, he turned his head as though searching out an unseen presence.

"We were discussing your contacts in Syria." Adam decided to try and push a little further while Knight was distracted. "The ones who work for the Reaper."

"I never said..." Adam had never heard Knight break off in the middle of a sentence. Never seen him get hastily to his feet. Certainly, never known him to raise a hand

and ruffle his carefully styled hair. "I don't know what is going on here, but I think it's time you left."

Never known him to lose his cool.

Adam took his time. "I'd like to say it's been nice, but it never is."

"You'd better start running and finding yourself somewhere to hide, because you have no idea what you're up against." And there it was. For the first time, he saw it all. The full extent of the venom in Knight's soul was on display. It almost sent Adam reeling backward.

Adam was about to turn away without speaking when Knight's empty chair went scooting across the room. It was like a scene from a horror movie, but Adam knew that no poltergeist was responsible for that sudden movement. As Knight turned to look at the chair, his huge desk flipped over onto its side. Seconds later, each piece of priceless artwork was lifted from its place on the wall before being dropped on the floor. Filing cabinets flew open, spewing their contents into the air.

Knight made a move toward Adam as though recognizing that this mayhem was linked to him. "Make it stop."

His lips drew back in a snarl and Adam decided he almost preferred this side of him. At least there was no longer any pretense. All those years of suspecting that a malevolent spirit lurked beneath his stepfather's cool exterior. Now he knew he had been right. What he had never been able to understand was why his beautiful, sensitive mother had married this man. Belinda Lyon was not the sort of woman who would have married Knight for his money, so what had the attraction been? No matter how much Adam wondered about the reason behind their marriage, he supposed he would never discover the truth.

Knight took a threatening step toward Adam. As he did, he was lifted off his feet and held suspended an inch or two above the floor. As he clawed wildly at the invisible hand around his throat, his face darkened until it was almost purple. Mewling sounds issued from his throat and spittle formed on his lips.

"Maybe you're the one who doesn't know what he's up against." With a final look into those dead eyes, Adam walked out.

He heard the thud of Knight dropping to the floor and the sound of the door closing behind Maja. He half expected to hear Knight coming after him, or to encounter security on his way out, but he reached the elevator unchecked. When he stepped inside, he leaned against the mirrored wall and exhaled.

"Are you here, Maja?"

"Yes." Her voice was hesitant. "Did I do the wrong thing? He made me so angry... I've never felt like that before, and I reacted without thinking."

Adam gave it some thought. It wasn't the way he'd planned for the meeting to go, but it had worked in his favor. Maja had jolted Knight out of his usual composure. Although Adam had been under no illusion about the man he had come to confront, now all his suspicions were confirmed.

"No, it wasn't the wrong thing." He smiled. "I'd love to be a fly on the wall in that office right now. Does he think I did all of that through mind control? Or perhaps he thinks there is a rogue spirit following me around?" He felt an unfamiliar tightening in his throat. "Maybe he thought it was my mother come back to haunt him for the way he treated her when she was alive?"

He felt Maja's hand on his arm. Even though she wasn't visible, her touch soothed him and he felt some of the tension ease out of his muscles. As he exited the elevator, he glanced around the lobby. There was nothing unusual. Knight had clearly decided not to pursue this…yet.

Maja waited until they were a block away from Valentine Tower, and in the midst of a fast-flowing crowd, before materializing. She linked her arm through the crook of Adam's right elbow. "You were right about him. That man is toxic."

"He meant what he said about running and hiding. He will come after me," Adam said. "And that means Tarek is in danger. Knight is not the sort of guy to let the presence of a child stop him."

"We made a promise to Tarek that we would look after him. And that's what we'll do."

Glancing down at her, he saw the steely determination on Maja's face. Adam might not have much respect for the great god Odin, but he was thankful to him every time he saw that look on his daughter's face.

"Instead of sitting back and waiting for Knight to come to us, we have to find solid proof that he is behind the Reaper consortium. At present, we are working on a hunch and the circumstantial evidence of what Tarek overheard. If Knight is running this as a company, he isn't alone. As hard as it is to believe, he must have persuaded other people to join him in this sick venture. I have to figure out a way to get the names of his associates."

"Where would he keep that information?" Maja turned back to look at the still dominant outline of Valentine Tower. "Getting back into his office will be difficult for you, but I could do it."

"It won't be there. I know exactly where Knight keeps his valuables and his secrets, and it's not in his office." Adam felt a cold feeling of dread track its way down his spine. The day his mother had died, he had walked out of his stepfather's home and sworn he would never return.

It looked like he was going to have to overturn that vow and walk back into Knight's Greenwich, Connecticut, mansion. Without an invitation.

Looking back at Maja, he felt his resolve harden as if a transfer of strength took place as they walked along that busy sidewalk. Adam knew his own strengths. He was a fighter. His determination and skill in business were legendary. Adam built up the Lyon brand by targeting failing businesses. Instead of closing them down, he brought them under his wing and made them thrive. His specialty was finding consumer discontent and turning that business into a success story. His loyalty to a cause was unswerving and his commitment to his employees and their rights won him accolades. But he was aware of his one weak point. Because it was also his greatest fear. Like the monster that lurked in the closet, Knight Valentine had assumed a larger-than-life persona in Adam's mind. The man who had dominated his teenage years had occupied a dark corner of his mind throughout his adult life.

Now, for the sake of the world, as well as his own sanity, he had to face him and defeat him. Looking into the endless blue of Maja's eyes, he felt he could do it. Today he had spoken to Knight without crumbling. That had been the first step. Now he was ready to destroy him…as long as he had Maja at his side.

Chapter 11

Over the following days and weeks, life settled into a routine. Tarek started school and Maja took him there each morning, collecting him at the end of the day when classes finished. It became their time. Although his anxiety at the change in his life occasionally showed through, his spirits remained high and he chatted about his teachers and his new friends. Maja worried about his reluctance to talk about his father, but Adam reasoned that it was still early. Having lost a parent at a young age, although in less dramatic circumstances, he sympathized with Tarek's silence.

"But I agree. It would do him good to open up about it." Maja wasn't sure if that was an admission. Did he wish he had opened up to someone about his own father's death? It was another reminder, if she needed one, that she knew very little about Adam. "If after he has settled into his new home and his new school you are still concerned, we can seek professional help."

Maja, having been thrust into an unexpected maternal role, found herself enjoying it. The responsibilities were huge, but so were the rewards. Having someone depend on her so completely was a new experience. Tarek had been through so much and she was determined to get this right for his sake. It wasn't easy. Not when he could fire a dozen questions at her, one after the other, without giving her time to think about the answers. Or when he could neatly trip her up with her own words. She quickly got used to dealing with the phrase "But you said..."

But she was falling in love with this little boy and this new life, and, when she stopped to examine the depth of her feelings, it frightened her. Despite his doctor's advice to the contrary, Adam returned to work almost immediately. It was a circumstance that left Maja feeling curiously bereft. Determined not to acknowledge, even to herself, how much she missed his company during the day, she decided to discover more of the mortal realm while he and Tarek were absent. Exploring the city on foot, she discovered a wealth of new experiences. And with each one, she fell a little more in love with this new world. A world that wasn't hers to love.

Shopping for clothes and other comforts she hadn't known existed became a daily delight. Department stores, coffee shops, food markets and outlets had her head spinning with the variety of wares on offer. She was conscious of the need to do something with her time. She had a new family and she wanted to care for them.

"I will cook tonight," she told Adam as he left for work on his second day back in the office.

He regarded her with a slightly wary expression. "You don't have to do that. We can eat out, or order in."

"I am a Valkyrie. One of my duties was to feed Odin's warriors."

"I guess you didn't do that on pizza or burgers?" he asked, referring to their recent diet of takeout food.

"No." She allowed her dignified facade to slip a little and gave him a teasing smile. "Although I am not sure if I will be able to get beached whale here in New York City."

He shuddered. "If you serve me beached whale…"

She laughed. "Go to your office, Mr. Lyon. Let me take care of your well-being."

He stared down at her for a moment, his expression becoming intent. She wondered what she had said to cause that look. It was as though he was seeing her for the first time, and his feelings were a revelation to him. It lasted only a second or two before he quickly brought the shutters down.

Maja had a feeling that traditional Viking fare would probably be okay with Adam, but it might not be popular with Tarek, who was rapidly developing a taste for fast food. She shrugged. He would soon learn to eat the hearty foods she intended to cook. Adam had given her a credit card, but she was still wary of it. Those machines asked too many questions that she couldn't answer. Instead, she snatched up a handful of the cash he had left her and stuffed it into her purse.

Leo pranced around her, begging to accompany her, but Maja had already learned the hard way that dogs were not welcome in food stores. Her only attempt to take him into one had resulted in a humiliating eviction for both her and Leo. Besides, Leo had already accompanied her on her morning walk to take Tarek to school, and he would go with her when she picked him up later.

"Your friend Sophie will be here soon." The little dog subsided into a pitiful heap.

When she reached the street, she headed in the direction of a farmer's market she had seen on one of her recent walks. She hadn't gone very far when a nagging sensation made her turn her head. The sidewalk was busy and, unsure what she was looking for, she scanned the faces of the people behind her. There was nothing that seemed out of place. But since she didn't *know* what she was looking for, that didn't chase away the feeling that something was wrong.

Shrugging her concerns away, she continued walking. What would Odin say if he knew one of his daughters could be so easily spooked? That after all her years of warrior training, she was paranoid enough to believe someone was right behind her? The Allfather was not a benevolent being. His response would not be kindly and reassuring.

He would have me whipped for my foolishness, and rightly so. I would be chastised for being not only the "rebellious one" but also the "imaginative one."

Yet the impression that she was being followed persisted, a sensation so real that she could sense eyes probing the back of her head, could even feel unwanted, unfamiliar breath touching her neck. It grew stronger with every step, piling on the tension until she wanted to scream. Not from fear. She was a Valkyrie and they didn't do cowardice. No, she wanted to cry out in rage and frustration.

If this was in her head, she wanted to get it out of there. If this was what having an imagination was like, she didn't want it. And if it wasn't all in her head, she wanted this unknown entity to fight fair, to show itself so she could deal with it her way. Lurking in shadows, blending into the crowd, stalking her... This way, there was nothing for her to fight. And fighting was what Maja did best.

"Scared yet, little Valkyrie?" The voice was close. Almost a whisper in her ear.

This time when she turned, she encountered the amused gaze of the man who had followed Adam into the lobby of Valentine Tower. He matched his strides to hers, walking alongside her as though they were together.

"No." She halted in her tracks, causing an obstruction to the people around her. *But you should be scared. You should be terrified.* She could kill him with an elbow to his throat or ribs, but she didn't think Adam would want her to draw attention to herself in that way.

Anyway, she wanted to know who this man was. How did he know she was a Valkyrie? And how had he been able to see her the other day when she had been invisible?

"Who are you?"

He grinned. "I work for your father."

That was what she had feared. Odin never ventured into the mortal world himself, but he sent his servants—the Valkyries and his warriors—into this realm to do his bidding.

"I don't know what you mean." She decided to act dumb in order to buy a little thinking time.

"I think you do. The Allfather's youngest daughter has gone missing and there is a reward for the one who returns her to him." His eyes traveled over her body. "I have seen you many times in the palace of Gladsheim, but you never noticed me. The Valkyries are too high and mighty to look in the direction of a lesser being."

Maja let his words sink in. It seemed likely, from what he had said, that Odin remained unaware of her whereabouts. This man had recognized her and was following her in the hope of taking her back to Valhalla and claiming the reward from her father. Travel between Otherworld and the mortal realm wasn't easy, but it could be done. Access to the mortal realm could be gained through a series of portals. While some hardy adventurers used these as a means of traveling regularly between the two, most beings remained within their own worlds. Those in Otherworld had an awareness of the mortal realm, but humans remained blissfully unaware that another world existed. She didn't know why this man was here. There was a thriving interworldly black market.

"I was here on other business when I caught sight of you. A daughter of Odin, once seen, is not easily forgotten." His words confirmed her fears. She was distinctive.

Whatever circumstances had led to this encounter, if she could stop this man, she could stay here. Her only problem now was whether to try and convince him he was wrong, silence him or to kill him. She didn't know if she could trust him, and killing him would be messy.

She raised wide eyes to his face. "I really don't know what you're talking about."

She may as well exhaust the alternatives before committing murder. Mortals seemed to have very strict rules about that sort of thing. She had watched some news programs. Killing was definitely not popular.

"Don't try that with me. You are Maja, youngest and most favored daughter of Odin, mightiest of all the gods."

"Please stop harassing me…" She continued with her helpless, bewildered act, hoping it would work. It seemed less likely with every passing minute. "I don't know who you are."

"I am one of Odin's servants." His grin turned nasty. "But why don't we put this to the test? If you're not who I say you are, why don't you cry for help? Or better still, why not call the police?"

He had her and he knew it. Maja wasn't going to risk drawing attention to herself. She tried to figure this man out. He knew who she was, yet he didn't seem to know how much danger he was in. He was quite close to her, yet apparently unaware of the full extent of her strength. She figured that meant he fulfilled a menial role in her father's palace. He would have seen the Valkyries and heard of their legendary strength, but never actually witnessed it firsthand.

It was time for him to get his own demonstration.

She weighed her options. If she struck him a blow to his temple, the bridge of his nose or his throat, he would drop like a stone in the middle of this busy street. Maja could become invisible in the same instant that she felled him, but there was a chance that someone would remember seeing her with him. It was unlikely a witness would be able to lead anyone back to Adam, but she wasn't prepared to take the risk.

If she grabbed him, became invisible and tossed him under a vehicle it would be unfair to the driver. Throwing him from one of the tall buildings posed a similar problem. She didn't know what, or who, he would hit when he landed.

Clearly unaware that she was weighing her options for the best method of killing him, he grabbed her elbow, almost earning himself a lethal knee in the groin. He might have supernatural abilities of his own, but he would be no match for a Valkyrie. "You are coming back to Valhalla with me."

She wasn't going to persuade this man that she wasn't the person he sought, couldn't persuade him to leave her alone, and certainly couldn't trust him to protect her identity. If he walked away from her now, he could go straight to Odin and tell him where she was. They were close to a park and Maja decided her best approach would be to get him there. She didn't have the time or the inclination to persuade him, so she took off at a run, trusting that he would follow her. His shout of annoyance confirmed that he was right behind her. It would have been easy for Maja to outrun him, but she slowed her pace, dodging in and out of the people on the sidewalk, allowing her pursuer to stay with her.

She was seeking somewhere quiet as she ran through the busy streets. Eventually, she came to an area she didn't recognize and turned into a narrow opening between two buildings. There were Dumpsters lining the alleyway and, seizing the opportunity while it was deserted, she swung around and faced the man, who was close behind her.

"Does Odin know the details of your business here?"

His look of surprise told her she was right in her guess. He wasn't here on any legal matter. If Odin discovered that, his retribution would be terrible.

With a growl, the man lunged toward her. Using the element of surprise, and his forward momentum, Maja jerked her fist straight out. The punch caught him fully in the face. Without pausing, Maja hoisted him onto her shoulder and tipped him into the nearest Dumpster. He was going to have a bad headache when he woke up, but at least he wouldn't be able to find her.

Breathing a little faster than usual, Maja retraced her steps. She was confident she hadn't been seen. If the man was found before he regained consciousness, he wouldn't be identified, because he didn't belong in this world. There was nothing to link him to her. Okay, his presence on her tail was a worry, because it opened up the possibility of others arriving in this realm in search of her. But she would deal with that if and when it happened. Odin thought he had offered a reward for her safe return. In reality, he had placed a price on her head.

What she didn't understand was the peculiar effect of the incident. As she walked toward the market, her limbs began to shake and nausea washed over her. Both were unusual for her. She was physically and mentally strong. She had never experienced any ill effects following a fight. Although she tried to overcome the feelings, it didn't work and the discomfort lasted until she reached home.

Still feeling shaky, she unpacked her groceries. Then, irritated at her own weakness, she lay on her bed until the feeling passed.

"Maja, that was delicious." Adam sat back, having eaten a huge portion of the chicken stew she had served with homemade flatbread.

"You sound shocked." Maja's smile was teasing as she began to clear away the plates.

He returned the smile as he shook his head. "Pleasantly surprised."

"And Tarek's reward for eating my home-cooked food is ice cream for dessert."

Tarek grinned. "And I can eat it while I watch TV?"

Maja pursed her lips. "Okay. But one hour. No more."

Tarek jumped up from the table, taking Leo with him as he ran to his room.

Adam joined Maja, gathering up serving dishes and carrying them through to the kitchen. "You hardly ate anything." She usually had a healthy appetite. And now that he looked closely at her, he realized she appeared pale.

"I wasn't hungry." He got the feeling there was something more to it. She sighed, leaning against the counter as she looked at him. "I had a problem today."

He tensed. "Was it anything to do with Knight?" If that monster had threatened her...

"No. I was followed. The same man followed us when we went to Valentine Tower. I was invisible, but he could see me. We had so much else going on and I didn't think much of it at the time, so I forgot to tell you about it."

"Was this guy dressed all in black with a shaved head?" Why hadn't he warned her about the man he'd seen in Times Square? So much had happened since then, but it was no excuse.

Maja nodded. "He was from Otherworld."

"You spoke to him? My God, Maja. When I think of the danger you could have been in—"

She held up a hand, silencing him. "I dealt with him."

Adam exhaled sharply, not knowing whether to be relieved or outraged. He supposed one of the dangers of living with a Valkyrie was coming home to the unexpected.

"You'd better tell me all of it."

"My father has offered a reward for the person who takes me back to Valhalla. This man had come to claim me. I've become some sort of prize." She wrapped her arms around her waist as though trying to warm herself. "Of course, what no one, including my father, knows is that I have committed many crimes. Once I get back to Valhalla, I will be held accountable for them."

"Maja, they will only know of these so-called crimes if you tell them. Must you do that?"

She looked astounded at his words. "Are you suggesting that I should lie?"

"Not that exactly. But only you and I know what has really happened. I'm not going to tell anyone. If you keep quiet as well, how will Odin know?"

She was silent for a moment or two. "The Valkyries are taught to always tell the truth."

Adam could see he had planted a seed, so he decided to leave it at that. "What did you do with the guy who followed you today?"

"I knocked him out and threw him in a Dumpster." She peeped up at Adam through the fan of her long lashes. "You are not angry with me?"

"At least you didn't kill him."

"I considered it, but I didn't think you'd like it."

He supposed he should be shocked at the ease with which he could hear those words. His priorities had changed. Syria had changed him. He had come away from there with a secret that would rock the world…and he was trying to figure out the best way to deal with it. He was living with a Valkyrie. Going about his daily routine made him feel like a fraud. Day-to-day business no longer interested him. In meetings, his mind was preoccupied with the details of how to expose Knight Valentine for what he was. He dreaded news of another Reaper attack, feeling the weight of responsibility behind his knowledge. And the only person who could help him was Maja.

But she was more than his partner in bringing down Knight. As much as his mind was preoccupied with thoughts of the Reaper, they were focused on her. Adam had never seen himself in a relationship, had never believed that life was for him. He didn't need anyone to tell him why that was. The memory of his beautiful, fragile mother was too painful. Her marriage to Knight had been the worst kind of nightmare and Adam had been old enough to understand what he was witnessing. Knight had broken her, systematically crushing her like a butterfly beneath his heel. Adam had been old enough to know there were secrets in their marriage, dark secrets, that had led to her decline. When she died, she had been fighting an ongoing battle against her twin addictions to drugs and alcohol, and depression had held her in its tight clutches for many years.

He had been dealing with his own problems at the hands of his stepfather. Knight, determined to crush Adam almost from the first day of his marriage to his mother, had commenced a regime of psychological and emotional abuse that still haunted him. At the age of thirteen, Adam had gone from having a loving relationship with his father to being thrust into a nightmare with a man who deliberately designed ways to torture him. If Adam had a fear, Knight would exploit it. If Adam had a favorite belonging, Knight would destroy it. If Adam wanted something, Knight would promise it and then withhold it.

In public, Knight's behavior toward Belinda, Adam's mother, was impeccable. It was only her son, watching helplessly, who could see the gradual decline in her. A decline that became dramatic for no reason that Adam could explain.

Belinda Lyon's death had been a blessed relief. Having seen what one person could do to another in a relationship, Adam was never going there himself.

Now he had been unexpectedly thrust into a ready-made family. His pristine apartment had been invaded by other people. There was mess and noise and laughter and nowhere to hide. His ordered life had been turned upside down. And he liked it. He liked the fun, the jokes... He even liked the goddamn barking. He liked coming home to the smile in Maja's eyes and hearing about what Tarek had done at school. He liked it when the three of them curled up on the sofa and watched a movie together. He *really* liked it when Maja took his hand as they walked up the stairs to bed.

He drew her into his arms, enjoying the feel of her body against his. "Just don't make a habit of knocking people out and throwing them into Dumpsters."

"I won't." She pressed her face into the curve of his neck. "Unless other bounty hunters come from Otherworld before I am ready to leave."

Adam found the subject of her leaving increasingly troubling. He knew it had to happen. He tested himself with that knowledge on a regular basis, steeling himself for the reality of it. Although his rational self knew it was coming, his emotional self was having a hard time dealing with it. Standing here, with Maja in his arms, her hair tickling his chin and her delicious scent invading his nostrils, he allowed himself a little daydream of forever. It was a screwed-up daydream. Because she was the only woman with whom forever really was impossible.

Maybe that was why his subconscious was taking this route? It was never going to happen, so tiny glimpses of might-have-been were safe. Maja would leave and Adam would return to safety and cynicism once more. His heart could retreat behind its iron-clad shield and he would be able to forget that it was ever in danger of being touched by a beautiful Valkyrie.

His life would never quite return to the way it had once been, of course. He had Tarek to care for now. Once Maja left, there would be the emotional fall out to deal with, and that shouldn't be underestimated. Tarek had bonded with Maja. He had already lost his parents. Losing her as well would be a huge blow, and Adam would have to handle it carefully. And, of course, he didn't know if, or when Danny would return. His brother might need care and support, whether physical or emotional, after his time in Syria. "I've been making some inquiries into Knight's plans. He is away visiting friends this weekend, which means he won't be going to his house in a town called Greenwich. It's a popular place for wealthy people to live and commute into New York to work." Although he didn't want to go back to the place where he had spent so many unhappy years, Adam knew Knight's secrets would be inside that elegant mansion. "I've checked with Sophie and she can stay overnight with Tarek on Saturday. She's promised to take him to a movie."

Maja laughed. "He may never want us to return." Her expression became serious again. "So we are going to go to this house of Knight's and break in to see if we can find any information about his partners?"

"That's the plan. Are you okay with it?"

He scanned her face. She really did look exhausted tonight. His Valkyrie had lost her glow. *Whoa.* Where did that thought come from? *His* Valkyrie? She wasn't his. She never could be.

She might be tired, but her familiar determination shone through her weariness as she nodded. "We have to stop him before he ruins any more lives."

Chapter 12

Valentine House was the largest waterfront property on the coastline between Greenwich and New York City, with incredible views across Long Island Sound. Although Adam had spent his early teenage years here, he had never taken the time to admire the beauty of the estate. His thoughts had always been on escape.

"If it hadn't been for Danny, I'd have run away." He had never said those words out loud and he surprised himself by saying them now to Maja. "I had to stay to look after him."

"What about your mother?"

"It's impossible to explain what happened with her. It was as if she became a wax model of herself. She looked the same, talked the same, but she was dead behind the eyes. I tried to talk to her once, but it was as if she didn't know who I was."

"Did Knight hurt you?" Maja asked.

They were viewing the property from the road. Not

that there was much to see from this angle. Adam could just glimpse the four octagonal turrets that were a feature of the house. Rising above the roof as they did, their purpose was more than decorative; they provided an ideal position from which Knight's security guards could observe the whole area. The turrets were the only part of the house that was visible from the road. Everything else was hidden by the protective pine and beech forest that bordered the estate.

"Not physically. His methods were far subtler." Adam lowered the binoculars he had been using. "Knight is a sadistic villain." Could he give her an example? Talk about it to another person after all these years? He wouldn't know unless he tried. "I've always been scared of the dark. It stemmed from when I was very small and I'd gone down into the cellar of the house where we lived. The door had closed behind me, and I'd been stuck down there in the dark for more than an hour before my dad—my real dad—found me."

"No wonder you were scared." Maja gripped his hand.

"My mom understood and always let me have a nightlight in my room. But when we moved in with Knight, he said I was too old for that nonsense and he refused to let me have one in my bedroom. Not only that, he insisted I should have blackout curtains so that my room was in total darkness."

Maja's hand tightened in his. "Hateful man."

"That wasn't all. When I couldn't sleep, he decided on his own form of aversion therapy." Adam felt his throat close at the memory. "He used to shut me in the cellar for hours at a time. He told me I would get used to it and overcome my fears. I never did."

"And your mother?" Maja's voice was hesitant. "She permitted this?"

"She had her own problems." He supposed it must be difficult for someone on the outside to understand why his mother hadn't come to his rescue. She'd been fighting her own battles. He wasn't sure his mother ever knew the full extent of Knight's abuse of her son, in the same way Adam never knew what was going on with Belinda. Danny was the only person who knew it all. By shielding his brother from the same treatment, Adam had drawn even more torture down on himself.

He supposed Knight believed he had broken the boy who hid in a corner of that cellar. He certainly hadn't expected to see Adam rise to become a business leader with an empire matching Knight's own. Adam's father had left him money, but he had made his inheritance work. And the perseverance and fire he brought to his business dealings had been forged out of a determination to ensure he was the only person who controlled his life.

Adam knew the layout of this estate better than anyone. Probably better than Knight himself. He had perfected the art of hiding away in its many nooks and crannies. It wasn't an easy place to get into without an invitation, but it could be done. Strolling up to the big double gates wasn't an option. Nor was scaling the eight-foot-high wall.

"We have to approach from the bay."

Maja looked horrified. "You know how you are afraid of the dark?" Adam nodded. "I don't like water."

He bit back a smile. Her Valkyrie training wouldn't allow her to admit to a fear, but it was written all over her face. The intrepid Valkyrie was scared.

He was glad to see her looking better. That curious fatigue had held her in its grip for a day or two, leaving her washed-out and pale. He had even found her resting once or twice, something he never thought he would see. On a normal day, Maja had more energy than an army platoon. Perhaps she was less invincible than she believed, and recent events had caught up with her. Today she appeared her usual radiant self.

"We don't have to swim. There is a point just along the bay where we can slip into the water and follow the edge of the shoreline until we come alongside the house. There is a blind spot where the security guards won't be able to see us. We can make our way through the trees and up to the house." He gave her a reassuring smile. "Only your feet will get wet."

She looked doubtful. "Promise?"

"Word of a Lyon."

When they reached the place Adam recognized, they removed their boots and socks and slid into the water. It was cold and Maja gave a little yelp of surprise as her bare soles connected with the slippery pebbles. Adam, who had used this method of sneaking on and off his stepfather's property many times, guessed his own feet had developed more of an immunity.

"You'll get used to it."

"If I don't, I'll make you warm my feet on parts of your body that don't like the cold." Her teeth chattered. "Word of a Valkyrie."

He laughed. "Let's go and find the names of the bad guys, so we know who we're dealing with."

By the time they were alongside the house, Maja could no longer feel her feet. Adam barely seemed to notice the cold as they paused, hunkering down below the level of the woodland that bordered the water's edge.

"If we keep going in this direction, we will come to the boathouse. There are steps nearby that lead down to the waterfront. Knight's guests sometimes swim here in the summer and that's how they access the water."

"Are they mad?" Maja shivered at the thought, not just because of the cold. The thought of striking out into these dark depths struck her as the ultimate act of foolishness.

"It's a pleasant experience. You should try it some-time."

Since it was never going to happen, she didn't answer. Let Adam cling to his eccentric mortal customs. She could tolerate his strange notions without having to engage in them.

"Once we reach the steps, we will be within sight of the house. Knight has security guarding the house 24/7." From his crouching position, Adam pointed upward. "This is the point where we have to climb up the bank. We will be hidden from view by the trees."

"If the place is so well guarded, how will we get into the house?"

"There is a way." His jaw clenched and she got the impression that he was momentarily looking back into the past. "It involves going through the cellar I told you about."

No matter where this led them, Maja wanted to make Knight Valentine pay for the pain in Adam's eyes when he said those words. She couldn't give him back the mo-ments of his formative years his stepfather had stolen from him, but she wanted to see Knight suffer. She wanted to stop him harming anyone else through his Reaper alias, of course, but right now, this was about Adam. The man who thought he was too damaged to care for others. Why couldn't he see that the opposite was true? He cared too much. His love for his brother had taken him into a war zone without a thought for his own safety. His compas-sion for an orphaned child had led him to bring Tarek into his own life, even though that action had turned his regulated routine upside down.

And she knew he was afraid of allowing himself to get too close to her because of what that might mean. No matter how close their physical and emotional bond might be, he was frightened of looking into his heart and finding it wasn't as tough and unbending as he believed. Afraid of letting himself care because it couldn't last…and he didn't know how to cope with any more emotional damage.

"I'll be with you this time."

When he didn't answer, she wondered if she'd said the wrong thing. Then he nodded, dropping a brief kiss onto her temple, before cautiously lifting his head above the level of the bank and looking around.

"The trees are just a few feet away. You go first. You just need to scramble up here, make a dash for the woods and wait for me to join you."

"What about your injury?" Maja eyed the bank dubiously. Although it was only about six feet high, it was steep and the rocky surface looked slippery. Getting up it was likely to be an undignified scramble. For someone who had recently sustained a serious injury, it could result in a major setback.

"I'll be fine." Adam flexed his shoulder as if to prove it. His mobility had been improving steadily and he was using his left arm and shoulder more and more. Even so, Maja wasn't convinced.

"I think I should wait at the top so I can help you up."

"If you do that you will be out in the open and risk being seen," Adam said.

"Not if I'm invisible." She pulled her woolen hat down farther over her ears, tilting her chin at him at the same time.

"You are one stubborn Valkyrie, do you know that?"

"Yes. Odin always called me his obstinate daughter." Among other things. She often wondered why she was the Allfather's favorite daughter when she had so many traits he disliked.

Handing him her boots, she started to climb. She had been right, it wasn't easy. Gripping the grass at the top of the bank, she hauled herself up, trying to find a foothold on the smooth surface of the rock. Adam's view from below would be of her ass thrust outward as she bungled her way to the top. It didn't feel dignified.

When she reached the top, she leaned over and Adam passed her both pairs of boots. Stooping down, she gripped his right hand. Since she was so much stronger than him, she could have lifted him one-handed without letting him make any attempt at climbing. Deciding to allow him his dignity, she reined in her strength and simply supported him as he scaled the bank.

The trees offered seclusion and semidarkness. Once the two of them had slipped their socks and boots back on, Adam led the way toward the house. Pausing before they emerged from the shelter of the woodland, he ducked low behind the cover of a lilac bush. From their secluded vantage point, they could observe the house without being seen.

"It's magnificent."

Maja made the admission reluctantly. The house was linked to Knight, and that meant it was tainted in her mind. Acknowledging its beauty felt wrong. Maja had once attended a feud between two warring factions of a noble French family. Her mission had taken her to a splendid chateau in the heart of the Loire valley. This three-story mansion reminded her of that grand structure. Its undulating swimming pool resembled the chateau's moat and its tennis courts mimicked the green fields. Like the chateau, this house had orchards and formal gardens.

"When Knight bought it, it was the most expensive

piece of real estate in the country. I don't think he had even seen the place when he made an offer for it. All that mattered was the price tag. He needs to be seen to be the best at everything. That includes being the wealthiest and most powerful man in the world."

"What made him that way?" Maja asked. "I thought it wasn't possible for a human to be born evil."

Adam appeared surprised by the question. "I've never really given it much thought. While I agree that people are not born with the evil gene, I think some are more susceptible to it than others. If those people are then brought up in a cold, mercenary environment, they may become immune to empathy and find it easier to commit terrible acts. By all accounts, Knight's family was a strange one. He was an only child and his parents worshiped money and status."

"Surely there are many children raised in similar circumstances? I cannot believe they all go on to commit horrible crimes."

"You're right, of course. It takes a unique set of circumstances, and we may never know what they were in Knight's case." Adam's lips hardened. "And I'll confess, I don't really care. That bastard is killing innocent people and terrorizing the world, and he's doing it for money. And we are here to find the evidence of that. How he reached this point doesn't interest me."

Although Maja could understand Adam's point of view, she didn't share it. Her dislike of Knight was equally strong, but she couldn't help wondering about his background. Something had molded the man capable of such foul crimes. Her prolonged stay in the mortal realm had piqued her interest in humans. She thought back to Adam's meeting with Knight in the other man's office. A strong feeling had assailed her then. That sense that Knight was human…and more. What had happened to him that was over and above the normal mortal experience? Adam had talked about his environment. What if something—she wished she could be more specific—had taken advantage of his uncaring parents and cold upbringing? Her thoughts were too vague to follow them through to a conclusion. But since she and Adam had a difficult task ahead of them, Maja had no more time to spend on speculation.

"There are steps over there leading down to the cellar." Adam pointed to the side of the building.

"You said the house is closely guarded, so surely security is tight all over? How will we get in there?"

Adam reached into the pocket of his jeans and withdrew a bunch of keys. "With these."

"You have the keys to Knight's house?"

"They were among my mother's belongings when she died. I always meant to dispose of them, but I never got around to it. Now I'm glad I didn't." There was a curious note to Adam's voice, one Maja didn't like. It was somewhere between sorrow and triumph.

"Will they still work?"

Adam appeared to weigh the distance between their hiding place and the house. "There's only one way to find out."

Steep stone steps led down from the garden to the cellar, and they descended these swiftly, having managed to cross from the trees to the house without incident. There was a heavy door at the bottom of the stairs and Maja reached for the handle.

Adam forestalled her. "It will be locked."

He sensed her impatience as he tried several of the keys before he found the one that opened the door. It swung inward with a creak worthy of horror movie special effects. When they were fully inside the cellar, Adam peered around him into the pervading darkness. There was a smell of mildew, cleaning products and gasoline.

"Where now?" Although Maja spoke in a whisper, her voice sounded unnaturally loud.

"There is another set of stairs that leads to a storage area at the back of the kitchens. Once we are there, we can make our way to the corridor where Knight's study is located." Adam led the way across the gloomy basement, guiding Maja around a series of obstacles.

"What about his security guards? Do they patrol the house?"

"I'm hoping they won't. Knight has security cameras, but their focus is on the exterior and preventing anyone from approaching. Since we've done the hard part by getting in, I don't think the guards will be looking out for intruders inside the house." He turned to smile at her, just making out her features in the dim light. "But if they do come after us, I'm relying on you for backup."

"You can count on me."

It occurred to him that she was the only person he trusted to really mean that. Danny, the only other person with whom he had ever been close, had always been too young for their relationship to be on equal terms. Although the two brothers cared for each other, Adam had always been the one looking out for Danny. For the first time, he had someone who was there for him. Maja had his back. She had demonstrated that over and over. He examined the warm feeling that brought with it. He had always viewed himself as solitary, believing it to be a preference rather than his destiny. Now he wasn't so sure. It felt good to know he wasn't alone.

It was particularly reassuring here in this cellar, the

place that had featured in so many of his nightmares. It was his own personal hell. He could still remember being pushed down the wooden stairs, still hear the sound of that door slamming, still feel the darkness wrapping its tentacles around him like a living thing as he curled up in a corner and wished for death. His fear of this place wasn't just pins and needles. It was daggers and razors.

Back then, fear had drained him of the ability to do anything. It hadn't just been this cellar. It had been the dozens of other things Knight had done to destroy the boy he had been. Fear had almost destroyed him. Even breathing had been hard, thwarting his ability to think straight.

Knight knew Danny was Adam's weakness. One day Adam came home from school and Knight met him in the driveway, his face serious. He told him Danny had fallen into the river, it didn't look good, they hadn't found his body... Choking back sobs, Adam had looked up at the house to see his brother waving at him from the playroom window. He had swung a wild punch, missed and fallen to his knees as Knight walked away laughing.

He had spent too much time over the years wondering why Knight treated him the way he had. All he could think was that Adam must have reminded Knight of his father.

Memories of minor cruelties came back to him. Being denied his dinner because of some imagined transgression was a feature of growing up in Knight's house. Adam could still remember being unable to sleep because of the twin torments of darkness and hunger. He had been old enough to have a strongly developed sense of right and wrong. He knew he was being treated unfairly.

Now, he was able to take those memories and use them as an energizer. In a curious way, they were part of his success story. Faced with the choice of fight or flight,

Adam had fought, and he had done it successfully. Although he didn't let anything stand in his way, fairness was his watchword. The companies he took over were happy to have him in charge. Unlike Knight, Adam didn't tear down; he built up. He took over businesses and empowered the existing teams to succeed. With his keen eye for trends, Adam had run one of the first organizations to spot the potential of streaming music digitally; as a result, the Lyon brand had been ahead of the market. He was never going to thank Knight for giving him the chance to transform terror into action, but it felt like a victory over his torturer that he had emerged the man he was.

The door at the top of the wooden stairs was locked and another search among the keys, this time in semidarkness, ensued. Maja, using invisibility as a cloak, emerged first. Once she had become visible and signaled that all was clear, Adam followed her.

They were in a storage area at the rear of the kitchen. The walls were lined with shelves and these were stacked with jars and cans containing every imaginable foodstuff. Adam paused to wonder why Knight still kept this amount of food in the house when he lived there alone. He supposed it was because his stepfather continued to entertain on a lavish scale. Appearances were what mattered to Knight. He had to be the best, had to win. The thought stuck with Adam almost as though it was an important thread in this whole nightmare.

He pointed out a door that led to the main corridor. This was the dangerous part. When they stepped into that corridor, they were in the heart of the house and exposing themselves to the possibility of discovery by one of Knight's security guards.

"Let me go first," Maja urged in a whisper. "If I'm invisible, I can take them by surprise and give you a chance to get away."

It made sense, even if it didn't suit Adam's sense of chivalry. He moved toward the door. "Once we are in the corridor, it's the third door on the right."

"Will we need a key?"

He shook his head. "The doors inside the house are never locked. With security guards monitoring the place, there is no need. And no one would ever dare go into Knight's study without his permission."

Opening the door a fraction, he glanced through the gap. The rich cream-and-gold decor of the corridor hadn't changed. He remembered the carpet, so thick it felt like it was gripping his ankles, and the tasteful paintings in their gilt-edged frames. Out of the corner of his eye, his glimpsed one of the crystal chandeliers.

"There's no one around."

Maja vanished and the door opened wider as she slipped through the gap. Adam followed her. Seconds later, he was inside Knight's study, his stepfather's sanctuary, and Maja was visible again. Although this room was serviceable, with its antique oak desk and bookshelves lining the walls, it had French windows with a view of the gardens that sloped down to the water's edge. There was a huge fireplace at one side of the room with a full set of tools.

Adam remembered that, on the few occasions he had been in this room in the past, Knight had made him clean the grate. His stepfather's argument had been that, although they had servants to do the job, it was an important life skill. Adam knew better. In his stepfather's eyes, he had never cleaned it well enough. Adam had spent hours on his knees in here, almost sobbing in frustration while Knight stood over him, finding fault with his efforts. He felt the wire-handled brush and the hot, soapy water that left his hands red and raw. Remembered the ache in his arms, the hard grate beneath his knees, and the dust in his nostrils.

You are not here to relive the past.

"He doesn't have a safe."

Knight's arrogance was going to work to their advantage. His conviction that no one would dare break into his home was so strong that he kept his private papers in his desk. It was made of solid oak, beautiful but functional. Its three drawers were locked, just as Adam had known they would be. He checked the room briefly for a key, but suspected it would be sitting safely inside Knight's breast pocket.

There was an ornate silver letter opener on the desktop and he tried to pry one of the drawers open with that, but only succeeded in scratching the polished wood.

"Let me try." Maja was clearly impatient to get into the desk.

He grinned at her. "If you get your hands on it, the whole desk will be a pile of firewood in seconds."

His eyes scanned the room and rested on the fireplace with its set of brass tools. Snatching up the heavy poker, he drove it into the drawer front, splintering the wood around the lock. When the drawer gave way, he repeated the process on the others, then cast the poker aside.

Each blow made a noise, and he hoped it wasn't loud enough to draw the attention of the security guards.

Once all three drawers were open, he removed the papers they contained and spread them on the desktop. He quickly discarded each of them as irrelevant.

Frustrated, he turned back to the desk. "There has to be something more."

Dropping to his knees, he checked beneath the desk, feeling for a hidden catch or compartment.

"Here." Maja beckoned him to the side of the desk. Adam's efforts with the poker had loosened the end panel.

"A concealed drawer. I remember Knight once boasting that he had paid a quarter of a million dollars for this desk at a German antiques fair. Now I know why."

There was only one item in the drawer. It was a plastic folder containing several printed spreadsheets. The top sheet contained a list of names and contact details. One name on the list jumped out at Adam.

He tapped a finger on the name, drawing Maja's attention to it. "Shepherd."

"Tarek said his father spoke to someone called Shepherd the night before he was killed."

Adam nodded. "If I'm right, the man Tarek's father called was General Rick Shepherd. He is the leader of the international task force that is hunting the Reaper."

"I don't understand. If Shepherd is hunting the Reaper, why would he kill Tarek's father for giving him his name?" Maja lifted a hand to her mouth as realization dawned. "Oh."

Adam felt his mouth thin into a grim line. "Exactly. The only reason I can think of is that Shepherd is in league with the Reaper." He pointed to a framed photograph on the mantel above the hated fireplace. It showed Knight shaking hands with another man. "It's not quite the conclusive proof we need. I'm hoping these spreadsheets will provide that. But that's a picture of Knight and Shepherd."

He placed the plastic folder in the back pocket of his jeans...just as a security guard walked through the door.

Chapter 13

The man who walked into the room was wearing a gun in a shoulder holster, but he didn't have time to draw it. He didn't have time to do anything before Adam punched him in the face and he dropped like a stone to the floor.

Maja was impressed. His reflexes had been faster than hers.

She had no time to offer her congratulations. Adam grabbed her hand and hauled her toward the French windows. They were locked, but Maja decided this was no time to fumble with keys. With one hard kick, she left the doors hanging from their frame as the two of them burst through and hit the grass at a run. She heard shouts behind them and shots rang out.

Realizing the direction they were headed, she gave Adam a sidelong look of horror. "I can't swim."

"It's time for your first lesson."

The grass sloped steeply down to a deck next to the boathouse. Still holding her hand, Adam launched himself from the wooden platform into the water. Maja was in midair when she realized this was something he must have done many times.

As the cold, dark water closed over her head, there wasn't much time for rational thought. *I am invincible.* It was worth a reminder. Because it sure as hell didn't feel that way right now. As shock drove the breath from her lungs and water replaced it, she felt sure this was the one thing that would destroy her invincibility. Although she knew there was no other way of escaping Knight's security guards—and she suspected now that Adam must have known all along this would be their escape route—she couldn't see any way of doing this. Not when she didn't even know which way was up anymore. She thrashed around, spluttering, kicking and holding on to Adam's hand like a lifeline.

"Keep still. I've got you." Adam's voice and his strong hands under her armpits as he pulled her to the surface went some way toward calming her fears. "Lie back and let me do the work."

Two opposing forces went to war within her. Part of her, the scared, irrational part, wanted to fight him, to try and get away. Another part, a deeper part, the one that felt connected to Adam, told her she could trust him despite her fears. That was the part she went with. Relaxing in his hold, she gave herself up and let him take over. It was a new sensation. Letting another person take charge wasn't Maja's way.

She felt Adam kicking out, propelling them along the shore in the same direction they had walked earlier. She heard more shots from the direction of the deck, and cringed each time in fear that Adam could be hit. Nothing happened. With every strong kick of Adam's legs, they were thrust further from the possibility of harm. Still trembling with shock and cold, with her throat raw from choking on the water she had swallowed, she was never going to call this a pleasant experience. But Adam was alive, so she had to consider it a positive one.

Adam kept going until they were out of sight of Valentine House. Then he kicked out strongly for the shore. Carrying Maja onto the pebbly beach, he sat on the stones and cradled her in his arms.

"I'm sorry." His breath hitched on the words.

She clung to him, her whole body shuddering. "I know why you did it."

"I couldn't think of any other way. If we'd stayed in the house or the grounds, they'd have shot us." He looked around. "We can't stay here. Even though we're no longer on Knight's property, they'll be looking for us."

There was no sign of Knight's men nearby, but she supposed it was only a matter of time before they caught up with them. They had seen them jump into the water and they knew which direction they had taken. The bank was less steep here than at the point they'd climbed earlier. Getting to their feet, they scrambled up it together, hampered by their wet clothing. Adam, who knew the area, quickly found the road that would lead them back to where they had left the car.

"I don't want to walk in plain sight, but we can go through these fields alongside the road. That way, we'll be hidden from view if Knight's guys come looking for us."

Maja decided it must be the effects of the water that were bringing on a renewal of the tiredness and nausea that had dogged her a few days previously. Just when she thought she had recovered, they came back with a vengeance. As she followed in Adam's wake, her whole body felt like it was made of lead. It was just as well they didn't encounter Knight's security guards, since she wouldn't have been able to lift a finger against them, let alone a fist or a foot.

There was a blanket in the trunk of the car and Adam withdrew it, wrapping it around her. "You look pale. Are you sure you're okay?" His face was a mask of concern.

"I think it's shock."

"Let's get you home."

She nodded, almost too weary to climb into the vehicle. *Home.* It was only a few short weeks since she had been scared of that elegant apartment. Now she did think of it as home. Although she suspected that had more to do with the man who lived there, and her new family, than anything else.

Adam was pleased his body had suffered no ill effects from their trip to Valentine House. Three days later, apart from some stiffness in his injured shoulder, he had never felt better. On this particular day, he had woken early, his mind on the spreadsheets they had retrieved from Knight's desk.

One of the sheets appeared to be a list of payments to someone called Berger. The payments were regular and the figures were eyewatering. *Berger?* The French word for *shepherd*? Adam's heart rate had kicked up a notch. He was certain these amounts would coincide with payments received by General Rick Shepherd.

Since scanning the contents, he had formulated and discarded several plans for next steps. Most of them centered around Shepherd, the man tasked with coordinating the Reaper hunt, the man Adam was now certain Tarek's father had called when he'd discovered the true nature of the world's most feared terrorist organization.

Shepherd was a four-star general and one of the most respected officers in the country. As soon as Adam had seen his name on the list of contacts he had found in Knight's study, his heart had sunk. He had suspected this all along. Now he had the confirmation he needed. It couldn't have been a coincidence that Tarek's father was killed the day after he'd called a man named Shepherd. The sorry truth was that the man the world trusted to bring down the Reaper was likely himself part of that consortium.

So not only do I have to get people to believe my story that Knight Valentine, billionaire businessman, is fronting a terrorist organization, I also have to convince them that a decorated war hero is in league with him, as well.

Turning his head, Adam noticed Maja was missing, and frowned. A faint sound drew his attention to the bathroom and he sat up, listening intently. There it was again. It was unmistakable. Throwing back the bedcovers, he rose and pulled on his underwear.

"Maja, are you okay?" He tapped lightly on the bathroom door.

A faint groan answered him. "I'm fine."

He hesitated. She clearly wasn't fine. So what did he do now? Respect her privacy, or go with his instincts and find out what was wrong?

"Can I come in?"

There was a moment's silence. "Yes. The door isn't locked."

As he entered, he paused in the doorway, taking in the scene. Clad in pajama pants and a camisole top, Maja was seated on the tile floor next to the commode. Her face was so pale it appeared translucent. As she tried to say something to him she winced and turned away. Leaning over the bowl, she clutched her stomach and retched.

Adam knelt beside her, pressing a hand to her forehead. Her temperature was normal. "Why didn't you tell me you were ill?"

She leaned her head against his shoulder gratefully. "With everything else that's been going on, it seemed like a trivial thing to bother you about. It's been happening every day. Just in the mornings. Then it goes away and I feel tired for the rest of the day."

The enormity of what she had just said hit him like a slap in the face.

"Maja." He spoke slowly. It was as if his brain was having difficulty processing his thoughts and translating them into speech. "This sounds a lot like morning sickness."

She nodded. "That's what I said. It only happens in the mornings."

"No." He tilted her chin up so she was looking at him. "Morning sickness is a very specific type of sickness. It's caused by a hormonal change that takes place in the bodies of women who are having a baby."

Her lips formed a soundless O as she stared at him. She looked about as stunned as a person could get without fainting. Then her eyes filled with tears.

"I'm sorry."

Although this had been at the back of his mind, Adam's initial reaction was one of disbelief. Could Fate be this cruel? That one time—the only time in his whole life he hadn't used protection—and this was the result? Two people from different dimensions now had to live with a consequence so huge it tilted both their worlds off course.

Even through his own feelings of shock, Adam was aware that how he reacted now was really important. Maja needed him. This was going to be hard on both of them, but what he said and did in the next few minutes would set the tone for how they got through it.

He took her hand. "I'm not."

The tears spilled over as she blinked. "Pardon?"

"I'm not sorry." He raised her hand to his lips. "I'll never be sorry we had that amazing night together, or the times that followed. And how can I be sorry we made a new life?"

Her lower lip wobbled and he could see her battling to get her emotions under control. She failed, and the next thing he knew his arms were full of weeping Valkyrie. It was some time later before she was coherent again.

"I'm scared." He could see how much it cost her to admit it.

"So am I." He reached for some toilet paper and dried her eyes. "But we're in this together. Every step of the way."

"What about Odin?" She looked around fearfully as though half expecting the mighty warrior god to be lurking in the shower cubicle.

"This is our baby. Odin can butt out." Perhaps saying it out loud would make it happen.

"You don't understand." Maja's voice was a fearful whisper. "This child is his grandchild. Living proof that a Valkyrie broke the code. Odin will never let that happen." She clutched his arm. "The Allfather will never let our child survive, Adam."

Her fear was palpable, communicating itself to Adam. He held her tighter against his chest. Before this instant, a baby might have been the last thing he wanted in his life. But this was his baby. His and Maja's. It was happening. The thought sent a new, unexpected thrill through him. Was it pleasure? Excitement? He didn't have time to examine it. All he knew for sure was nothing was going to threaten this child. Not Knight Valentine and his terrorist organization. Not a four-star general who was prepared to sell out his country for however many million dollars

Knight was paying him each month. Not even a mighty Norse god with a mean streak.

Sitting on a cold floor in his underwear might not be the best place for the most momentous vow of his life, but Adam made it anyway. "Maja, I don't care who I have to fight. No one will harm our child."

It was real. Maja walked out of the doctor's office in something approaching a trance. The day after Adam had found her on the bathroom floor, eight weeks after the night they had spent together in Syria, it was official.

I'm having a baby.

Adam had arranged for her to see a female obstetrician, a partner of the doctor who had been treating his injured shoulder. Although Maja had told Adam her body was that of a mortal woman, she had gone into the initial consultation worried that Dr. Blake might notice something unusual. Her fears had been laid to rest. Although some of the questions and tests seemed intrusive to someone unused to discussing intimate details, the doctor had been pleasant and approachable. She had not denounced her patient as an otherworldly warrior woman. She had, however, confirmed that Maja was quite definitely pregnant.

Maja had been telling the truth when she told Adam she knew nothing about how her body worked. Since it was never going to happen to them, the Valkyries had no need to know about sex. That meant they also didn't need to know about pregnancy. Maja had never met anyone who had been pregnant. The Valkyries had been kept apart from other women at Asgard. She had never listened to stories of what it was like to carry a child or to give birth. She had never even held a baby in her arms. Tarek was the first child she had ever known.

If Dr. Blake had been taken aback at her patient's lack

of knowledge, she had kept her surprise to herself. Talking to Maja and Adam together, she had explained what they could expect from the coming weeks and months, recommended books and websites, and told them to call her if they had any questions. They had made an appointment for an ultrasound scan during which they would be able to see an image of the baby.

I don't know how to feel about this.

The baby was on Maja's mind constantly, her feelings wavering between soaring elation and total devastation. Bitter, bittersweet. She wanted this child. And that frightened her more than anything else. The fierceness with which she wanted it was like a fever burning its way deeper into her with every passing minute. But the fear of what this meant was a barrier to her feelings of joy.

Maja didn't know if a child had ever been born to a Valkyrie. She couldn't believe it had ever happened. She was fairly sure she was the first of Odin's daughters or stepdaughters to commit a misdemeanor of this magnitude.

Adam had said he would not allow anything to harm their child. And she believed him. He had said the words with a conviction that would not be shaken.

But where does that leave me?

She didn't know how to approach that question. They existed in different worlds. Worlds that had briefly and magically collided. But they both knew she couldn't stay here. So how did Adam see the future? Did he picture her leaving their baby with him soon after its birth? Because the illegitimate child of a Valkyrie had no place in Valhalla.

Maja ran a hand over her still-flat stomach. *How can I leave the child who already means so much to me?*

The answer was simple. She couldn't. Even if Adam

could keep his promise and ensure their child's safety against Odin's wrath, what sort of future would there be for a child who was half mortal, half Valkyrie? She didn't know what the future held. All she knew for certain was that she would turn both worlds upside down to ensure there was a future for her child.

Just as Adam had made a vow, this was Maja's. In order to see it through, she had to stay alive. And that meant she had to remain hidden from those seeking to return her to Valhalla.

"Dr. Blake said the morning sickness will pass." Adam watched her face closely as she nibbled on a piece of dry toast, the only thing she felt able to eat before noon.

"But possibly not for some time." She set the toast aside and reached for a glass of water instead.

"We couldn't ask her about dropkicking bad guys, but I'm guessing that's banned." His voice was serious. "Or let me put it this way. It *is* banned."

"I read some of the information the doctor gave us on exercising, and it suggests continuing with your usual routine. Even if that is martial arts." She took a breath, guessing what his reaction to her next words would be. "Or kickboxing."

"Not a chance, Maja. I know what you are capable of. You don't have to tell me you can take on anyone and win, but you are not getting in a fight that might result in an injury to you or our baby." When she didn't answer, he moved closer to her, gripping her hands in his. "I feel bad enough that I made you jump in the water the other day. We're not taking any more chances with your safety. If you exercise, you do it in the gym, not face-to-face with a living, breathing, unpredictable opponent. Am I making myself clear?"

Maja wasn't sure how to respond. She wanted to be

angry that he was taking over, telling her what to do. She was Odin's daughter. Was she going to bow to the will of a mortal? Yet part of her felt Adam's words enveloping her like a warm, protective blanket. And she liked it. The doctor had talked about pregnancy hormones. Maybe they were responsible for this desire to rest her head on his shoulder and let him take charge. Of everything.

Instead of objecting to his high-handedness, she simply nodded. "Yes, Adam." Changing the subject, she asked a question that had been bothering her. "What shall we tell Tarek?"

"I don't think we should tell him anything yet." It was clear Adam had also given it some thought. "He's still settling in at school. We'll give him this time to adjust before we drop this new bombshell on him."

"I'm worried about what it will do to him," Maja said. "On the surface, he's coping well, but he's been through so much. We're his family now that the adoption process has started, but he may feel a baby will push him out."

"It's our job to see that doesn't happen, even if we have to get professional help to do it." Adam dashed back the remains of his cup of coffee. "I've arranged for him to attend weekend classes at his Arabic school and to go to a mosque."

"Does Tarek remind you of Danny?"

The question was asked before she had time to think about it. She winced slightly at how it sounded—intrusive and abrupt. Adam rarely talked about his brother, but she knew he was on his mind all the time. He watched the news from Syria each day and emailed Edith Blair regularly for updates. Now and then, Maja would catch a faraway look on his face and she guessed he was thinking of the idealistic young man who had gone away to help, and gotten caught up in a war that wasn't his. She was surprised when Adam answered readily.

"In some ways he does. I think I was initially drawn to Tarek because he reminded me of Danny. They both have that smartness and determination to overcome their difficulties. And something more." He shook his head as if he was struggling to explain. "It sounds like a cliché, but it's a simple enjoyment of life. Something I was missing for so long."

The words struck Maja as odd, making it sound like he was no longer missing his own pleasure in life. Yet she didn't want to interrupt what he was saying by questioning him about what he meant.

"But I don't want Tarek to grow up thinking I brought him here to be a Danny substitute. Or out of pity. I love him and I'm proud to have him in my life."

"That's what he needs to know. From both of us." Bright tears stung the back of Maja's eyelids. These pregnancy hormones were a killer. "When we tell him about the baby, those are the first words he needs to hear."

"I suspect we will, then we need to follow the news with 'let's get pizza.'" Adam laughed, drawing her into his arms. "Tarek has adapted to some aspects of Western life remarkably quickly."

Maja leaned her forehead on his chest for several long, still moments, grounding herself in his warmth and delicious scent. When she lifted her head, she didn't want to break the ambience, didn't want to ask the next question. But there was no avoiding it. "And Knight? What happens next?"

"We've got the evidence that he was paying Shepherd, but we need more before we can take this to the authorities. You got me thinking when you asked about his background. I don't know how much it will help to have an insight into the mastermind behind the Reaper, but if we can understand his motives, maybe we can find his weakness and get more evidence. With that in mind, there is someone I need to talk to. Someone I haven't seen for a very long time."

Maja could sense he was subject to a torrent of conflicting emotions as he spoke. There was some residual anger in his eyes, but she could also see reluctance and a trace of pain. He didn't want to do this. Whoever he needed to see clearly aroused strong feelings in him.

"Who is this person?"

"My mother's aunt. Elvira was her only close relative at the time of her wedding to Knight. She hated and mistrusted Knight and caused a scandal by doing that dreaded thing and standing up during the wedding service—" Adam broke off with a smile before Maja could tell him she didn't know what he meant.

"It's a mortal thing," he explained. "There's a point in a marriage when the person performing the ceremony asks if anyone knows of a reason why the bride and groom shouldn't marry. It's always a tense moment and it has become a popular trope in films and books. You know, someone bursts in and dramatically spoils the wedding. Usually an ex-partner."

"And your mother's aunt did this during her wedding to Knight?" Maja liked the sound of Elvira already.

"Yes. Elvira got to her feet and denounced Knight in front of the hundreds of his socialite friends who were gathered at Valentine House for the occasion. I can't remember exactly what she said after all this time, but it was quite a speech. It even included a statement that Knight had sold his soul to the devil. Even though my mother and Elvira had been close until that point, it caused a rift between them that was never healed."

"I might not be Knight's biggest fan, but I can understand why that would happen." It was the sort of family split from which there could be no going back.

"I'd like to talk to Elvira. My mother married Knight within weeks of my father's death. I was quite young and still grieving, but it seemed so strange, so callous. Yet my mother was almost in a trance. It was as if Knight had her under his spell and nothing was going to change her mind. How did Elvira get to a point where she hated him so much in such a short space of time? She was known to be a snob. Was it simply that Knight didn't come from old money—his family wasn't elite enough to suit Elvira's tastes—or was there more to it?"

Maja thought she could understand the storm of emotions she had sensed in Adam. If he talked to Elvira, he would have to speak of his mother. Adam was a complex tapestry, comprising many interwoven strands. She sensed that Belinda Lyon was the golden thread running through it. His mother completed the picture, so when you stood back you could see it all. But so far, no one had seen the whole image. Not even Adam. And he was frightened that, when he spoke to Elvira, the final stitches would be placed in the canvas. His tapestry would be complete.

"Can I come with you?"

He smiled. "I was hoping you would say that."

Chapter 14

"The book Dr. Blake gave me said sex is fine." Several days after her visit to the doctor, Maja had become a walking, talking pregnancy encyclopedia. She blushed. "If you want to."

"How can you even ask that question?" As they lay naked in bed, Adam drew her closer so she could feel his erection pulsing against her belly. "Surely you know by now that, with you, I *always* want to? Even when I'm not with you, when I'm walking down the street, when I'm in the middle of a high-powered meeting, taking a call from an overseas client, supposed to be one hundred percent focused on business...part of me is thinking about how much I want you."

It was more the look on his face than the words he spoke that instantly had her nipples hardening, her clit throbbing and her whole body thrumming in response to the blaze of need in his eyes.

He pressed his mouth against hers, parting her lips by flicking his tongue lightly over them. Wrapping an arm around her waist, he pulled her closer again and deepened the kiss. It was soft, yet there was a hint of the hunger that always burned between them. Heat infused her senses, sweeping over her body. It was addictive, a buzz tingling through her bloodstream, more powerful than any drug.

His hand was warm on her breast, cupping it gently. A new sensitivity made Maja shudder at his touch and press into his palm. Her nipple was hard, and ultraresponsive as his thumb rasped back and forth over the tip. It tightened even further, causing a feeling somewhere midway between pleasure and pain, until she murmured a soft protest and drew his head down to her.

The warmth of his mouth on her nipple was sweet torture. Rich sensation poured over her like cream and honey mingling in a heady concoction.

As if there was all the time in the world, he moved a hand down to part her thighs, slowly stroking a finger around her clitoris, causing it to swell and throb beneath his touch.

"Feels good." She wasn't sure the words were audible.

Adam must have caught the essence of what she was saying because he leaned on one elbow, watching her face as he pressed a finger inside her. Maja's flesh burned, clenching around the impalement.

"I want my cock inside you. So deep I can't tell where I end and you begin."

"Yes." She could barely pant out the words as she gripped his finger, grinding her hips against him. "I want that, too, Adam. So much."

"But first I want to watch as you come around my fingers. I want to be sure this feels okay."

Okay? If she had been capable of further speech, she'd

have assured him it felt like perfection. Her inner muscles spasmed around his fingers as she lifted her hips in time with his pumping motion. Each thrust was heaven and hell. Rapture and torture. Each breath that left her lips was a moan of pleasure as she quickened her movements. The warning waves of her release started at her core and began to ripple outward. She tightened around him, arching her back and straining toward him.

Adam moved faster in smooth strokes as he buried his fingers inside her flesh. Each caress touched sensitive nerve endings and she cried out between attempts to draw enough air into her lungs. And then it hit. Savage and out of control. A ragged wail left her lips and she clung to Adam's shoulders as she was flung through a dark tunnel and out the other side into brilliant, blinding light. The violence of the sensations buffeting her body robbed her of any remaining breath as she tensed and shuddered through the storm.

She was still trembling as Adam turned her so she lay on her side with her back to him. His chin was pressed into the curve of her shoulder, his lips caressing the shell of her ear. "This is what we'll do when the baby gets bigger."

"Are we practicing?" Her breath hissed sharply as he pressed up against her tight entrance.

"Why not?" He pushed forward, opening and stretching her. "We may have to do it a lot to make sure we get it right."

He held her hips, cushioning her spine against the hard muscles of his chest and resting the back of her thighs on top of his as he eased into her. Maja could feel his heart pounding between her shoulder blades as his lips found the sensitive spot at the base of her neck. Excitement fizzed through her blood like bubbles in soda as she moved her hips in time with his.

The world narrowed to the point where their bodies joined, and the intensity built to a crescendo, vibrating through them, demanding release. Gasping, breathless moans issued from Maja's lips as Adam used the fingers of one hand to tease her nipples while the other circled her still-sensitized clit.

"Too much." She clawed at the sheets, squirming wildly against Adam's pelvis.

"Do you want me to stop?" His voice was a growl in her ear.

"Don't you dare."

Seconds later, she was convulsing again, gripping him tightly as another mindless orgasm tilted her world off course. With him buried deep inside her, holding her close against his heart, she felt the blistering heat of Adam's own climax as he murmured her name.

Later, when she turned to face him and lay in his arms, she wished she could smooth away the line of tension that pulled his brows together. Although she knew its cause, it worried her.

"What time do we need to set off?"

"Straight after we drop Tarek at school," Adam said. "The retirement home where Elvira lives is only an hour and a half away, so we will be there and back in time to pick him up again."

"Is she expecting us?"

"No." A flicker of a smile crossed his face. "Elvira is the most stubborn, contrary woman in the whole world. With probably the nastiest tongue. If we turn up unannounced we retain the element of surprise and there's less chance of her refusing to see us."

The Preserve was nothing like Adam's mental image of a retirement home. It was more like a high-class hotel.

The concierge informed them that they would find Ms. Perlman in the solarium where she would be finishing coffee, having returned from her morning round of golf.

Elvira hadn't changed. That was the first thought that struck Adam. He hadn't seen her since he was thirteen, but if he'd passed her in the street, he'd have known her instantly. She was tall and stick thin, with piercing blue eyes and strong features. As they approached her table, Elvira glanced up from the newspaper she had been perusing and gave Adam a long, cold stare.

"Do you need money?" Her voice was perfectly calm.

"No, but thank you for offering."

She gave a snort of laughter. "You'd better sit down." She indicated a chair on the opposite side of the table before turning a hard stare in Maja's direction. "Which are you? A secretary or a gold digger?"

"Neither." Maja took the seat next to Adam. "But I'm glad I was warned that you have a nasty tongue."

Elvira gave a single bark of laughter. "I like her," she told Adam. "You should keep her."

"It's not that simple." He flicked a smile in Maja's direction and caught her startled glance. "But we're not here to talk about me."

"Why are you here? It's almost twenty years since I last saw you."

"I want to ask you about Knight Valentine."

He didn't know what he'd expected Elvira's response to be. Anger, possibly. Outrage that he would bring up the subject of the man who'd been at the heart of the family rift. Even sadness.

Not fear. That was the last thing he expected to see. Yet for a moment or two, that was what he saw in the depths of her pale eyes. It shocked him. Somehow, he had never imagined Elvira would be capable of feeling afraid.

"No." She shook her head, and he heard a faint tremor in her voice. "You can go now."

"Elvira..." he lowered his voice "...this is important. We have reason to believe he is involved in something very bad, and I want to discover anything that I can use against him. You objected to his marriage to my mother very strenuously. You must know something. I need your help."

Her eyes scanned his face. He didn't know what she was looking for, and he wasn't sure what she found, but after a moment or two she pressed her lips together tightly. Giving a brief nod, she folded the newspaper and pressed a napkin to the corners of her mouth.

"Not here. We'll go to my room."

Her elegant, third floor room overlooked rolling hills and Elvira served coffee in bone china cups that seemed vaguely familiar to Adam. They made him think of his mother and he wondered if Elvira had used this set when he'd been a child. The thought stuck on a loop in his mind. *My mother could have drunk from this cup.* Why did it matter so much? He did know why. It just did.

Elvira took a seat in a wingback chair. "Let me be very clear about this. I don't want to talk about that man. I don't even want to think about him. I prefer to fool myself that he doesn't exist. But you are Belinda's son. I tried to help her and failed." A shadow crossed her face. "If I can help you, I'll do it. For her sake."

"Thank you." Adam was amazed at the depth of emotion in his voice. What was even more amazing was he didn't care his feelings were on show. If Elvira could talk openly about his mother, maybe he could, too.

"What do you want to know?"

"I don't remember much about the speech you made at their wedding. All I know is you spoke out about what a bad person he was and why my mother shouldn't marry him. I remember you said he'd sold his soul to the devil. Can you be specific about what you meant by that? Maybe give me some examples of the sort of dirty deals he'd done that made you use that expression?"

Elvira lifted her saucer from the table at her side and the cup rattled as her hand shook. Instead of taking a sip of her drink, she placed it down again. "You don't understand. I thought perhaps you did." Her gaze traveled from Adam's face to Maja's and back again. "When I said that, it wasn't a metaphor. Knight Valentine really did sell his soul to the devil."

Since Adam had been frozen into immobility by Elvira's words, Maja decided to take over his role and direct the conversation. "How did you learn of Knight's transaction with the devil?"

The question seemed to rouse Adam from his dazed state. "Surely you are not taking this seriously?" He scrubbed a hand over his face as though checking that he was awake. "Either of you?"

Elvira answered Maja's question as though Adam hadn't spoken. "Adam's father, Robert, and Knight were best friends. Right through school and into adulthood. Although I found it difficult to believe, it was Robert who told me the story." She cast a wary glance in Adam's direction. "Just before he died."

"I can't believe I am listening to this." Adam got to his feet and went to the window, standing with his back to the room.

"Go on." Maja nodded to Elvira.

They had come to hear the truth, no matter how farfetched or gruesome. She understood that it was easier for her to be open-minded about what Elvira was saying.

She came from another world. A place inhabited by gods and demons. A realm in which werewolves fought vampires and the evil faerie king had just been overthrown. Pacts with Satan were rare, but they were not unheard of. Throughout history, there might have been only a handful of mortals who had taken the devil's hand and walked a dark, dangerous path at his side. But it had happened. As a child, she had listened wide-eyed to the stories. They never ended well.

"Robert told me that Knight always had this fiercely competitive streak. He said his family was odd. Knight once said he didn't know why his parents had a child, since they weren't interested in him. They just wanted an heir. Someone to carry the name." Although her hand still shook, Elvira managed to lift her cup to her lips and take a sip of her coffee. "Robert said it started as a game. Knight had to be the best at everything. It started with little things. They were practicing before a basketball game and Knight, who wasn't the best shooter, jokingly said, 'If I get this next shot, the devil can have my soul.'"

Maja cast a glance in Adam's direction. His shoulders were hunched and his head was bent. Everything about his stance spoke of despair. She leaned forward and gripped Elvira's hand. To her surprise the unyielding old woman returned her clasp gratefully.

"It became Knight's thing. His catchphrase. Anything they did, he would use the same words. When they played pool, he would say the devil could have his soul if he pocketed the next ball. The devil could have his soul if he flipped a coin and it came up heads. The curious thing was, every time Knight used that phrase, he got what he wanted."

Adam swung around. "So he's lucky. I don't like the

guy any more than you do, but that doesn't mean he's in league with the devil."

"Do you want to hear this story, Adam?" Elvira had regained some of her strength and her voice was compelling.

After what appeared to be an internal battle, he gave a curt nod and returned to his seat.

"When he went into business, Knight was ruthless. Still is from what I hear. Robert told me he was seeing less of him at that time, but he met him for lunch. All Knight could talk of was this deal he was involved in. It was a make-or-break thing. And Knight said it again. 'If this deal goes through, the devil can have my soul.' Robert told me something about the way he said the words that time made him shiver." She gave Adam an uneasy look. "You father was not a man who scared easily."

"And the deal went through." Maja felt herself drawn into the story.

"The deal went through. It launched Knight as the man he is today, the world's leading deal maker. The man who owns more luxury properties across the globe than any other. A brand name to be reckoned with. Robert didn't see him again for several months, but when he did, he was shocked at the change in him."

"Don't tell me. He had horns and a pointed tail?" Maja knew what Adam was doing. He was severely jolted and needed to stay in control. Nevertheless, his mocking tone introduced a discordant note that unsettled Elvira.

"I didn't ask you to come here and dredge up old memories." Her finger shook as she pointed toward the door. "Don't let it hit you on the way out."

Maja caught Adam's eye, conveying a message to him with her expression. *We are here to listen.* For a moment, their gazes locked. Strong brown eyes clashed briefly with hers. Then he relaxed, his body language changing. The tension left his frame and he nodded, acknowledging that he understood what she was attempting to communicate.

"I'm sorry," he said to Elvira. "I'm struggling to take this in, but that's no reason to behave like an ass. Please continue."

The outcome appeared to be in doubt for several seconds. Then she gave a tight-lipped nod. "Robert got a call from Knight out of the blue, asking if they could meet up. When they did, he was shocked at Knight's appearance. He said he looked thin and gaunt, like a man who was terrified. Over lunch, he told Robert he had made the worst mistake of his life. He had done something he couldn't undo. That deal he'd wanted so badly had looked like it was going to fall through at the last minute. Knight had used his old maxim, calling on the devil to see it through and offering his soul in return. The next day, everything was back on track. But Knight woke up that day and something within himself had changed. He said it felt like a part of him had gone missing. Like there was a giant hole in the center of his being."

"But he didn't talk about any specific interaction with the devil?" Maja asked. She was aware of Adam watching her intently as she spoke. "No vow of eternal servitude or pact signed in blood?"

"That was the exact question Robert asked. Knight laughed and said that wasn't how it worked. When Robert asked him how he knew, Knight told him what had happened the day after he'd signed the contract on his big deal. He was woken by an unusual sound in his bedroom. Lying still, he tried to figure out what it was. When he recognized it, his blood ran cold. It was breathing. Heavy and ragged, as though from someone who had run a long distance…or the panting of a wild animal. Of course, Knight thought someone had broken into his apartment.

He was scared, but he kept a gun in the dresser at the side of his bed. As he slowly reached for the drawer, something moved across the room and he saw a figure coming toward him."

Elvira gulped down the remains of her coffee. She seemed to Maja to have crossed an invisible line. It was as if she was no longer here in the room with them. She had stepped back into the past.

"Knight saw a creature with the upper body of a man and the lower half of a goat. It had cloven feet, horns and eyes that glowed red in the darkness. If that wasn't bad enough, it was the tail, the awful pointed tail, swinging back and forth, that convinced him. The devil was in Knight's bedroom."

"Could it have been a dream?" Adam asked. "Brought on by Knight's insistence on using that expression about selling his soul?"

"That was what he hoped. He said he even tried a prayer as he lay there with his gaze fastened on the beast. As it moved toward him, he gave up hoping and praying and started screaming."

Elvira had started shaking again and Maja decided it was time for a break. "Shall I make more coffee?"

Both Adam and Elvira appeared grateful for the offer. As she gathered the cups together, Maja noticed a photograph in a silver frame on the table at Elvira's side. It was of a laughing young couple. The man could only have been Adam's father. The resemblance was striking. Which meant the slender woman with the cloud of dark hair must be Belinda Perlman, the woman who had married Robert Lyon and then Knight Valentine. Even in that picture, it was possible to see that Adam's mother had been incredibly beautiful. She had delicate features and an air of fragility. One woman and two friends who both loved her. Robert Lyon, the man in the picture, and Knight Valentine, the shadowy figure in the background. There had to be a story there.

When she returned with the coffee, she was pleased to observe that Adam and Elvira had been making conversation on neutral topics instead of staring into space as they had been when she left them. She knew from her interactions with the warriors who had joined Odin's army that mortals had a dread of the supernatural. They remained largely oblivious to the existence of Otherworld. Sometimes the two realms overlapped. Ghosts were the most obvious example. Vampires and werewolves persisted in causing problems for those who defended the borders of this mortal realm. Her own interaction with Adam was an example of how thin the veil between the two worlds really was. Because Otherworld was hidden, with only occasional glimpses, Maja could see why it was feared.

The devil, of course, was a whole other problem. He was feared in both worlds. Satan was the angel who had rebelled. Now, he was everyone's enemy. He had only one mission. To destroy. When it came to humans, he was prepared to achieve his ambition by killing or enslaving them.

With a fresh cup of coffee in her hand, Elvira was ready to continue. "Knight knew he wasn't dreaming when the devil spoke to him. Just two words. The same two words every time. *Pay me*."

"Every time?" Adam asked.

"He told Robert the beast came to him every night from then on."

Chapter 15

It was like listening to the most ridiculously far-fetched fairy tale. Yet Adam could tell that Maja believed it. Elvira certainly did. And she was recounting a story that had been told to her by his father. Could he force his skepticism aside and open his mind to it? He had to try. Had to suspend belief and imagine that Knight had been visited every night by a horned being who was half man, half goat, because he had sold his soul to the devil.

"Robert said he did everything he could to put Knight's mind at rest. Told him he was working too hard, suggested he take a holiday, recommended he see a doctor who could give him something to help him sleep. Knight just laughed. The two men didn't meet again for several months. During the intervening time, Robert said the rise in Knight's fortunes was meteoric. Everything the man touched turned to gold." Elvira drummed her fingers on the arm of her chair as she glanced at the picture in its silver frame. "By the time he saw Knight again, your father had met Belinda."

Adam followed the direction of Elvira's gaze. He hadn't seen that particular picture of his parents until today. Now he was glad he had come here, if only for that. It gave him a brief glimpse into who they had once been. Robert, big and strong, was staring at Belinda with such love it was obvious even through the lens of a camera. And it was good to see his mother looking happy instead of the sad, broken woman he remembered...

"When Robert did see Knight, it was only on social occasions with other people present. They barely got a chance to speak privately. Knight seemed happy and Robert assumed the strange dreams had ended. When he snatched a moment to ask him about it, Knight was flippant. He said his nocturnal visitor still showed up every night. Still uttered the same two words. *Pay me.* But he had laughed and said he thought it was worth it for the benefits." Elvira grimaced. "*Worth it.* Those were the words he used. He told Robert he was on the way to his first billion. That was the price of Knight Valentine's soul."

Adam supposed the story had value even though it couldn't be true in any literal sense. Knight had told Adam's father about it. It had taken a grip on his imagination. He truly believed he had a pact with the devil. That had to have screwed up his head. It explained why he thought he was indestructible. It also answered Maja's question about Knight's motives. She was right. He hadn't been born wicked, but had convinced himself that he was evil because of this imaginary pact. He had the perfect excuse. *The devil made me do it. The devil made me lock you in the cellar when you were a child. The devil made me drive your mother into an early*

grave. The devil made me create a terrorist organization
as a front for wiping out my business rivals.

"After that, Knight was so wrapped up in business, their friendship dwindled to nothing. They met now and then, but never in private. There wasn't another opportunity for the sort of confidences they'd previously enjoyed. If anything, Robert felt Knight was embarrassed by the things he'd told him. Years passed and Robert put it to the back of his mind. He assumed Knight had gotten counseling or other treatment for what must have been a delusion brought on by stress."

"But you didn't believe that," Maja said. "When you stood up to Knight at Belinda's wedding to him, you told everyone about his pact with the devil."

"No, I didn't believe it. For one simple reason. Knight Valentine always got everything he wanted in life." She took a deep breath and looked at the photograph again. "And what he wanted more than anything was Belinda."

Adam jerked as though an electric shock had been applied to his spine. "What are you suggesting?"

"I'm not suggesting anything. I'm telling you. As soon as Knight set eyes on your mother, he wanted her. She didn't feel the same. Not then. But soon after your father died her feelings changed." His aunt's eyes challenged him. "Knight Valentine gets what he wants."

"Elvira, this is nonsense. Are you trying to say that the devil killed my father so Knight could marry my mother?"

"Yes." That simple word hung in the air, cutting through any ambiguity or doubt. "And what's more, your father believed it. He told me all this as he lay dying. He begged me to take care of Belinda, and of you and Danny. He asked me to make sure she didn't marry Knight." She covered her face with her hands. "I let you all down."

Maja went to her and knelt before her chair, gripping

her hands in her own. "You are one woman. You couldn't fight the devil."

Elvira raised a tear-streaked face. "At first, like you, I thought Robert's story was far-fetched. Then I saw how quickly Belinda fell under Knight's spell. I tried to dissuade her from marrying him. She'd always listened to me, but his hold over her was too strong. I decided I needed to do something drastic to stop the wedding. I wanted to denounce him publicly because I thought he wouldn't come after me that way, but I just made a fool of myself. And I lost Belinda. She refused to see me after that day. She wouldn't take my calls and my letters came back unopened. Oh, I know Knight was behind that. Belinda didn't have a malicious bone in her body. I should have done more, pushed harder. But I was a coward." Her voice trembled. "I feared what he could do, so I hid myself away. I'll admit it. I tried to pretend it wasn't happening."

"Did he come after you?" Maja asked.

"Not directly." Elvira's lips twisted into a half smile. "He didn't need to. I'd lost everything that mattered to me. Family. Friends. My reputation. I'd been written off as a crazy woman after my outburst at the wedding. But he sends me a warning now and then."

"What sort of warning?" Adam frowned. Knight took the time to threaten an old woman?

"The sort of things that would get me locked up if I ever spoke of them to anyone. Fingernails scraping on my bedpost in the middle of the night. A demonic chuckle in my ear just as I'm dozing off to sleep. Glowing red eyes in a darkened corner of the room. Little reminders that Knight has friends in hot places." The smile was genuine this time. "I can read your thoughts, Adam. You're thinking you've wasted a morning on a crazy old woman. Hell,

you only have my word that Robert told me that story. I
could have made it all up."

Adam tried for a polite protest. "I wasn't—"

Elvira held up a hand, cutting across his words. "Don't
worry. I'd be thinking the same thing in your place. But
I have something that may persuade you."

Adam frowned, meeting Maja's eyes across the room.
What proof could Elvira possible produce to convince him
of the truth of something that must surely all be imagination?

Getting to her feet, Elvira went to a bureau under the
window. Producing a key on a chain around her neck, she
unlocked one of the drawers. "Your mother wrote me a
letter from the nursing home where she was being cared
for. It arrived the day after she died." She held the folded
pages out to him. "Maybe Belinda's words will convince
you where mine can't."

Although he remained perfectly still, Adam's reluctance to take Belinda's letter from Elvira was coming off
him in waves. Maja felt his fear as though it was a black
cloud descending on the room. And she understood its
source. He didn't want to know what Knight had done to
break his mother. He had been thirteen when she died,
and Maja supposed that was the reason his father had
told Elvira the story of Knight's pact with the devil instead of him. Robert would have reasoned that Adam was
too young to be burdened with such a horrific tale. The
part of him that took the burden of responsibility onto
his own shoulders, that cared so deeply, was afraid of
what he would find. The man who had traveled to Syria
to find his brother was scared that the boy he had been
could have done more. Even though he had been a child,

subjected to his own nightmare at his stepfather's hands, he was weighed down with guilt at his mother's decline.

Maja wanted him to find the truth, and to do it he needed to read that letter.

She moved to sit next to him and took his hand. "Let's do this together."

He gave her a grateful look and nodded, holding out his other hand to Elvira. "I guess it's time."

The first thing that struck Maja was the precision of Belinda's handwriting. Adam smiled as he traced the first line with one fingertip.

"She was always such a perfectionist. My handwriting is untidy and she spent hours trying to get me to be neater. It was a losing battle."

The first few paragraphs contained a personal message to Elvira, an apology for the breakdown in their relationship. Without making any direct reference to Knight, Belinda implied that dark forces had been at work to keep them apart. She hoped Elvira would forgive her. There were splashes on the page. Belinda had shed tears as she wrote.

Maja rested her cheek lightly against Adam's upper arm as he read. She scanned the words with him, feeling the tension in his body as he followed his mother's final thoughts. Elvira returned to her seat and watched them, her hands gripping the arms of her chair so tightly that her knuckles gleamed white.

The next part of the letter developed into a story, and Maja supposed at first that Belinda's mind must have been wandering as she wrote.

"This is the story of a man who sold his soul and thought to gain riches in return. And he did. But what was the price? When the devil came for the debt, he asked a favor so great it brought the man to his knees, howling in pain.

"'Pay me.' They were the words the devil spoke in the darkness of the man's bedroom.

"The world is a dark place these days. The devil needed to call in the favor. Azrael, the Angel of Death, the one they call the Grim Reaper, was overworked. Death needed a helpmate.

"The woman in the corner of the room recoiled in dread as her husband's skin and muscle melted like candle wax and dripped from his body, and his blood boiled. She watched as all that was human about him was driven out with such force that he screamed and writhed on the floor, begging the devil to end his life rather than torture him this way. He died a thousand deaths that night, as his terrified wife looked on, helpless to do anything.

"When he rose, all that remained was a skeleton. The devil held out a black robe for him to cover his hideous appearance and handed him a scythe taller than himself, with a blade as sharp as a razor.

"'Join Death in his grim task. Find the ones whose time has run out and cut them down.'

"The devil's command echoed inside the woman's head. She thought she was going mad, but the foul-smelling smoke he left behind was a reminder that this was real.

"Silently, the man obeyed the devil's command. In the morning, his body was restored to normality. But each night he would assume his skeletal form once more and take up his robe and scythe to reap the souls of the dead alongside his grim master. He had sold his soul without questioning the detail of the contract. Now the devil was exacting his awful price.

"And that's my story, Elvira. When Death comes for me—maybe tonight, maybe tomorrow. Who knows the exact hour? I only know it will be soon— I will be the only woman to stare at that hooded figure and know she is looking into the blank eye sockets of her own husband."

Adam's own eyes were bleak, dark pools as he lifted them from the page and looked at Elvira. "She has been dead eleven years. If I hadn't come to you, would you ever have shown me this letter?"

"No." Elvira flinched as his expression hardened further. "Think about it, Adam. Your mother died in a nursing home. As far as the world was concerned, she was being treated for an affliction of the nerves. We know better, and so did most of her acquaintances. In addition to suffering from chronic depression, Belinda was addicted to alcohol and drugs. That was what Knight drove her to." Elvira pointed to the paper in his hand. "That letter explains why. But no one would have believed what she was saying. They would have dismissed it as the sad ramblings of a confused mind. And if I'd brought that letter to you, that's what you would have done. You wouldn't have taken the time to listen to me and hear the rest of the story. Admit it."

Because Maja was still leaning against Adam, she could feel the tremor that ran through him. Could sense the conflict gripping him. Knew how close he was to walking out and turning his back on this. Because the truth was in danger of breaking him apart.

She also felt the moment he capitulated. The stiffness went out of his body and his breathing relaxed. Although she knew what it cost him, this was the man she knew. She understood his hurt and knew why he wanted to deny what he was hearing. But Adam was stronger and better than that. He was the bravest man she had ever met. And coming from a Valkyrie, that was quite an accolade. The only men Maja met were heroes, but Adam surpassed them all. He would not walk away from a difficult message, even if it tore him in two.

She heard his indrawn breath catch in his throat. "You're right, Elvira. Without a new chapter to this story, I wouldn't have come here today. If you'd told me your story of Knight's deal with the devil, I would have dismissed you as a bitter old woman." His expression was hard to read as he glanced down at the paper in his hand once more. "And even though it hurts me to admit it, if I'd read my mother's letter at all, I would have written it off as the ravings of the troubled mind of an addict."

"A new chapter?" Elvira sat up straighter. "What do you mean?"

Adam shook his head. "I think it's better if you don't know. The fewer people who are in danger the better. We are talking about the man who killed my father." His expression darkened as he spoke. "And who caused my mother's death, as well. I know what you are about to say, Elvira. You have borne this by yourself for almost twenty years, and now I'm taking over and making the decisions."

"Believe, me, Adam, I was going to say something far less polite." There was a snarl in Elvira's words.

He laughed, and although the sound was shaky, Maja was relieved to hear a trace of genuine amusement in there. "I promise we will come back and tell you how the story ends."

Evening had become Adam's favorite time. In the past, it had simply been an extension to his working day. An annoying interruption to his routine when other people stopped responding to messages and emails and didn't answer calls. Now he got it. He understood why people valued this part of the day.

It was a time to enjoy his new family. Maja sat curled up on the sofa next to him with her head resting on his shoulder. Adam kept his arm around her waist. He liked the feel of her close to him. Soon Tarek would be safely tucked up under his duvet with his furry bodyguard beneath his bed. This was their world. It belonged to the three of them...

Adam smiled and corrected himself. Five of them. Leo and the baby were part of this cozy bubble of theirs. If only they could keep the apartment door closed and stay this way forever.

Upon leaving Elvira's apartment the previous day, Adam had heaved fresh air into his lungs, binging on it like a man rescued from drowning. The dramatic atmosphere had begun to stifle him, and with his promise that they would return and tell her the outcome of their fight against Knight, he had grabbed Maja's hand and left.

Adam still felt the grief of his father's death. He knew the trauma of his loss had made him the person he was today. He figured he was like a jigsaw puzzle. At the age of thirteen, all his pieces hadn't been in place. When Robert Lyon died, he took one of the pieces of his son's puzzle with him. Adam was incomplete without it. There were memories, private jokes, conversations...hundreds of moments in his life that he had shared with his father. No one else knew about them. There was no one else to turn to when something triggered a reminder. He had no one to go to with his silly questions, the ones his dad would always answer. There was no one to tell him silly jokes. He would never again hear that deep rumbling laugh... He had lost his hero as well as his parent.

His start in life had given him the perfect role model for the sort of father he wanted to be. The greatest gift his father had given him was his time. When his own child was born, Adam would be there for him or her in the same way. The love he already had for the unborn infant was an extension of everything he felt for Danny and Tarek. The same strength of emotion, the same urge to protect.

He had been older when his mother died, and watching her decline had been the hardest thing he had ever done. Belinda had been incredibly beautiful, but she appeared fragile. Looking back on her life before Knight, Adam could see the difference, and it hurt him to know what had caused it. Her life with his father had been happy. She had been loved and nurtured. Adam had always suspected that the decline in her health, the depression, accompanied by her addiction, was caused by her unhappy second marriage. To find out he had been right—spectacularly so—gave him no satisfaction.

Would a stronger woman have walked out on Knight when the devil came to exact his price? Or did what she saw unhinge Belinda so that she couldn't leave? Adam hoped she hadn't stayed because of him and Danny. He didn't think that was the case. When Robert died, he'd left them well provided for, and Belinda must have known she could have gone to Elvira. He suspected that Belinda *couldn't* leave, no matter what she saw. For the same reason that she had married Knight in the first place. The same reason she didn't see how he was abusing her son. She was under his spell. She was one of the prizes Knight had been granted by his master.

Blackness clouded Adam's mind when he thought of Knight. The man whom, he now knew, was responsible for the deaths of both his parents. The man whose greed had forged a path of death and destruction, trampling on anyone who stood in his path.

No more.

Although they hadn't discussed the contents of his mother's letter any further, it had been hanging in the air between him and Maja ever since. Adam knew she had been giving him space, allowing him to digest the awful details of what he had read. It was part of that unique way she had of picking up on his mood. Now, as Tarek went to watch a TV program in his room—part of his pre-bedtime routine—Adam felt it pressing down on him further.

He needed to feel Maja tight against him. He pulled her into his arms and, turning in his embrace, she molded her body to his. Her warmth and scent comforted him. Her heartbeat and breathing in time with his were exactly what he needed. When he found her lips opening beneath his, he lost himself in their sweetness, and some of the horror of his thoughts receded.

"I believe it." He rested his head forehead on hers.

"I know." He loved that he didn't need to say anything else. She picked up on the rhythm of his speech instantly.

"He is doing the devil's work and reaping souls at the same time." He gave a shaky laugh. "How arrogant do you have to be to call your organization after the Reaper when you *are* the Reaper?"

"He never thought anyone would find out," Maja said. "It was his private joke against the world."

"Elvira knew." Adam clenched his fists. "She must have been in hell all these years."

"You said it yourself. No one would have listened to her. Knight knew that. He was safe from Elvira." Maja took his hand. "But he's not safe from us."

"How can we fight him, Maja? He's the right-hand man of the Angel of Death."

"Aren't you forgetting something?" She laughed at his bemused expression. "I do the same job as the Reaper. I collect souls. We just obey different masters. I'm not afraid of Knight." Her brilliant smile lit her face. "He should be afraid of me."

"If we could just find a way to expose him. Elvira had the right idea. Exposing him publicly is the way to hurt him. Knight is a narcissist who thrives on his reputation. If we can damage that, expose him as the brains behind the Reaper, he's ruined. I can't even begin to think of how we can do that, let alone show the world the truth about his pact with the devil. I'd do it if I could, but right now I can't think of a way to get close enough to him to do anything. What we have still isn't enough. If I published this story in one of my newspapers, it would cause a stir, but it wouldn't ruin him."

"For now, let's concentrate on the first part. If we can end the terrorism and the killings, we will have achieved what we set out to do. While we are planning that, we may also think of a way of exposing his deal with Satan."

Adam shook his head. "I still can't get used to talking about it as reality. It's like we've stepped into a nightmare."

"Not everything that has happened to us has been bad," Maja reminded him.

"God, no." He pressed a hand to her stomach with a smile. "And I won't let him detract from the best thing that's happened to me."

Maja returned the smile, holding his hand in place with her own. "What we need is a plan."

"You're right. Any plan would be better than the big, fat nothing we have right now." Adam grimaced.

"We could use some reinforcements. A small army would be useful."

"Sorry I can't oblige." Adam grimaced. "You are the one with the warrior contacts."

"Unfortunately, I don't think Odin will allow my sisters to come to our aid." The expression in her eyes was shy as she raised them to his. "I liked the way you said our baby is the best thing that's happened to you."

He gazed down at her, drinking in the beauty of her features. How would he have dealt with this situation with Knight if she hadn't been here at his side? It was a silly question. Without Maja, Adam would be dead. She had saved his life and now she was dragging him through the most bizarre crisis he had ever experienced. His mind had already been opened by the arrival of a Valkyrie into his life. It had been flung even further open with the news that his stepfather had engaged in a pact with the devil. If that wasn't enough, he then had to contend with the information that Knight, in repayment of his debt, had entered into partnership with the Azrael, the Grim Reaper. All in all, for a man who didn't believe in the paranormal, Adam was having something of a wild initiation.

"Our baby is one part of the best thing that's happened to me," he said, enjoying the blush that stained her cheeks. "And here is another."

At that moment, Tarek emerged from his room to remind Maja that he needed to take something for show-and-tell the next day. It looked like persuading him that it couldn't be Leo might take some time. On reflection, Adam didn't know whether to be sorry or relieved that the moment of intimacy was lost. With every minute that passed he felt himself drawn to Maja. But nothing had changed.

A thought flitted through his head, futile and frustrating. *If only she could make me immortal...or I could make her human.*

If only one of them could break down the barriers and join the other's world. It wasn't going to happen. They had more chance of Knight repenting and giving up his evil ways. Which meant each time Adam answered the powerful tug that was pulling him closer to Maja, he was making it harder for himself to break away when the time came for her to leave.

It didn't matter. He could tell himself that over and over. He could get it as a tattoo. Make it his ringtone. He was already in too deep. He was powerless to resist her. Which meant that as well as finding a way to expose Knight Valentine to the world, he was just going to have to find a way to make sure he didn't lose his family.

Chapter 16

The department store was busy and Tarek trailed behind Maja with a long-suffering expression. The video game he wanted had been out of stock, and although they had ordered it, as far as he was concerned the shopping expedition had lost its appeal.

Trailing around a busy store with a reluctant eight-year-old in her wake was not Maja's idea of a pleasant way to spend an afternoon, and she was about to suggest they leave when Tarek took her by surprise.

"Are you having a baby?"

"What makes you ask that?" She stalled for time.

"You are sick every morning." She had hoped she'd hidden that from him. Clearly her attempts had failed. "And you look at baby clothes. A lot. In catalogs. On Adam's laptop. Here in the store."

"Would you mind if I was?"

Tarek appeared to give the matter some thought. "Will you send me back to Syria when the baby comes?"

"No." The words brought a lump to her throat. Ignoring the other shoppers around them, she stooped and wrapped her arms around him. "That will never happen. I love you, Tarek. So does Adam. Your home is here..." She wanted to finish the sentence by saying "with us" but she couldn't. There was no "us" and it would be unfair to give him false hope that she would be part of his life forever. "This is where you belong, and the baby will be a new brother or sister to you."

"In that case, I don't mind." He sounded cheerful. "If it's a boy, do you think you might call him Thor?"

"Probably not."

He sighed. "I thought you might say that. It's the name of my favorite character in the game we just ordered. Can we get ice cream on the way home?"

Once again, his resilience amazed her. Laughing, she took his hand and they made their way to the escalator. They were almost there when, out of the corner of her eye, Maja caught sight of something that made her pause. Two women were browsing through a pile of sale items, but they were watching Maja and Tarek.

Maja knew all the Valkyries.

Which made it almost laughable that these two would imagine that she wouldn't recognize them as they stood in the middle of a New York department store and pretended not to be following her. At least they had dressed in mortal clothing instead of their traditional garments. Maja thought back to her first encounter with Adam, when she had been clad in her Valkyrie attire. No wonder he had believed he was dreaming.

Aurora and Lotus were dryads who had joined the Valkyries recently enough to still retain some of their wood nymph characteristics. In fact Maja had overseen their combat training. The thought made her want to

laugh. Clearly, they needed more work on covert sur-
veillance. Unless someone wanted her to know she was
being watched. Someone? She knew exactly who had sent
these two. None of the Valkyries operated without direct
instructions from Brynhild.

Odin ruled Valhalla, but Brynhild was his general.
Maja's eldest sister was powerful in her own right, but
she delivered Odin's will with loyalty and determination.
Known for her strength and courage, Brynhild demanded
nothing less from the Valkyries who served her. Maja
had to wonder why she had sent these two on this mission. Aurora and Lotus were the most inexperienced of
the shield maidens.

That didn't make them less deadly. They were still capable of delivering a lethal blow to anyone who stood in
their way. But even together, they were no match for Maja.

And Brynhild knows that.

Maja's mind was racing. She could only conclude that
someone must have seen her here in the mortal realm and
recognized her. Unlike the man she had tipped into the
Dumpster, whoever it was had reported back to Brynhild. And her sister had sent Aurora and Lotus to do...
what, exactly? They wouldn't be able to force Maja back
to Valhalla with them—she could resist them with one
hand tied behind her back—and they weren't doing a very
good job of spying on her.

This could mean only one thing. It was a message from
Brynhild. Her sister's way of telling Maja she knew where
she was. That there was no place to hide.

It should scare her. On one level, it did. But on another, it triggered the first stages of a plan in her mind. A
crazy, daring plan that would likely fail before it even got
started. What had Adam said? *Any plan would be better
than the big, fat nothing we have right now.* She would

take crazy and daring over nothing. As long as it didn't endanger the baby.

"Wait here a second." She motioned to Tarek to remain by the escalator.

Aurora and Lotus looked startled when she strode over to them. Clearly, they had not been expecting this.

Smiling, Maja leaned close to them. "Tell Brynhild if she wants me, she'll have to do better than this. My sister will have to come and get me herself."

"There are eight names on this list. That means, with Knight, the consortium consists of nine people. Apart from Shepherd, they are all leaders in the business world." Adam placed the spreadsheet they had taken from Knight's desk on the coffee table in front of him. "I've done some checking, and none of them have ever been affected by a Reaper attack. On the contrary...they have all benefited when rival companies have suffered from a terrorist strike."

He drew Maja's attention to one name. "Charlie Hannon, CEO of Associated Review. Remember how I told you about the Reaper bomb attack on my Boston office? After that, the building was a pile of rubble and my company could no longer print our local newspaper in that city. Hannon's rival publication saw its digital subscriptions increase by 40 percent as a result." Adam shook his head. "They blew up my building for the sake of his profits. If it hadn't been for the quick thinking of a security guard, hundreds of people would have been killed that day."

"I wonder how Knight recruited these people," Maja murmured. "It's hard to believe they've all made a pact with Satan."

"Knight can be very persuasive. And looking down this list, I'd say we're not dealing with the nicest group of men and women. Although I have to agree. I don't imagine Knight has mentioned his silent partner. Even this little group would run screaming from the room if they knew they were dealing with the devil. They can turn a blind eye when it comes to killing and maiming innocent people for the sake of money, but add in horns and a tail and I'd imagine they would freak out." Adam flipped the top sheet over. "This next spreadsheet is interesting. It's a list of dates, past and future, each about six months apart."

Maja wrinkled her nose. "You find that interesting?"

He laughed. "Not in itself."

They had once again waited until Tarek was asleep before discussing the problem confronting them. Maja had told him that Tarek had figured out the news about the baby. When they'd sat him down and discussed it, he had surprised Adam by being mildly pleased. Apart from pushing strongly for a superhero name, and expressing a desire not to share a room, he had appeared unperturbed.

"You won't make me wear anything that says Big Brother, will you?" Tarek had directed a searching look at Maja. "There was a kid at school whose parents had a new baby, and his mom made him do that for a family picture. He was teased for days."

Laughing, she had assured him it was never going to happen.

Now it was late and staring at spreadsheets wasn't helping Adam overcome a feeling of intense weariness. "It got interesting when I checked out the social media activity of each of the people on the first list against the dates on this second one."

"You've been busy." Maja nodded approvingly.

"It wasn't too difficult. Like Knight, this group is made up of narcissists. They all like to let their followers know how wonderful they are, what they are doing and where they are. But around the dates on this sheet—the ones that have already passed—they were much quieter. So I suspected that these were the dates of meetings." He indicated his laptop, which already had several browser tabs open. "Although the Reaper consortium were quieter, they weren't silent. And some of them didn't switch off their location sharing."

"Pardon?"

"If you have a mobile device, it transmits a signal to your service provider, sharing your location. When you post to social media, you can either choose to let other people see your location, or you can keep it private. If you usually share it, the device will continue to do that, unless you purposely change the settings and make it private."

"I see. These people may not have wanted the ones who follow them on social media to know where they were on a particular day, but they didn't change this function?"

"Exactly." Adam pulled his laptop forward. "In May last year, Suzanne Sumner shared a picture with her followers." On the screen was an image of a pile of papers balanced on a woman's lap as, on a table close by, a full glass of champagne fizzed temptingly. The caption beneath the picture read No Rest for the Wicked. "As you can see, her location was Greenwich, Connecticut, USA. The time and date match this spreadsheet exactly."

"Greenwich? You think she was at Valentine House?" Maja asked. "That's where they meet?"

"I checked it out. None of the other people on this list have homes there, or any affiliation to the area. No reason to be there that I could discover. But Knight's house would be the obvious place to meet," Adam pointed out. "Knight controls the environment. You saw how difficult it is to get in. Security is rigid and privacy is guaranteed."

He went to another tab. "This is Alain Dubois, head of

one of the top French retail companies. His chain of high-end clothing stores dominates the market. I've met him once or twice. The guy would sell his own grandmother if the price was right. A few hours before Suzanne was sharing her champagne picture, Alain was complaining about jet lag." Adam pointed to the screen. "Although his post is in French, the translation is straightforward. 'Transatlantic flights are the worst. Now facing a thirty-mile cab ride. But looking forward to catching up with friends in a beautiful, waterfront setting and a productive meeting.' Again, he shared his location. When he posted that, he was at JFK Airport."

"That doesn't prove they were at the same meeting," Maja said. "All it tells us is that he was in New York that day. We don't even know for sure that he went to Greenwich."

"No, it doesn't. Except Greenwich is about thirty miles from JFK. And Suzanne and Charlie Hannon both 'liked' Alain's comment. Again, it proves nothing. But it gives me a gut feeling about their connection to each other. If nothing else, it says they were checking out each other's social media feed that day." He opened another tab. "Finally, we have the four-star general himself. Shepherd doesn't use social media."

Adam indicated a picture of a tall, straight-backed man with iron-gray hair descending the steps of a helicopter. He was dressed casually in jeans, leather jacket and distinctive blue-and-tan cowboy boots. "This was snapped at Westchester County Airport around the same time that Alain was arriving at JFK. You can see that the photograph was taken with a long-distance lens. It featured in an article written by a reporter who is highly critical of what he calls Shepherd's 'inactivity' over the Reaper. The article questioned what Shepherd was doing in New York when there had been a Reaper attack in Sweden the day before. Since Shepherd was appointed to lead the international force against the Reaper, there was strong feeling that he should at least have made an appearance at the scene." Adam shifted position so he was facing Maja again. "In case we were in any doubt about what we were up against, the guy who wrote that article was found dead the day after it was published."

"Didn't anyone ever connect his death to Shepherd or the Reaper?"

"He left a suicide note," Adam said. "Just as I'm sure I would when the time came."

Maja's hand crept into his. "That time will not come." Her voice shook slightly and Adam raised her fingers to his lips.

"This was what finally convinced me." He went back to Suzanne Sumner's picture. "Look here." He pointed to the top corner. Above the champagne glass, a man's crossed leg could be seen on the opposite side of the table. He was wearing jeans, and part of a distinctive blue-and-tan cowboy boot could also be seen.

"Adam." Maja raised wide eyes to his face. "You should be a detective."

He laughed. "Has Tarek been getting you to watch daytime TV with him?"

She nodded. "But none of those cops are as good as you."

"There are clues for some of the other dates, but none of them are as conclusive as this." Adam closed the lid of his laptop. "Of course, it only means something to us. To anyone else, including the authorities, it's meaningless." He pointed to the spreadsheet. "But it does give us the date of the next meeting."

Maja leaned over to read the information. "That's only two days from now."

"We have to act fast." He pushed a hand through his hair. "I run one of the biggest media organizations in the world. If we could get a recording of their meeting, I can broadcast it worldwide. That would stop them in their tracks. But getting past Knight's security? I'm struggling with the logistics of that."

Maja remained silent, but something about her expression intrigued him. It was just a little too innocent. "Maja, are you up to something?"

"No."

"I don't believe you."

She smiled, smoothing a hand over his chest. "I promise not to do anything you won't like."

Adam groaned. "So you *are* up to something?"

"I have an idea, but right now I don't even know if it will become a plan. Trust me, if it ever gets that far, I'll tell you."

He gazed into the endless blue of her eyes and nodded. "I'll trust you. But promise you'll tell me if this idea of yours starts to develop into action?"

Her expression became serious. "I think it will be obvious if that happens."

Adam took Maja's hand and led her into his dressing room. It was a large space lined with shelves and hanging rails. Adam had a lot of clothes. All of them were expensive. All of them had that delicious Adam smell.

"I've been considering having this space converted into a nursery. I thought we could talk to the designer together at the weekend."

The slight smile on his face changed to a look of astonishment as she started to cry.

"Maja, what have I said to upset you? I thought you'd be happy."

"I am happy. It's just…"

How could she explain it to him? He knew as well as she did how uncertain their future was. How could they consider something like a color scheme for a nursery when they didn't know where their baby would be living? Didn't Adam know her heart was breaking every time she thought about it? There didn't seem to be any way out of this dilemma. Every time she tried to focus, her thoughts became bricks in a wall, piling higher and higher and then tumbling down, burying her beneath their weight.

She wanted to stay here with Adam and their child. And with Tarek. And Danny, if he returned. This felt like her home in a way Valhalla never had. She knew why that was. She loved Adam. Loved him with a certainty and fierceness that was never going away. Despite her tears, the admission made her heart soar. She, the hard-hearted Valkyrie, had succumbed to a range of emotions so vivid it was like she had hurled herself headlong into a rose garden. The color, scent and texture of her feelings for Adam were overwhelming.

But there were thorns. She knew he cared for her. Of course he did. He held her in his arms every night. There was no escaping the tenderness in his touch and in his eyes. But forever wasn't for them. And even if by some miracle they could wave a magic wand and make it happen, Maja didn't know if that was what Adam would choose. They were having a child together, but would he want her, that baby's mother, to be a part of his life? Would he prefer to look back on this as a sweet interlude? Or possibly not even that, since their time together would always be interwoven with the horror of the discoveries about Knight and the Reaper?

"Just…?" Adam prompted.

She took a deep breath. "What does this mean, Adam? How do you see our future unfolding?"

He took her hands, drawing her to him and running a palm along her spine. "I wish I could give you an exact answer to that question. Instead, I'm going to tell you how I hope our future looks. After we defeat Knight, we are going to come back here and live happily ever after. You, me, Tarek and—when he or she is ready to make an appearance—our baby."

Happily ever after? Maja knew what that would mean to her. It would mean they could live together just the way they were now. It would mean Adam didn't need any other women, because he had her. She blinked back a fresh rush of tears. It would mean he loved her as much as she loved him. She didn't know if she could presume that much. But she suddenly knew that she couldn't take half measures. If by some miracle she found a way to stay in the mortal realm and raise her baby here, she wasn't going to settle for anything less.

"Because you want our baby to have a family?"

Adam leaned back slightly so he could look at her face. "Yes, I want our baby to have a family. I want our baby to have all the things I had until my father died. But if there was no baby, I would want you, Maja." Her heart began to thud loudly at the warm look in his eyes. "Because I love you."

Unable to speak, she made a little choking sound and rose on the tips of her toes. Wrapping her arms around his neck, she pressed her lips to his in a kiss that lasted for a very long time.

"I hope that means you love me, too?" Adam murmured when he raised his head.

"More than you will ever know." What was it about

crying? It happened when she was sad *and* when she was happy. She was going to blame baby hormones. "But we don't know if I can stay here."

His arms tightened around her waist. "Maja, all I know for sure is that, while there is breath in my body, I will never let you go."

Chapter 17

Adam loved the feel of Maja's silken heat clasping him, her inner muscles tightening around him. The tiny gurgle she made as he thrust deeper into her. He was caught in a whirlwind of sensation, feeling it swirling around him, sinking into it, letting it tear him apart.

A day had passed since he told her he loved her, and he hadn't tired of the reality. He just wondered what had taken him so long.

Pleasure like this was once-in-a-lifetime. He knew that now. That was what made their lovemaking so sweet. She belonged to him. There were no barriers between them. Because he loved her, he would never stop needing her. The feelings she aroused in him were so powerful it felt like wildfire spreading through his bloodstream.

The emotional intensity of what he felt when they made love was more extreme than the physical pleasure. Opening his heart to another person after years of believing it could never happen was a unique sensation. It had frightened him when he hadn't recognized it, made him feel vulnerable. Now he knew what it was—knew it was love and it was reciprocated—it thrilled him, taking his arousal to new heights.

He kissed her long and deep, drugging kisses that swept them further into rapture and had Maja writhing to press closer to him.

"Don't stop." The words came out in a ragged groan.

His hips jerked as she clenched around him, drawing him farther into her, holding him tighter as if she never wanted to let him go.

He slid a hand between their bodies, pressing the pad of his thumb against her clit, and Maja cried out, her whole body jerking wildly. Adam rolled his thumb, pressing the little bud, feeling it swell further.

"Oh, that feels so good." She lifted her legs, gripping his hips with her knees and arching her back as he pumped harder and faster.

She was so hot and wet, it was like she was stroking him with fire, possessing him with her tight muscles. Adam's cock throbbed and grew even thicker inside her, stretching her, opening her to him.

He watched her face, drinking in every tiny movement. Her eyes widened and her body tensed as he paused, buried fully inside her. Pulling back, he drank in the flare of pleasure in the depths of her eyes, giving in to the perfection of the moment before surrendering to the hunger tearing through him. With a thrust of his hips, he drove back into her, pushing into the tight clasp of her vagina. Each stroke was a new arousal, each thrust took him closer to perfection, each jerk of his erection pushed him closer to the edge of his control.

Locking his gaze on hers, he filled her, throbbing as

he impaled her. The flames inside him burned brighter, searing his balls, scorching a path up his spine and triggering explosions along his nerve endings.

Maja tensed and cried out with her own climax as release erupted inside Adam in a wave of destructive rapture. It stripped everything from him. He had no energy, no breath, no senses and no thoughts. All that remained was this wild power overtaking him, storming through his veins, along his nerve endings like a thousand-volt electrical shock. Maja was shaking in his hold, gripping his shoulders tightly and crying out his name, as he continued to drive into her, riding the crest of the wave until they were both spent.

Gradually, the tremors stopped and Adam eased out of Maja, moving to lie at her side and wrapping his arms around her.

"This feels like a very decadent way to spend an afternoon." Maja stretched her arms above her head lazily.

Tarek and Sophie, with their shared love of gaming, had gone to a convention. Although Maja had made a halfhearted attempt to get Adam to accompany her on a walk in the park, he had dragged her off to bed almost as soon as the door closed behind the two.

"I am about to be even more decadent and go in search of coffee and cookies. Join me?" He reached for his boxer briefs and T-shirt, which were lying at the side of the bed.

"Luckily, since it would be bad for the baby, I have never succumbed to the mortal obsession for caffeine. But cookies sound good." Maja also pulled on underwear and a T-shirt.

In the kitchen, Adam wrapped his arms around her and rested his chin on the top of her head. "As crazy as it seems to say , with everything that's going with Knight... I'm happy. I can't remember the last time I said that. I don't know if I've ever said it."

Maja lifted her head to look at him. The smile in her eyes corresponded with the one in his heart. Before she could say anything, there was an almighty crash and the sound of Leo howling in terror.

"What the...?"

Adam dashed into the entrance hall of the apartment, with Maja at his heels. The door was open and the whole area was filled with smoke. Standing in the center of the tiled space, an impressive figure placed her hands on her hips and glared at him. Leo, crouching low so that his belly touched the floor, bustled up to Maja, and she scooped him into her arms.

Adam recognized the woman's clothing. It was identical to the outfit Maja had been wearing when he first met her. This Valkyrie looked like Maja. Her hair was a darker shade of gold and her features, while still beautiful, were slightly harsher. This must be one of Maja's sisters.

"Here in the mortal realm, we have a custom you might want to try next time. It's called knocking." Adam closed the door as he spoke.

The frown that descended on her face was clearly intended to terrify him. In other circumstances, it might have worked. If it wasn't for pacts with the devil and Grim Reapers, he would have feared this apparition and her scowl. Now he had gone beyond terror and shock. He was in a state of supernatural overload.

"You dare address the daughter of Odin? Kneel before me, mortal, and tremble at my feet."

"Oh, stop being so dramatic." There was a note of amusement in Maja's voice. "Adam, I think it's time you were introduced to my sister. This is Brynhild."

It took some doing, but Maja persuaded Brynhild to join her in the sitting room.

"This is not a social call. Your hiding place was revealed to me by one of Odin's servants who saw you here. I am here to escort you to Valhalla."

Clearly threatening the man who had followed her, punching him and tipping him into a Dumpster had not been enough to deter him after all.

"Just listen to me, please?"

Beneath her fierce exterior, Brynhild had a kind heart, Maja knew. Possibly the kindest she had ever known. Although Brynhild's devotion to duty was legendary, Maja was hoping to tap in to the love she had for her sisters. Valkyries weren't supposed to have feelings, but Maja could see with hindsight just how deeply Brynhild cared for her siblings. She was the one who'd brought them up, taught them the skills they needed to survive, developed them into powerful warriors. She protected them from Odin's wrath, often at the expense of her own well-being.

Maja wasn't fooling herself. The magnitude of the task ahead of her was enormous. Asking Odin's devoted general to go against his wishes? Just the idea of it made her blood run cold. But she thought of the sister who had raised her. The sister who understood her. The sister who, even now, looked at her with affection. Maja knew she had to try. She pressed a hand to her stomach.

Not just for myself. For all of us.

Although she handed Leo to Adam and signaled for him to leave them, she was conscious of his presence just outside the room. The knowledge that he was there strengthened her resolve.

"Who is that mortal?" Brynhild's voice was outraged. "And why are you here with him? Interacting with him. In this state of undress. Maja, you know the Code…"

"His name is Adam Lyon." She took a steadying breath. "And he is the father of my unborn child."

Until that moment, Maja had never seen Brynhild at a loss for words. Her mouth opened, but nothing happened. When she tried again, a tiny croak emerged. In that instant, Maja felt sorry for her. She could almost read her sister's mind. The reputation of the Valkyries rested on Brynhild's shoulders. Odin might have conceived the idea of the female fighters who escorted the fallen to Valhalla, but Brynhild was the one who had built them into the elite force they were today. She was the one who would ultimately be blamed if they were disgraced.

"Sit down." Maja patted the place next to her on the sofa.

Moving mechanically, Brynhild obeyed. "This is my fault."

"What do you mean?"

"I should never have sent you to Warda. You were inexperienced. And this rebellious streak of yours was always there. Just like—" She broke off, appearing to think better of whatever she had been about to say.

"Just like?" Maja prompted.

Brynhild shook her head. "It doesn't matter. I should have known better. I am to blame."

Maja laughed. "This isn't about fault or blame. I'm having a baby. You are going to be an aunt. Can't we be happy about that?"

"You know we can't. The Allfather's rage will be like nothing we have ever seen." Brynhild took Maja's hand in her own. "I don't know if I can save you from it."

"Must you tell him?" It was a suggestion Adam had made, and it had taken a hold on Maja's newly discovered imagination.

There was that look again. Brynhild was stunned. Throughout her life, Maja had believed her sister was indestructible. Today she was discovering that Brynhild was just another woman. A woman who didn't always have the answers. It was quite an eye-opener.

"Deceive the Allfather? How can you suggest such a thing?"

"It's not deceiving him if you don't mention that you know where I am. If you take me back to Valhalla, he will have me and my unborn child killed." Maja paused and watched Brynhild's face as that information sank in. She saw the flare of emotion in the blue depths of her sister's eyes and relished it. That momentary lapse told her Brynhild would do all she could to prevent that. It told her she was right. Maja wasn't the only Valkyrie who could experience love. "While you think about it, there is something else with which I need your help."

"You don't think asking me to save you from Odin's rage when you are carrying a human child is enough?" Brynhild's lips curved into a smile.

Maja returned the smile with relief. Her sister was on her side. Life had just gotten a little bit brighter. "This might score points with Odin. You know how much he loves mortals, and my plan involves helping humanity."

"You make it sound huge."

"It is." Maja bit her lip. Would Brynhild agree to her next request? "I need Adam here to help me explain."

Brynhild held up her hands in horror. "I cannot interact with a mortal."

"Brynhild, there is a consortium of humans posing as a terrorist organization, and Adam can prevent them from killing more people, but he needs our help."

"This is outside of the Valkyrie Code. You know our task is to escort the souls of the fallen to Valhalla. Interfering in mortal problems is not part of our job." Brynhild's expression was closed. This was the great general doing what she did best, refusing to be swayed from her position.

"The leader of this group is in league with the devil and he reaps souls on his master's behalf. He may be taking those intended for Valhalla." Maja didn't know if that was true. But she didn't know it wasn't... She saw the moment Brynhild wavered. "What harm can it do to listen? Odin will never know, and you may be able to save many brave warriors from the Reaper's scythe."

"Very well." The words were issued through a jaw that was clenched tight.

When Adam came into the room, Maja was pleased to see he had donned a pair of sweatpants. At least her sister's sense of decency would be appeased.

"You don't have any cause to love me." As he sat down and took Maja's hand, he spoke to Brynhild's averted face. "But we both love your sister, so I hope we can put aside our differences and do what's best for her."

Since there was no noticeable thaw in Brynhild's manner at his words, Maja decided to outline what they knew about Knight Valentine. Her sister listened in silence, speaking only when Maja had finished her explanation.

"Your plan is to unmask this group by—" Brynhild flapped a hand as though seeking the right words "—producing a moving picture with sound that reproduces their meeting? You will then distribute this throughout the world so that everyone can see exactly what they are doing?"

"Yes, but the problem will be getting past the security guards at Knight's house. It's heavily guarded. And of course, they are not going to conduct their meeting willingly if they know they are being filmed," Adam said.

"It seems you have set yourselves an impossible task."

Brynhild had thawed slightly and was actually facing in Adam's general direction now.

"That would be the case." Maja looked from Adam to Brynhild. "If we didn't know a small army of people who can make themselves invisible."

Adam started to laugh. "This was the idea you had?"

She nodded. "Now you know why I didn't tell you. I needed Brynhild to come here so I could ask her to make it happen."

"Since I *am* here—" Brynhild's frosty tones cut across their conversation "—maybe someone could explain to me what you are talking about?"

"We can use a group of Valkyries to get past Knight's guards and into Valentine House. If we are invisible, we can hide in the room and film the meeting." She turned to Adam. "Maybe on cell phones?"

He nodded. "That would work. Even better is we use high-tech hand cameras and stream it live."

"I hate to interrupt your plans, but the Allfather will never allow this," Brynhild said.

"Does he need to know about it?" Maja asked. There. She had dared to say it. To suggest that Odin could be defied. Not once, but twice. Not only could Brynhild hide the fact that she knew where Maja was, but she could go a step further and help bring down Knight and the Reaper consortium. "Once it is done, there will be nothing he can do about it."

The question hung in the balance. She could see Brynhild weighing the two sides of the argument. She could choose to save human lives and defeat evil. Or she could do what she had always done and be Odin's loyal general, afraid to make a move without his approval.

"If I do this without his consent, his fury will move mountains." Brynhild's voice sounded different. Breathy and excited. That was the moment when Maja knew she was considering it.

"There will be other Valkyries involved. He can't kill us all," Maja said.

"He can't, can he?" A flicker of a smile crossed her sister's lips. Maja got the feeling she was thinking of other times when the Allfather's temper had moved mountains. Maja might be the only Valkyrie with a rebellious streak, but maybe Brynhild had a few scores to settle.

For the first time, she looked directly at Adam. "I will do this."

One of the most surprising things about the apartment being filled with Valkyries was the way Leo quickly became resigned to the situation. The little dog seemed to feel that if Adam and Maja were okay with this number of visitors, he should accept them, too. After sniffing around their feet in curiosity, he wandered off to Tarek's room and curled up on the rug.

Tarek was at school and the arrangement was for Sophie to collect him and take him out for dinner and to see a movie after he had done his homework. Adam had made the excuse that he and Maja were going to see his elderly aunt again.

"We will take you to see her one day." Adam had felt guilty about the lie and hoped he had done a good enough job of convincing Tarek.

Clearly, he had failed. The boy's bright eyes had scanned his face for a moment or two. "Will you tell me all about it when it's over?"

"What do you mean?"

"I know this is about the Reaper. That means you can't tell me now, but I'd like to know what happens when it's finished."

Adam recounted the conversation afterward to Maja. "Is he very perceptive because of what he's been through, do you think? Or is it something unique about him?"

"He's supersmart." She said it with a note of pride. "But he's also tuned in to you and me—what we're thinking and feeling—because he's scared of losing us the way he did his father. I hope he hasn't been worrying about this."

"It will be over soon."

And one way or another, it would. Adam had never given a thought to the future. If anyone had asked him, he would have said—vaguely—that if anything ever happened to him, Danny would inherit everything he had. He still hoped to find Danny, of course, but until recently, he'd had no other responsibilities, so no reason to care beyond that. Lately, the situation had changed. Last week Adam had met with his attorney and made a more formal arrangement. Now, he had ensured that Tarek would be taken care of. He was now his adopted son and Elvira and Sophie were named as the boy's legal guardians if anything should happen to Adam. It was more difficult to make provision for the unborn baby, mainly because Maja didn't officially exist. Instead, Adam had inserted a clause in his will bequeathing the bulk of his fortune to his children, including Tarek and any yet to be born. His attorney had agreed that the change was legal and had assured Adam that it would be upheld.

There were twelve Valkyries in the apartment, including Maja. These were the true daughters of Odin. Although they all looked alike, Adam was able to view them critically and decide that none of them were as beautiful as *his* Valkyrie. He knew, of course, that he didn't have a warrior princess fetish, but it was nice to have this confirmation. These blue-eyed blondes were all good to look at, but they didn't move him in any way. There was only one Valkyrie for him, and how he felt about her had nothing to do with her shield maiden status. His connection to Maja was about who she was inside. And who she was inside was perfect for him.

Although his visitors looked like a group of catwalk models, they acted more like a squad of GIs. Having abandoned their Valkyrie garb in favor of casual, human clothing, they were being briefed by Maja on what to expect when they reached Valentine House. Although they weren't quite standing at attention, there was nothing relaxed about their stance. Clearly, they had been told by Brynhild to interact as little as possible with Adam, since they treated him as if he was the one with the powers of invisibility.

He didn't like the feeling of being an outsider in his own home. Maja, obviously picking up on his discomfort, gave him a sympathetic smile once or twice and he shrugged in response. He would do whatever it took to end this. The disdain of a few Valkyries was nothing in comparison to what was at stake.

Whatever gets us through this day and out the other side with a recording of the Reaper meeting.

This plan of Maja's was all they had. Even if it didn't get them the recording they sought, it might shake up the Reaper consortium by letting them know someone was onto them.

When Adam mentioned the logistics of transporting a small army of shield maidens to Greenwich, Brynhild gave him a pitying look. "We are Valkyries. We will make our own arrangements."

Maja's older sister was beginning to seriously get on his nerves. Although her help on this mission was invaluable, Brynhild was determined to put Adam in his place. She never missed an opportunity to sneer at him, or remind him of his lowly status in comparison to her and her sisters. He got it. His parents were mortal; their father was a god. He wanted to point out that there was no comparison. He'd take Robert Lyon over a moody deity any day. But getting into a petty argument with Brynhild wasn't going to make the task ahead of them any easier. No matter how much it might feel like a good way to relieve some of the pressure cooker of emotions building inside him.

"The meeting is scheduled to start in three hours. Since I don't have the benefit of a winged horse, I'm going to head out to Greenwich now and watch the house as the members arrive."

Although he spoke to Maja, it was Brynhild who answered him. "Very well." She gave a dismissive wave.

Maja took Adam's hand as she faced her sister. "We will see you there."

"We?" Adam had an expensive heating system, but Brynhild's expression was doing its best to override it as she looked at their clasped hands. "You will come with us, Maja. You are a Valkyrie."

"I'm going with Adam." Maja's chin had that willful tilt to it. The one that always made him want to kiss her. He decided against it on this occasion.

It was a declaration. Maja was telling Brynhild loud and clear that she might be a Valkyrie, but her loyalties had changed. The atmosphere shifted in that instant. Adam saw a flicker of emotion in Brynhild's eyes. There was sadness, but it was followed by respect. He thought there was something more. Something that had stirred up memories Brynhild would have preferred to let lie.

She nodded. "You have made your decision and I will respect it."

Chapter 18

From their vantage point in the trees, Adam and Maja watched as the members of the Reaper consortium arrived at Valentine House. The security had been stepped up since their last visit; this time, they evaded guards and dodged new cameras before they reached a point from which they could view the house. Adam got no satisfaction from being right about this. Some of the most powerful men and women in the world had signed up to this alliance.

He wondered how Knight had recruited these people. It wasn't the sort of subject a person could ask over a business lunch. *"Hey, how would you like to make billions by joining me in a new venture? The catch? Well, we have to finance a terrorist organization that will commit atrocities as a front for wiping out our business rivals."* It needed just one slip—to ask one person with a conscience who was willing to go to the police—and Knight's cover would have been blown wide-open.

But he had clearly selected these people carefully. Adam couldn't think of a nastier group. A conscience? They couldn't raise one between them if they tried. Adam had a reputation for ruthlessness, but each of these people he observed made him look like a Boy Scout.

Knight stood on the sweeping gravel drive, greeting his guests. General Shepherd was the first to arrive. Adam felt a knot of cold, hard contempt tighten his gullet as he watched the two men shake hands. Shepherd had been decorated for bravery. Had led his men in action countless times. Served his country with loyalty and honor. At what point had he become *this* man? Every day Shepherd had to look the leaders of the free world and his fellow soldiers in the eye and tell them he was no closer to finding the Reaper. Adam hoped the words choked him. Even if they did, the sensation was likely soothed by the thought of the billions he had probably stashed in an offshore account.

Designer-clad Suzanne Sumner arrived next. Adam had almost done business with her a few years ago. He recalled her kittenish smile and relentless flirting. They hid the venomous fangs of a snake. And that was probably unfair to snakes. He had pulled out of the deal when he discovered one of Suzanne's companies used child labor. She had proceeded to bad-mouth him, telling anyone who would listen he was bitter because he had made sexual advances and she had turned him down.

Charlie Hannon, a guy whom Adam was sure had crawled out from under a rock, was next to emerge from a cab. Adam had to fight the impulse to break his cover so he could punch the self-satisfied grin from Hannon's face. The Englishman had made his money through internet porn and webcam services before moving into the more mainstream role of running a public relations firm.

Now the lines had become blurred as Hannon himself regularly appeared on reality television programs, while managing the careers of some of the highest profile celebrities in the world.

Alain Dubois shared a ride with Donna Webb, founder of the world's second largest sportswear company. Adam bit back a smile. *Second* largest. He knew from experience how much she hated being reminded of that.

The final three were people he didn't know personally. A Saudi Arabian oil executive, an Italian hotel magnate and a Silicon Valley technology genius.

"They are all here." Adam watched as Knight followed the last of his guests inside the house.

"The meeting isn't scheduled to start for another hour," Maja said.

"It's lunchtime. I expect they'll eat first." Adam led her farther into the trees, finding the midpoint where they had arranged to meet Brynhild and the other Valkyries.

Maja shook her head. "They will be filling their stomachs and then planning mass murder?"

"That about sums it up. Knight might be the only one who made it formal, but each of those people is in league with the devil. The others just don't know it yet."

Adam and Maja had followed the same route they had taken the last time they had come to the house, following the shoreline until they reached the shelter of these trees. Because Adam was hampered by his inability to become invisible, his task would be to coordinate the activity of the Valkyries. He was frustrated at the thought that he couldn't take part in the action, but he had planned this carefully. He knew the layout of the house and had directed Maja's sisters until they were word perfect and could recite his directions back to him.

His concern was about Maja's role. Because of the

baby, Adam didn't want her involved at all, but she was the only other person who had been inside the house. She was also the only Valkyrie he really trusted to use a camera. When he had given the others a training session in how to record a video on the tiny cameras he had passed out, the results had ranged from poor to nonexistent. He was relying on Maja to get him the footage they needed.

He had initially been worried that, although the Valkyries would be invisible, the cameras would not. How would that look? Twelve cameras floating around Valentine House? There was no way that wouldn't arouse attention, and he couldn't think of any way to disguise them. Luckily, Maja had explained how it worked.

"As long as the items we carry are small, they become invisible, too. If they didn't, our swords and daggers would give us away."

His lack of knowledge of all things paranormal had let him down yet again. It made things a hell of a lot easier. The plan was for the Valkyries, all of them invisible, to get into the house, each carrying a small backpack containing the things they would need for this mission. Their first task was to take out the security guards.

"You are under strict instructions to stay out of any fighting. The baby comes first, remember?" he told Maja.

"You have told me that several times already."

"I thought it was worth another reminder." He knew his feisty Valkyrie only too well. If there was trouble, she would be in the thick of it.

Once the security guards were no longer a threat, Brynhild would lead her warriors into the meeting room. Maja, cloaked by invisibility, had sneaked over to the house and checked out the room where the meeting would be held. This was in a separate building from the main house. Situated near the pool, it was a single-story, purpose-built annex. Adam remembered Knight always used it for business meetings. It was comfortable and completely private.

On her return, she had confirmed that the room was already set up for a meeting. The six French windows were unlocked and three of these were open, affording a view of the gardens and the water beyond. It was a beautiful day and there was no reason to suppose anyone would lock the windows before the meeting started. To be absolutely sure, Maja had followed Adam's instructions and filled the locks with superglue, ensuring that the doors would remain open to admit the Valkyries.

Although all twelve of them would be in the room and filming, the focus was Maja. The others were there as her bodyguards. Since she was the most experienced, she was the one who was to film the meeting from start to finish, come what may.

Although Adam was near crazy with worry when he thought about Maja in close proximity to Knight, she reminded him that she would be invisible. Her pregnancy gave his fears for her safety an added edge, but the thought of the other Valkyries acting as her protectors helped calm his nerves.

Adam had configured the cameras so they would be live streaming their recordings to social media as they were filming. His job would be to use an electronic tablet to edit the stream and direct traffic to that site from other places. Adam had a vast social media presence. He would be able to use that to generate a huge amount of interest in the meeting, particularly once he mentioned the Reaper.

He still wasn't happy at the idea of sending Maja into that room without him, but Brynhild would be there. He had to have confidence in the Valkyrie leader's ability to take care of her sister. Anything else was unthinkable.

* * *

The Valkyries arrived with over an hour to spare before the meeting, and they talked through the plan one last time. Although Brynhild had no idea what Adam was talking about when it came to the technology, she had a clear grasp of her role. She would lead her sisters to overcome the security guards, while ensuring Maja's safety. They might not agree on anything else, but Adam and Brynhild were both focused on those twin outcomes. If they could ever be brought to see it, they were actually quite alike.

"I want you to do something for me." Maja had been waiting for the opportunity to get Brynhild alone.

"If this involves keeping any more secrets from the Allfather, I'm going to stop you right there."

"It's nothing like that. Did you ever find the warrior called the American Lion?" Maja cast a look over her shoulder to where Adam was crouched in the shrubs, watching the house from his hiding place.

"No, he has disappeared from my charts, much to Odin's annoyance. He really wanted that hero to join his army. Why do you ask?"

"I think I may know his identity." She threw another glance in Adam's direction. *Leave my brother out of this.* That was what he had said to her when they first met. But he was no closer to discovering Danny's whereabouts. And Brynhild might be able to help. "If I'm right, his name is Daniel Lyon and he is Adam's brother. Could you find out where he is, or what happened to him?"

"I'll see what I can do, but you know it isn't always simple."

"If you can try, I'd be grateful."

Brynhild followed the direction of Maja's gaze. "This thing with you and the mortal…it's serious, isn't it?"

"I love him."

There was genuine curiosity in Brynhild's expression. "How do you know?"

"Because I couldn't live without him." Maja didn't have to think about her answer. She continued before Brynhild could respond. "Do you think I don't know how much easier it would be *not* to love him? Loving Adam is hard. If there were ever two people who were not meant to be together, it's us. We come from separate worlds—our paths should never have crossed. The only things we have in common are an orphan and a dog. It would be so much easier if we could *not* love each other."

"So why don't you just stop it?"

"Because my first thought when I wake up in the morning is of Adam. Throughout the day, whenever I think of him, I smile. Every time I hear his voice, even if he's just talking on the phone to someone else, my heart skips a beat with pure joy. If he's not in the room, I glance up every time I hear a sound in case it's him coming through the door. When I go to bed at night, I hope I'll dream of him. If I say something that makes him laugh, I feel like I've won a prize." A smile trembled on her lips. "Those are a few of the reasons why I can't just switch off my love for him."

Brynhild was silent for a moment. "I didn't know it was like that."

"Nor did I. And although it is hard, I would not miss a minute."

"And you will have his child."

Maja straightened her spine. "Proudly. No matter what the Valkyrie Code says, I am not ashamed of loving Adam."

"Do you wonder if your child will inherit your magical abilities?"

Maja laughed. "If our child takes after Adam, he or she will be magical."

Before Brynhild could reply, Adam tapped his watch, signaling that it was time for them to move.

"Remember, the security guards are based in the turrets." He indicated the four towers, one at each corner of the house. "They will be watching the grounds for any signs of intruders, but they won't see you coming, of course."

He turned to Maja. "You remember how to use the camera?"

"Yes, Adam. Because you have shown me at least five times." She grinned mischievously. "And unlike my sisters, I have used a camera before. Tarek likes me to take photographs or videos of Leo while he is at school so he knows what his dog has been doing during the day."

He returned the smile. "I'm sorry. Was I being obsessive?"

"Maybe just a little." Ignoring her sisters, she stepped up close, enjoying the way his arms instantly closed around her. "I love you," she whispered.

"I love you more."

"Not possible." She pressed her cheek against his chest briefly before pulling reluctantly away.

She was aware of Adam and Brynhild staring at each other over the top of her head.

"Look after her." She had never heard that note in Adam's voice before. It was almost a plea.

"I intend to," Brynhild said.

Although they would get into the meeting room from the garden, they would have to go into the main house to access the turrets.

Maja led the way through the cellars using Adam's

keys. Because the whole group was invisible, the only problem she could foresee was the point when they would emerge from the cellar into the storage area at the back of the kitchen. If Knight and his guests were dining here at Valentine House, someone must be cooking for them and serving their food. That meant the kitchen would be in use.

No one would see the twelve Valkyries, but they would notice if the door to the cellar suddenly opened. There was a possibility a witness might be spooked by that rather than believing it to be evidence of a break-in. But Maja didn't want to take a chance. She didn't want to do anything that would mean Knight might cancel his meeting. Today was the day they were going to expose him and his evil consortium. She was determined about that.

The second danger point was the door from the storage room into the main hall of the house. Once again, they risked someone watching the door. Brynhild was ready to move in and silence anyone who did notice anything.

Maja felt a fierce sense of pride at the way her sisters had responded to her call for help. She knew they were obeying Brynhild's orders, but any one of them could have gone to Odin and told him what was going on. Instead they had chosen to risk his anger and support her. Brynhild had made it clear to them that the Allfather knew nothing of this venture. Odin was likely to be pleased at the outcome, since he would welcome the downfall of a group that brought harm to the human race. He would not willfully cause bloodshed, even if it meant more warriors for his great army. But he would not be impressed to learn of his daughters' defiance.

Stealth wasn't usually a priority for the Valkyries. Their environment was the battlefield, where noise and fury were normal. When they used invisibility to disguise their intentions, they had no real need to be furtive. Now, despite their invisibility, they had to work together to keep their presence secret. For the first time, it felt like all of them were a team.

At the same time, Maja felt sad. Because no matter what happened here, she was no longer part of this. While she didn't want to be, she wished they could have reached this point without having to face the threat of Knight Valentine. This sense of sisterhood shouldn't have been so hard to achieve. And now that they had it, could it last when their number was about to be depleted by one? That shouldn't be Maja's problem, but they were still her sisters. She would always be a Valkyrie, even if she wasn't a practicing member of the team. It had taken a problem to bring them together. She'd have liked to know how things worked out for them in the future.

When they reached the stairs that led to the storage room at the back of the kitchen, Maja went first, with Brynhild following close behind. She didn't need Adam's reminders about taking care of herself. Nothing was going to stop her doing this, but she was going to be careful for the baby's sake. Using the key to open the door at the top of the steps, Maja slowly turned the handle. The storage area appeared different from the last time she had been here. Then the house had been empty. Now, she could hear noises coming from the kitchen, and the aroma of food filled the air.

Even so, the storage area was empty. Maja released a sigh of relief as she beckoned Brynhild forward. The others followed. The last Valkyrie to emerge from the cellar closed the door behind her.

It wasn't just the sounds and scents from the kitchen that made this visit different. Maja felt it as soon as she left the cellar. The whole atmosphere had changed. It wasn't about her. It was nothing to do with being here with her sisters instead of Adam. It wasn't pregnancy hormones. It wasn't nervousness about making sure she got the recording right.

This impression was like a bad smell. Once imprinted on the nostrils, it was immediately recognizable again. She knew exactly what it was. Knight Valentine was in this house, giving off his own unique air of evil. The devil had marked him, and no amount of expensive cologne could disguise the underlying aroma.

Maja reached for the next obstacle. Her fingers closed over the handle of the door that led to the main corridor. She told herself it was ridiculous for her heart to be pounding so loudly. Even if she opened that door and Knight was standing on the other side, he couldn't see her.

It didn't matter. She had an image of those eyes boring into her. How she had felt in his office, that sense of undiluted malice, came back to her, sharp and bright. Her nerves were jangling so wildly that she had to wait until she stopped shaking.

She had known this plan would involve seeing Knight. Yet being closer to him again brought the reality of what that meant into focus. This man had brought so much misery into Adam's life. Had caused him so much personal damage. She had to focus on the way Adam had risen above that. He was strong and good and true, despite the things Knight Valentine had done to him and his family. Maybe, in some ways, because of them.

Was that going to stop her being horribly afraid when she looked into Knight's dead eyes once more? No. Would it stop her from wanting to place her hands around his throat and squeeze until his face turned blue or his devilish master turned up to save him? Again, the answer to that question was a resounding negative.

Brynhild placed a hand on her shoulder, checking that she was okay, and Maja nodded. *I can do this.*

With a hand that no longer shook, she turned the handle and opened the door a fraction. A glimpse of the corridor revealed that it was deserted, and she beckoned her sisters through into that part of the house, closing the door behind them. Last time she had been here, she and Adam had followed the passage to the right and entered Knight's study. This time, they needed to turn left and into the main entrance hall. They would have to climb the sweeping central staircase to access the turrets.

As Maja placed her foot on the first stair, she heard a burst of laughter coming from a room to her left. There was a buzz of conversation emerging from that direction. Adam had sketched a plan showing them the layout of the house. Maja recalled it now. The noise was coming from the dining room. It sounded like lunch was proving to be an enjoyable occasion.

As the Valkyries began their ascent of the stairs, the dining room door opened and Knight stepped into the hall. Although she was invisible, Maja instinctively pressed her body tight against the wall. Aware of Brynhild's surprise at this reaction, she used her fingers either side of her head to mimic a pair of devil horns.

Brynhild looked down from her vantage point several stairs above Knight as he crossed the hall. Turning back to Maja, she grimaced. Maja released the breath she had been holding. It wasn't just her. Her sister could feel it, too. The aura of evil that hung about him was tangible.

When she had attacked Knight in his office, Maja hadn't known what he was. If she had, she might have thought twice about her daring behavior. Maybe not. Her impulsiveness had always been the subject of much eye rolling from Brynhild over the years.

But Knight didn't know what I was, either. She had scared him. His deal with the devil conferred some gifts upon him, but it didn't make him all-knowing. Right now, he was striding across his hall, calling impatiently for someone to bring more wine, unaware that twelve Valkyries were standing on his stairs. She used that knowledge to strengthen her resolve. *We know what he is now, but he still has no idea what he is up against.*

Chapter 19

The turrets were accessed through the attics. The Valkyries split into teams of three, each team taking one of the four turrets. Since Maja was under strict instructions not to take part in any fighting, she accompanied Brynhild and Eir, the two most experienced Valkyries.

They entered stealthily. It was a circular room with windows all the way around. The view across the gardens was spectacular. Maja could see why Knight had chosen this house. For a man who wanted to maintain his privacy, this was perfect. Nothing could move on those grounds without the people in these towers knowing about it. Unless, like Adam, you had grown up in this house and, as a frightened child, found hiding places and ways to avoid detection.

In addition to the view over the grounds, the turret also contained a bank of monitors showing images of the interior of the house. Maja recognized the staircase they had climbed to reach these attics, and the meeting room in the grounds. She noted with relief that the French windows were still open.

There were two men inside the circular room, and that fitted with the information Adam had given her. He said Knight employed sixteen security guards, working in two teams of eight. This was the day shift. The setup was identical in each turret.

Brynhild and Eir stepped forward in a concerted movement, grabbing the men from behind before they could move. Adam had been uncompromising in his instructions. No killing unless it was unavoidable. Brynhild had curled her lip slightly when he gave that order.

"No killing? How very mortal."

"I am mortal and proud of it. Not killing my fellow humans is what raises me above Knight Valentine and his terrorists," Adam replied.

"It would be so much easier if we could break their necks." Brynhild had placed her hands on her hips, prepared to argue.

"I'll tell their families that, shall I?" Adam had faced her, his own expression equally immovable. "Maybe I'll do it at the graveside." *This was more convenient than tying them up and gagging them.* "I'm sure they'll understand."

The unthinkable had happened— Brynhild had backed down. Which was why the Valkyries' backpacks contained rope and duct tape.

It was over in seconds. Moving with superhuman speed and strength, Brynhild and Eir had the two men trussed up like a pair of turkeys ready to be roasted. Adam had decided that leaving them in these rooms would be a bad idea. It was unlikely anyone would come up here, but he didn't want to take any chances. Brynhild picked up one of the security guards and tossed him over her shoulder as easily as if he had been a child. Eir did the same with the other.

One of the attic rooms was large and well ventilated, and they carried their captives to this space. The other Valkyries met them there and they deposited all eight inside. Maja found the key on the bunch Adam had given her and locked the door.

Extracting her cell phone from her backpack, she checked the time. "The meeting is scheduled to start in fifteen minutes. We need to get into position."

Firing off a quick message to Adam to let him know the first part of their mission had been successful, she replaced her phone and they made their way back down the stairs.

Once they were out of the house and crossing the garden toward the pool, the feeling of dread lightened. Maja knew it was because she was no longer as close to Knight. The air here was not contaminated by his poison. She thought of Belinda, Adam's beautiful, frail mother. No wonder she hadn't survived. Exposed to Knight's malevolence, up close to it every day, it must have been like standing within range of the heat from a blast furnace.

The Valkyries entered the meeting room. A central table occupied much of the space. One chair had been placed at the head of the table, with four others at each side. Bottles of water had been set in front of each chair, along with pads of paper and pens. There were also bowls of candy in the center of the table.

"I'll stand here." Maja took up a position at the far end, directly opposite the head of the table. That was where she knew Knight would sit. She wanted to keep her eyes— and her camera—on him all the time. Every word, every expression, everything that would tell the world who he really was...she didn't want to miss anything.

Directing her sisters to their places, she explained what she wanted from them. One camera on each of the other consortium members. The other three Valkyries would have an overview of the meeting. Each camera's footage would be live streamed directly to Adam. This way, she hoped he would get everything he needed.

Adam. She thought of him waiting back there in the trees. He would be almost out of his mind with worry, wishing he was here with her, wishing he didn't have to put her through this. It was all made so much worse for him because it was *here*. This house, the scene of so many awful memories for him. The place that had clouded so much of his young life. He couldn't allow himself to hope that anything would go well here. Like Belinda, he had been exposed to the toxins that Knight gave off for so long it had affected his whole outlook. Everything had become so much worse now that he knew the truth. It was only now that he might finally be able to get the poison out of his system.

And with that thought, she felt an icy finger claw its way down her spine. Knight was approaching.

Impatience felt like a giant rodent sitting on his chest, gnawing at his flesh. The fibers of his woolen sweater felt like tiny razors scratching his arms, and Adam tugged the garment over his head, flinging it down on the damp grass. The birdsong was overloud, making the blood pound in his ears until he wanted to find something to cover his head. Overhead, sunlight breaking through the canopy of leaves was too bright, stinging his eyes like shards of glass, forcing him to bend his head and stare at the wet leaves between his bent knees. Behind him, the tree trunk against which he leaned pressed its gnarled knuckles into his spine, adding to the teeth-clenching, jaw-grinding, swearing-under-his-breath restlessness that spiraled higher with each passing second.

He spent most of the time staring at the blank screen of his tablet, telling himself Maja would be okay. She was a fighter. Before she met him, her life had been about going into combat zones and plucking warriors out of the middle of scenes of death and destruction. She was better equipped than he was to face Knight.

Adam's lectures didn't work. He wanted to be at her side, caring for her and protecting her. Skulking in a forest while the woman he loved placed herself in the line of fire? That didn't suit Adam's idea of chivalry. He could tell himself he had an important role to play in the fight, but it didn't feel right.

Right would be leading from the front. Right would be looking Knight in the eye while he brought him to his knees.

When his phone buzzed with a text from Maja, he allowed himself to breathe normally again for a few minutes. Then the tension ratcheted back up to stratospheric. The Valkyries would be on their way.

The silent screaming inside his head began again as he waited. Forcing himself to calm down, he concentrated on his breathing. Wasn't that what you were supposed to do? Trying to block out the negative thoughts, the images of what could go wrong, he kept his mind on each next inhalation.

Until an image appeared on the screen of his tablet, of Knight entering the meeting room.

"Maja, I love you." Adam whispered the words in the gloom of the forest. Even the birds stopped their singing and listened. Or maybe now that he had something to do, his irritation at every little sound was gone.

Adam watched as Knight checked out the room, moving around the table, pausing to straighten items on its surface. The quality of the recording was good. Inserting his headphones, Adam checked out the sound quality. Although there was no talking, Adam could hear Knight's footsteps, the rustle of paper and the scrape of water bottles.

He checked his signal and connection to the internet. He was logged in to the social media sites he would use to share the live stream of the video of the meeting. Everything was ready. The guards were patrolling the area around the house and grounds, but they hadn't penetrated this far into the trees.

As if in answer to a cue, he heard Knight's voice in his headphones.

"Come in. Sit down."

Adam switched from Maja's view to Brynhild's. She was facing one of the open French windows and, on Adam's screen, he saw the other eight members of the Reaper consortium enter the meeting room. He was pleasantly surprised by her technique. Her hand was steady and she got a good shot of each face as they took their seats. It would be easy for the police to identify them from these images.

Changing back to Maja's recording, he watched as Knight took his seat at the head of the table. Adam had to get a grip on his emotions as he observed the smiling face of the man who had thrown his life into turmoil over and over. Now was not the time to let those feelings get the best of him. Defeating Knight would never wipe out the past, but it would help to redress the balance.

The group around the table got straight down to business. Adam listened carefully as he started to direct his social media followers to the live stream. There wasn't any specific mention of the Reaper in Knight's introduction, but there were references to recent successes.

"Our allies have delivered a high standard of service on every occasion, with the result that each of us has seen an unprecedented increase in profits." There was a ripple of agreement around the table. "We owe a debt of thanks, of course to the general—" Knight nodded to Shepherd, who was seated on his right "—for his hard work. He faces a difficult balancing act. Not only must he appease the international forces of law and order who are breathing down his neck, demanding results, he must also protect our allies from the risk of discovery."

"Come out and say it, you bastard." Adam muttered the words to the screen as he typed a commentary for his followers. "Instead of saying 'allies,' say 'terrorists.'"

"With that in mind, and before we discuss forthcoming projects, I have a recommendation to make." There was a ripple of interest around the table. Clearly, this was unexpected.

Adam checked the figures on his screen. People were beginning to follow the live stream. He had called it *Reaper Video* and encouraged his followers to watch. Although there were bemused comments asking what was going on, Adam's name and his own comments were maintaining interest. Adam Lyon, media mogul, had said the identity of the Reaper was about to be exposed live. Was it a scam? If it was, it was worth a few minutes to see how it panned out. If it wasn't…no one wanted to miss the final reveal.

"The general has been in touch with our allies in the Middle East. Given our recent triumphs and the increased focus on our ventures, they, and he, have requested an increase in their payment."

There was a momentary silence before Charlie Hannon leaned back in his seat, tapping a pencil on the table. The sound seemed unnaturally loud through Adam's headphones.

"How much?" The Englishman's voice was not encouraging.

"That would be a matter for negotiation."

Hannon cast a glance around the table. "I'm not denying that the general here does a good job of throwing the politicians off the scent. And we couldn't do this without the guys who plant the bombs and fire the bullets—"

Yes! Adam checked the live stream again. The number of people viewing the meeting was skyrocketing and, thanks to Adam's comments, *Reaper Video* was trending on other social media sites.

"—but I think we already pay enough."

A heated discussion ensued and it was clear that there were two distinct sides in the room. Those who felt the rewards they gained meant the general and the terrorists had earned a pay raise, and those who didn't want to part with any more cash.

After a few minutes, Knight intervened, his cool tones cutting across the conversation. "My friends, in the interests of efficiency, may I suggest we put this to a vote? Just to remind you of our protocols… I will refrain from voting, but in the event of a tie, mine will be the final decision."

There was silence as Knight outlined the proposal again. "Raise your hand if you are in favor of an increase in the amount we pay to the general and our allies in the Middle East."

Four hands were raised and four remained down. Knight

spoke again. "Since the final decision is mine, I vote that we increase the payments—"

"Hold it right there!" Charlie Hannon, who had voted against the increase, interrupted. "The general shouldn't be able to vote on this."

"He's right," Suzanne Sumner said. "It's a conflict of interest."

This was not what Adam wanted. A group of people fighting among themselves was not what he wanted his followers to see. He wanted the Reaper consortium to expose themselves by talking about their involvement in terrorism. He wanted to hear examples. Hard, cold facts.

The general slammed a hand on the table, bringing the argument to an abrupt end. Glaring at Charlie Hannon, he got to his feet. "Do you want to take a turn at doing my job, sonny? You want to negotiate with terrorists and murderers, then show up at the United Nations after the next Reaper attack and explain why nothing is happening?" His icy glare took in each person around the table. "Each one of us is the Reaper. We are all equal partners— maybe with Knight running the show—but I'm the one who gets my hands dirty. You get the benefits when your rivals topple after a terrorist attack. I don't have that. The least you bastards can do is pay me what I deserve."

Adam exhaled a long, relieved sigh. That was what he needed. The general might almost have been reading from a script. Adam checked the screen of his tablet. Within a few seconds of the military man's speech, social media was going crazy. Initial reactions ranged from disbelief— *was this for real?*—to outrage.

"Knight." Alain Dubois spoke in a slightly bored voice. "You're in charge here. You are the person who thought up the Reaper and recruited us all. The largest terrorist organization in the world is your master plan. Now can you please get this meeting back on track so that we can do what we came here for and plan our next attacks? I want to make some money from my investment in the Reaper."

"Guys…" Donna Webb held up her cell phone, drawing her companions' attention to its screen. "We have a bigger problem right now. I just got a message from my PA telling me to check out what's happening on the internet. I don't know how it's being done, but we're being filmed."

The room descended into chaos as the other members of the consortium checked their own cell phones. The awful truth began to dawn on them. They had been exposed. Their meeting had just been streamed live to hundreds of thousands, maybe millions, of viewers. While the others went into full-blown panic mode, Knight sat very still at the head of the table, his hands gripping the arms of his chair. He seemed to be staring at a point just past Maja's head. Fascinated, she continued to film him, wanting to capture his reaction—or lack of reaction—to what was going on.

"How can this be happening?" Suzanne Sumner's voice was high-pitched with fear. "There must be a hidden camera in here. Knight, didn't you check the place out? Can't you shut it down?"

"You were supposed to take care of security." The general seemed to have aged ten years. "That was the reason we came to your house. We trusted you."

"Get out." Knight didn't move as he spoke. His face remained expressionless. "All of you. Just leave."

There was a moment's hesitation. The snarl on Knight's lips as he turned the full force of his fury on his companions was truly terrifying. "Go…or suffer the consequences!"

The other eight members went from inactivity to an

undignified scramble for the French window within seconds. Brynhild caught Maja's eye and jerked her head toward the exit. The message was clear. Should they leave? They had done what they came here to do. The Reaper consortium had been exposed. Adam had his recording.

Maja wavered. Yes, they had everything they needed, but something was going on with Knight. It was as if the air around him was beginning to boil.

Just a few more minutes.

Even though the toxic atmosphere was stifling her, she wanted to keep recording. To let the world see exactly who this man was. Brynhild gave a slight shrug, but the message in her body language was clear. She wasn't happy to stay.

Maja turned her attention back to Knight. His face was deathly pale, those soulless eyes bigger and darker than ever, as though all the light in the room was being drawn into their depths. The strangest illusion seemed to be taking place, almost as though a reflection of his face was overlaid on top of the original. There was just a hint of another image. It shifted and then disappeared so quickly that Maja was unsure if she had seen it at all.

Even though he couldn't see the Valkyries, Knight looked around the room as though he was aware of their presence. His expression was menacing, his lips drawing back in a grotesque snarl.

"Is this your doing, Adam Lyon?" His voice sounded different. Low and guttural, it rasped like a foul echo in the beautiful room. Although she knew he couldn't see her, he looked directly at Maja as he spoke. "You should have listened to me when I said you didn't know what you were dealing with."

Knight began to chant. Softly at first, then his voice gradually became louder. He was speaking a language

Maja didn't recognize. The room filled with static and dark, swirling energy. Wisps of white mist began to curl up from the point where Knight's fingers gripped the chair.

"Maja." For the first time in her life Maja saw fear on Brynhild's face. "He is invoking a demon. We need to leave."

Maja nodded. They had seen enough. Was Knight summoning *any* demon? Or was he calling on a specific occult guide, one with the skills to help him in this situation? Maybe he was invoking the greatest of them all... the master to whom he had sold his soul? Would the devil himself answer a summons at will? Did Satan do house calls? Maja didn't think they should hang around waiting to find out.

She gestured toward the open French window, indicating for the other Valkyries to go ahead of her. It felt hard to leave. The air in the room was thick and cloying. Something within it was pulling them back. With each word Knight spoke, the sense of malice increased, stretching tighter like the skin of a drum. Maja watched in relief as, one by one, her sisters left through the French window.

Maja was the last to approach the welcome exit. Fresh air greeted her like a kiss when she was within a foot or two of escape. She turned to get a final look at Knight, just as he rose from his seat. Crouching low, his eyes gleaming red, he looked at her and smiled as he licked his lips.

The cell phone slipped from Maja's hand as the window slammed closed, trapping her inside the meeting room with the beast that was now inhabiting Knight Valentine's body.

Chapter 20

Adam was running across the grass toward the house as soon as Knight began to chant. Why was Maja still inside the meeting room? It was all over. The Valkyries needed to get the hell out of there as fast as they could.

Why had he let her do this? Allowing her to head into that meeting without him had gone against every instinct he possessed. It wasn't about some macho gene that said he was a man and he had to be in charge. It was because Maja and their baby were the most precious things in the world to him, and he was handing them over to the devil.

It was also because this was his fight. It was Adam's life Knight had screwed up. He wanted to be the one to look into those shark eyes when the tables were turned.

Adam had seen the other members of the consortium leave the meeting room through the French windows. Now, they were making their way across the garden toward the front of the house as he sprinted past them. They huddled together like a group of lost souls. Which, he decided, was exactly what they were. It didn't matter where they went now, or what they tried to do to cover their tracks. The authorities would deal with them. They would get what was coming.

He didn't have time to waste another thought on them. Didn't even have time to feel a flicker of satisfaction. As he rounded a corner of the house, his heart almost stopped. Brynhild, having abandoned her invisibility, saw him and ran across the grass toward him, her face a mask of terror.

"He has Maja. The demon could see her." She choked back a sob. "He is hurting her. We can hear her cries, but we can't get back in there."

The other Valkyries were trying everything they could to get the French windows of the meeting room open. Nothing they did—kicks, punches, even patio furniture thrown at the doors—made any impression. Something other than wood and glass was keeping the Valkyries out of that room.

There is superglue in those locks to stop them working; those doors shouldn't stay closed.

"Let me try." Adam stepped up to the door. "It's me he wants."

As soon as he touched the handle, the French window flew open. He stepped inside. Although Brynhild pressed close behind him, attempting to follow, she was forced back again by the window slamming in her face. Her cry of fury was drowned out by a hoarse cackle from within the room.

Adam's blood froze as he took in the scene. Knight was seated in the chair at the head of the table. His face was vampire pale and his eyes had lost their dark sheen. Instead they glowed from within. Red sparks danced in their depths. His bloodless lips were drawn back in a terrifying smile. Whatever demon he had summoned was inside him, but the man still retained control. This was Knight Valentine, but supercharged. Scarier than any demon.

Maja was curled in a fetal position at his feet. She wasn't moving. As Adam took a step toward her, Knight raised a hand. "I wouldn't."

"If you've hurt her…"

Knight's laughter was like fingernails on a chalkboard. "What will you do? Pay me back? I'd like to see you try."

"Let her go, Knight. This is between you and me."

"You've made it more than that." Knight's voice was petulant as he held up his cell phone. "You've made sure it is between me and the whole world."

"You did that yourself." The words came out before he could stop them.

Knight's foot connected with Maja's ribs in retaliation and she cried out. Relief, fury and fear stormed through Adam in equal measures. Relief that she was still alive. Fury at himself for provoking Knight. Fear, because if anything happened to her…

"Take it out on me, not her, you coward." He took a step closer to Knight, his fists clenched.

"Why would I do that, when it's so much more fun this way?"

He knew why Knight had called upon this demon. He didn't want to relinquish control, but Adam knew that deep down his stepfather was a coward. He needed this boost to his psyche and his strength. He wanted to know he could defeat Adam in spectacular style, rather than risk a fair fight. The glowing eyes, the rasping voice, the ability to keep the Valkyries out—they were all part of the show.

"What happened to the man who wanted to be the best in his own right?"

"Stalling for time, Lyon? Are you scared? The way

you used to be when you went into the cellar?" Knight's smile widened.

"My dad used to talk about his best friend. An honorable guy. A guy who fought fair, never took a cheap shot and always paid his way." Adam was making this up as he went along. Robert Lyon had never spoken to him about his friendship with Knight. But when he was fighting for his life, and Maja's, Adam guessed a few liberties with the truth were permissible.

"Your father was a loser."

"The sort of loser you used to be? The sort who could look in the mirror and like what he saw? Would you like your reflection now, Knight?" Adam looked at the antique mirror on the wall. "Shall we find out?"

"My reflection hasn't changed." Even though the words were confident, the snarl wavered. "I'm not playing your games."

"But you like games, Knight. You like to be the best at them." Adam wasn't sure if Maja could hear him. If she could, he hoped she knew what he was doing. *Hang in there. I'm here for you. We can do this...together.* "Remember how you used to say the devil could have your soul if only you could make that shot, sink that pool ball, make that money?"

"My deal with the devil was the best I ever made."

"If that's true, and you truly believe it hasn't changed you—that you are still the same guy my dad knew—you won't be afraid to take a look in that mirror." Adam tried out a smile to go with the words. "The Knight Valentine who was my dad's best friend would never back down from a challenge."

"You think your pathetic mind games will work on me? That I'll be scared of what I see in the mirror? You think I can't look at my own reflection and live with what I've done?"

"Prove it."

Knight got to his feet and moved toward him. At the same time, Adam saw Maja press her hands to the floor as she attempted to get to her knees. His heart gave a thud of gratitude. His brave Valkyrie knew what he was trying to do. Could a demon multitask? Was the one inside Knight strong enough to pit its wits against Adam while still keeping those French windows locked against the Valkyries? There was only one way to find out. And to do it, Adam had to keep Knight's attention focused on him.

Side by side, the two men moved toward the mirror. Being so much shorter, Knight came up only to Adam's shoulder. It meant he not only couldn't see as much of his own reflection, but he also couldn't see as much of the room behind him.

"What am I supposed to be looking at?" Knight's voice was mocking. "Are you expecting me to be shocked because my face is pale and my eyes are glowing?"

"What is the name of the demon inside you?" Adam tried not to fix his attention on what was going on behind them.

The abrupt change of subject brought a slight frown to Knight's brow. *Damn.* Adam didn't want to make him too suspicious. "Why do you want to know?" The gravelly note in his voice was more pronounced.

Behind him, Adam was aware of Maja crawling toward the French windows. Was she going so slowly because she didn't want to alert Knight to what she was doing, or because she was badly hurt? His head was spinning at the notion that she could be injured and he couldn't go to her. It felt like a giant hand had been thrust into his chest and was slowly drawing out his heart inch by painful inch.

What if she tried the handle and couldn't open the French window? If the demon's power was still too great for her and the other Valkyries together to override, what then? Adam had no plan B. This was it. This was all he had.

That's why you have to make this one work.

"Because I prefer to talk to the puppet master rather than the puppet."

Knight's fist, powered by the full force of the demon's strength, connected with Adam's jaw. Even though he was expecting the blow, it rocked his head back. That whole seeing-stars thing was a myth. It was more like being underwater. Everything became blurred, including sound.

Knight was talking, but the words came to him as though spoken in a wind tunnel. Adam caught the most important ones: *"...impertinent jerk with a death wish..."*

Maja had reached the window. Adam had to buy her enough time to try and get it open. He swung at Knight's stomach. It was like punching a brick wall. Pain shot up from his knuckles through his wrist and flared into his elbow. He barely had time to register the shock before Knight grabbed him by the neck, pinning him against the wall. Dark spots appeared before Adam's eyes as he clawed at the hand around his throat.

"What do you think you're doing?"

Adam was on the verge of blacking out. No matter how hard he fought for his next breath, he couldn't draw even a gasp into his lungs. As blackness invaded the edges of his vision, he saw Maja scrabbling to get the French window open. His senses became supercharged. He could hear Brynhild yelling encouragement from the other side of the door.

Knight, becoming aware of what was happening, swung around, a growl issuing from his lips. He released

Adam, who slid to the floor, gulping in air. As Knight dashed across the room, Maja used both hands to pull on the handle, and Brynhild crashed through the window with the other Valkyries behind her.

The demon fought like—well, he fought like a demon—but eleven Valkyries would have been a match for the devil himself. Knight disappeared under a blonde onslaught.

Staggering to his feet, Adam lurched to where Knight had placed his cell phone on the table. With fingers that felt like they belonged to someone else, he called 911.

"I need police and paramedics. Yes, it's an emergency."

He gave the operator the details as he stumbled across to where Maja was sitting propped against the wall. Stooping low, he managed to lift her into his arms. Without speaking, she linked her fingers around his neck and rested her head against his chest.

Slowly, Adam carried her outside and sat on the grass with her cradled in his lap, until he heard the sound of sirens.

Brynhild placed a hand on Adam's shoulder. "We have to go before your mortal authorities arrive. Knight is still alive…but only just."

"Thank you." His voice was gruff with emotion.

She bent her head to kiss Maja's cheek. "You were right. We both love her." The Valkyries disappeared and Adam and Maja were left alone as the emergency vehicles appeared.

When Maja spoke, her voice was so quiet he had to lower his head to catch the words. "You fought a demon for me, but you never did find out its name."

"I didn't need to." He pressed his lips to her temple. "There was a demon inside his body, but the thing I feared the most was the man called Knight Valentine."

* * *

Maja tried to focus on a part of her body that wasn't experiencing pain. It was no good. There wasn't one. As soon as he was alone with her, Knight, his strength enhanced by the demon within him, had launched into an attack so ferocious she thought she was going to die. No amount of Valkyrie training had prepared her for it. It didn't matter how hard she tried to fight back; the onslaught was relentless. Though vaguely aware of Brynhild and the other Valkyries desperately trying to get back inside to help her, she'd found her only thought had been to protect the baby.

When Adam arrived, she had been barely conscious. Even so, her first emotion had been relief that he was there. It had been swiftly followed by fear. Adam was a mortal. He had no defense against the demon residing inside Knight's body. If Maja, with her strength and Valkyrie training, could be so easily defeated, Adam would be crushed like a moth between a careless thumb and finger.

She didn't know how she had dragged herself to the French window. The memory was a blur. All she could remember was the overwhelming feeling of joy as Brynhild rushed into the room. After that, the only thing she could remember was Adam's arms around her.

Now, as she lay in the hospital bed, one thought persisted. Her whole body was a mass of bruises. An initial examination had reveal that she had two broken ribs and a fractured wrist. That diagnosis didn't tell her the most important thing. She pressed a hand to her stomach.

"Dr. Blake will be here any minute." Adam, interpreting her thoughts, took hold of her uninjured hand.

"What if…?"

"No." He shook his head, and she could sense how hard it was for him to say it. It was hurting him as much as her. "Let's not do 'what if.' Not yet. Let's hear what the doctor has to say."

Maja leaned closer and rested her head on his shoulder, feeling the tension of his muscles beneath her cheek. They stayed that way until Dr. Blake arrived. Her manner was brisk. Clearly, she knew that was what they needed.

"I'm going to conduct a pelvic ultrasound examination. That should show us if, and how, this attack has affected the baby." An orderly wheeled a trolley into the room. "This is the machine I'll use."

When the orderly had left, she looked from Maja to Adam, her expression grave. "Your injuries are serious, Maja. It will also allow me to diagnose a potential miscarriage."

Maja tightened her grip on Adam's hand. That was the word she hadn't wanted to say. Hadn't even wanted to think. It was what had sustained her through the attack. *Stay alive. Protect the baby.* She had used her fear to keep her focused. Initially trying to fight back, when she realized she was up against a superior power, she had used her own strength to defend herself, curling up and shielding her abdomen and pelvis. Had she done enough? That metal wand the doctor was holding in her gloved hands was about to reveal the truth.

"I thought an ultrasound was done abdominally?" Adam's question surprised Maja. She had believed she was the only one who had been obsessively reading all the literature.

"Normally it is," Dr. Blake said. "But this is an early ultrasound and doing it this way will produce a clearer picture." She gave them a reassuring smile. "Don't worry, it's perfectly safe. There is no risk to either Maja or the baby."

The feeling was mildly intrusive rather than uncomfortable, and Maja watched the screen, feeling as though her heart didn't dare risk its next beat. She wanted to look at the doctor's face for a clue to what was happening, but it was too daunting. What if she caught a glimpse of something she wasn't meant to see? A frown or a pursed lip? Adam kept a hand on her shoulder and her whole world seemed focused on the grainy image before her eyes and the warmth of his fingers through her hospital gown.

Dr. Blake pointed to the screen. "This black area here is your uterus, Maja." She turned her head and smiled. "And this—" she pointed to what looked to Maja to be a gray blob inside the larger black area "—is your baby. You can just about see his or her limbs developing."

Maja wanted to say something, but she burst into tears instead. It wasn't a good move. The action caused pain to rip through her injured ribs and she gasped, clutching her uninjured arm around herself in a defensive gesture. Doing her best to stem the flow of tears, she gazed at the screen in wonder. There it was. Their baby. She and Adam hadn't been the only ones fighting Knight in that meeting room. The tiny life inside her had survived, as well.

The emotions welling up inside her felt like a dam threatening to burst. The tears came again, less violent this time. Tears of pure joy. This baby was going to be okay. She knew it in that instant. Like its parents, it was going to be a fighter...and a survivor.

"Can you see the heart?"

Dr. Blake nodded. "It's very clear." She pointed. "You baby's heart is beating normally. Everything else is fine as well. If you come into my office in two weeks, we can repeat this procedure, and by then we will be able to hear the heart as well as see it."

Even though the movement caused her more pain, Maja turned her head to look at Adam. There were tears in his eyes as he bent his head to kiss her.

Dr. Blake removed the probe. "Now, both of you need to get your injuries checked out. Then I believe the police are waiting to speak to you."

Adam had repeated his story about half a dozen times to different agencies. Now he was telling it again to two officers, one male, one female, from the Department of Homeland Security.

"Explain to me again how your girlfriend—" the woman, Agent Glenn, who was clearly senior to her partner, consulted her notes "—Miss, er...?"

This was what he had tried to avoid. Given that she didn't actually exist as a mortal, too much scrutiny of Maja could give them a problem. "Odin." Maja would hate it, but it was the first word that came into his head. "Maja Odin. She's Scandinavian."

"Okay. Just explain one more time how Miss Odin came to be inside Mr. Valentine's meeting room."

"She was looking for me."

Once he had been checked over, Adam had not been admitted to the hospital. His jaw wasn't broken, and although his throat had taken a beating, there was no lasting damage there, either. All he wanted to do now was getting back to Maja's bedside. These interviews were formalities. He knew that. So did these expressionless people opposite him. They had the video evidence from that meeting. They had all the members of the Reaper consortium in custody, including Knight Valentine. Although whether Knight would survive the injuries inflicted on him by Maja's sisters was not a foregone conclusion. The live-streaming of the meeting had been illegal, but Adam knew as well as Agent Glenn did that her investigation into that wasn't going anywhere.

"You didn't arrive at Valentine House together?" Agent Glenn asked.

"No. It's well known that my stepfather and I don't get along. I was going to Valentine House to confront him. When Maja found out what I was planning, she followed me with the intention of trying to stop me." Adam was surprised at the ease with which he had come up with the story, and the calm way he was able to deliver the lies. But he could hardly tell the truth. Valkyries, deals with the devil, the Grim Reaper and demons? He didn't want his child's only experience of its father to be visiting a secure mental facility.

"That doesn't explain how Miss Odin came to be in the meeting room with Mr. Valentine and his associates."

"I'm sure Maja already told you this herself." *Because we concocted this story together.* "She couldn't find me in the house or grounds, so she went into the meeting room. When Knight and his colleagues arrived, she was scared that she was trespassing. Knight is a scary guy." Adam fingered his jaw reminiscently. *You should see him in action.* "So she hid behind one of the potted palms. When she realized what they were discussing, she started to film the meeting."

"And you live streamed it?" Agent Glenn, double-checked her notes.

"She live streamed it." Adam guessed they had ways of checking that, so he decided to keep it factual. "I was on the grounds of the house, making my way to her. When I saw what she was doing, I shared the recording digitally."

"Wasn't that a little...unheroic of you?" Agent Glenn gave a disapproving cough. "Your girlfriend was trapped in a room with a group of dangerous criminals. In the time it took to share that recording, you could have called the police."

"You think I don't regret that now?" Adam gave her back look for look. *Unheroic?* She could tell that to his aching knuckles.

"What I'm having a hard time understanding is who tied up Mr. Valentine's security guards and locked them in the attic, and who beat Mr. Valentine to a pulp while you and your girlfriend escaped." Agent Glenn peered at him. "Both you and Miss Odin are pretty vague about that."

"Probably because we were fighting for our lives at the time." Adam came back at her with a touch of acidity. "Have you asked Mr. Valentine or his security guards these questions?"

"Mr. Valentine is not able to answer questions. It's possible he may never be able to do so." Adam wanted to ask a few questions about that, but he got the feeling Agent Glenn wasn't the type to be forthcoming with answers. "And none of his security guards saw their attackers."

"So we're not the only ones who can't answer your questions about these mystery assailants?"

"No." She seemed disappointed at the admission. "But they overpowered eight guards without a fight, and the attack on Mr. Valentine was delivered by a number of people in a particularly ferocious manner."

Good. Adam might have a few issues with Brynhild, but if he ever saw her again, he would enjoy thanking her all over again.

"The doctors have no idea how he survived," Agent Glenn continued. "He must be incredibly strong to have put up any kind of fight, but he's waning fast now."

Adam wasn't going to enlighten her about what had really happened. It was the demon inside Knight that had done the fighting, but he guessed it had made a quick getaway when it realized the Valkyries were winning. He might not be an expert in the paranormal, but even

Adam could guess that demons weren't renowned for their loyalty. As for the devil, would the deal still stand now Knight was no longer able to pay his dues?

Agent Glenn closed her notebook and got to her feet. "If you remember anything else, particularly about these mysterious vigilantes, please get in touch, Mr. Lyon."

Her voice wasn't hopeful. And she was right not to indulge in any false confidence. *We gave you the Reaper; what more do you want?*

Intense weariness overcame Adam as he watched them walk away. But he knew the perfect cure for that. With a smile, he walked along the corridor to Maja's room.

Chapter 21

Tarek had made Maja a "get well soon" card and he and Sophie had brought her flowers and cookies. Dr. Blake had said Maja could go home the following day, as long as she promised to rest, and Sophie was staying in the apartment until then. Once Tarek was satisfied that Maja would recover from her injuries, he began to plan a marathon gaming fest for the duration of Sophie's stay.

Sophie grinned in response to Adam's rolled eyes. "I enjoy playing games with him. Honestly."

"Remind me to give you a pay raise." He escorted them to a cab and watched as they departed.

When he returned to Maja's room, she was half sitting, half reclining, propped against her pillows with her eyes closed. Adam paused just inside the door, watching her.

He was overwhelmed by the strength of the connection that drew him to her. It was always the same. Her beauty hurt his heart. But Adam had seen many beautiful women. Maja's physical characteristics couldn't account for a yearning so fervent it made him tremble. Was it stronger because his life had been so dark before she had come along to brighten it? Had this burning intensity been caused by two worlds colliding? He didn't know the reasons, and he didn't care. It just *was*. That was all that mattered.

Adam had found out early, and learned the hard way, that life was cruel. Those lessons had encased his heart in steel. They had focused his mind, making him ambitious and determined. For a long time, hatred and fear had been his driving forces.

Maja had dissolved his pain. She had given him a different reason to be resolute, and a new focus. Money, power, ambition, all the things that had once mattered, were nothing now. The only reward he wanted was her smile. His riches were her happiness. His goal for the future was to stay wrapped in her love.

He had proved over and over that he could do anything if he put his mind to it. Now there was only one thing on his mind. A future with his family.

"I know you're there." She didn't open her eyes, but a slight smile lifted the corners of her mouth.

"I want to kiss you, but I'm scared of hurting you," Adam said, as he pulled a chair up as close to the bed as he could get.

"I'll risk it." Just when he thought he couldn't feel any more emotion, she opened her eyes and his heart did a backward somersault.

Even though her lips were bruised and swollen, Maja's smile made it all okay again. All the hours of interviews, of reliving the horror of what they'd been through, of trying to convince people who blatantly didn't believe him that he was one of the good guys, faded away as he gently touched his lips to hers.

"Our baby is alive." Her whisper was filled with wonder. "Knight tried to destroy another part of your family, but this time he failed."

Adam lightly placed a hand on her stomach. "We made ourselves a fighter."

He was still overawed by the memory of the images they had seen on that screen. Of the life that had started in the midst of chaos, violence and confusion. When he had been at his lowest ebb, searching for Danny but not finding any trace of him. Injured, scared and confused, he had found Maja and they had made this new life. With every fiber of his being, he vowed to nurture that tiny person. He hadn't been able to protect Danny, but he would devote everything he had, everything he was, to ensuring that nothing ever harmed this baby.

"He takes after his parents."

"He?" He cocked an inquiring brow at her.

"Or she." Maja placed her hand over his. "But I think it's a boy."

"Do Valkyries do intuition?"

She shook her head. "It's just a feeling."

They remained still for some time, Maja resting her head against his shoulder. Although neither of them spoke of it, he knew they were thinking the same thing. Knight had been neutralized, the Reaper had been brought down, but there were still some hefty roadblocks in their way.

When the door opened, Adam expected to see a nurse. Instead, Brynhild stepped into the room with her usual, confident stride.

She approached the bed, her brilliant eyes scanning Maja's face. "You look like someone who has danced with the devil."

Adam winced. "No matter how grateful I am to you for saving our lives, can we dispense with the dark humor?"

Brynhild raised her brows. "I am a Valkyrie. I don't do humor."

He held up a hand. "I forgot."

"I came to see how you are, and to tell you what happened when Odin discovered what we had done." Brynhild took a seat on the opposite side of the bed from Adam. Clad in jeans and a hooded sweatshirt, she still managed to maintain an air of authority. Adam imagined she was an unstoppable force as the Valkyrie leader.

"Did you tell him?" Maja asked.

"Of course."

Adam recalled what Maja had said. The Valkyries couldn't lie. Even when he had suggested omission or telling a half-truth, the concepts had been alien to Maja. He wondered briefly what it would be like to live in that world. Would life be better if truth always prevailed? His own world had been rocked recently when hidden secrets had been revealed. Maybe there was something to be said for absolute clarity.

"Was his anger very bad?" Maja's eyes were round with anticipation.

"It was one of the worst rages I have seen. The whole of Gladsheim and beyond shook with its force."

Maja bit her lip. "I'm sorry."

"It burned itself out eventually." Brynhild smiled. "And I am still alive. You were right—even in his fury, Odin saw that he couldn't condemn his finest Valkyries, including their leader, to death."

Maja swallowed. "Did he issue a pardon?"

"To all except one." Brynhild's voice lacked emotion and Adam decided that was probably the best way. If she'd done this with drama and sympathy, it would have been harder for Maja to hear. Cold, hard facts—the Valkyrie way—might sound harsh, but they were quicker and easier to listen to. "When he learned of your other crimes, he could not spare you, Maja."

"So he knows it all?"

"He knows what I told him." Was Adam imagining it, or did Brynhild look ever-so-slightly guilty? He definitely didn't imagine the quick glance she cast over her shoulder. "I said due to your inexperience, you had made an error of judgment and interacted with a mortal man while leading your first mission."

"You didn't mention the rest of it?" Maja reached for Adam's hand. "That I saved Adam's life? Our relationship…the baby…?"

There was no mistaking it. Brynhild, fearsome Valkyrie general, was blushing like a naughty schoolgirl. "I may have skimmed over some of the details."

"What did he say?" Adam could barely get the words out, he was breathing so hard.

"For once, the Allfather was lost for words." Brynhild gave a reminiscent smile. "I don't think that has ever happened before. He said he always knew that this day would come. Then he asked what I thought should happen to a Valkyrie who had broken the Code in such a manner. I pretended to give it some thought, although in reality I had already prepared what I wanted to say. I told him that although your crime was serious, your innocence was a mitigating circumstance. However, if you were pardoned, it could send a message to the other Valkyrie, suggesting that such a violation of the Code was not taken seriously."

"You urged Odin not to pardon me?" Maja voice was barely a whisper. "You, my own sister, deprived me of my freedom?"

"I did, but it is not as bad as it sounds. I suggested a

punishment other than execution. And Odin took my advice." Her voice became formal. "I am here as the messenger of Odin, father of the gods. You, Maja, Valkyrie and shield maiden, are henceforth banished from Otherworld and cast out from the presence of the Allfather. From this moment on, your Valkyrie powers, including your immortality, are revoked and you are condemned to live out the rest of your days as a mortal woman."

Maja blinked, her grip on Adam's hand tightening. "That is my punishment? I am to become human?"

"It is decreed and cannot be reversed." Brynhild's expression was wary as she looked from Maja to Adam. "I thought you would like it. Was I wrong?"

Maja choked back a sob, lifting Adam's hand to her cheek. "You weren't wrong."

"How can I ever thank you, Brynhild?" He wanted to hug her, but he got the feeling her response could be a death punch to his larynx.

Her eyes blazed blue Valkyrie fire. "By taking care of my little sister."

Adam nodded. "That's my plan." He bent closer to Maja. "You know what this means?"

"We can take Tarek to Florida?"

"I was thinking more that I can finally ask you to marry me—" her expression of surprise was followed by a rosy blush "—but we can do Tarek's Florida vacation, as well."

"Before I leave, there is one more thing." Brynhild's voice dragged him back to reality. "Maja asked me to find out what I could about the man called Daniel Lyon."

Maja's blush faded as she turned to look at Adam. "I didn't tell you because there wasn't time with everything else that was happening. Brynhild consults the Norns to discover where the bravest and strongest fighters will be, and I thought she might be able to use her charts to discover where your brother is."

Adam's heart gave a thud of anticipation so violent it felt like it was trying to escape from his chest. After all this time, all the fruitless searching and disappointment, was he finally going to find out where Danny was?

"I'm afraid it is not good news." Brynhild's calm voice plowed on, cutting through the turmoil of his thoughts. "Daniel Lyon was killed in Syria two years ago."

The words were like a knife to his heart, an organ that had already been subject to considerable mistreatment in the last twenty-four hours. But Adam couldn't simply accept what he was hearing. He owed Danny more than that. A horrible image intruded into his mind. What if Brynhild was wrong and Danny wasn't dead? What if he should one day lie injured in the red Syrian dirt, calling his brother's name, but Adam was no longer searching for him because he listened now and believed Danny *was* dead?

"How can I be sure we are talking about the same Daniel Lyon?"

"I am talking about your brother," Brynhild said. "The man who had more heart and feeling for his fellow humans from the day of his birth than most men acquire through a lifetime of interaction."

"Did you tell her this?" Adam turned to Maja. Even as he asked the question, he knew he had never described Danny in those terms to her. Yet Brynhild had described his brother's personality to perfection.

"No." Maja's eyes were sympathetic, as if she could sense his distress. "I simply asked Brynhild to help find your brother."

"How did he die?" The words were easier than he expected. Finally, he had questions, even if they were not the ones he wanted to ask.

"He met a group of men. They tricked him into believing they shared his beliefs, but in reality, they were vicious mercenaries. Their numbers were depleted and they hoped to persuade Daniel to join them. He accompanied them to a town where they carried out some appalling atrocities. Daniel was horrified and fled. His aim was to get to the peacekeeping forces in the area and report what he had seen. The mercenaries captured and killed him before he could reach the peacekeepers."

"I don't understand." Maja sat up straighter in her agitation. "Odin sought the American Lion, one of the bravest fighters ever known. I went to Warda in search of him. It was Adam's brother, Daniel Lyon."

"Daniel was not the American Lion," Brynhild said. "It is most confusing. My charts show me that the man we seek is still alive. He is now in America."

Maja's cry of surprise drew Adam's attention back to her. "Don't you see?" Her eyes were shining as she looked at him. "*You* are the American Lion."

He shook his head. "I'm not a warrior."

"You are the bravest man I have ever known. You saved Tarek from the Reaper without sparing a thought for your own safety. Then you brought him here and gave him a home. You fought Knight Valentine and saved so many lives." A smile trembled on her lips. "And you rescued me. You made me into a person with real feelings, hopes and dreams."

Brynhild nodded. "Maja is right. Bravery takes many forms. It does not have to be courage in battle. The valor you have displayed is greater than that of many of the fighters who now reside in the great hall of Valhalla."

Adam quirked a brow at her. "If you think you are going to drag me off to Valhalla just as your sister is able to stay here…"

Brynhild shook her head. "I can only claim the souls of those who die in conflict."

Adam raised Maja's hand to his lips. "If that means I must live a peaceful life from now on, you and I are taking our family to a new home in the country as soon as you leave this hospital."

"I must go." The sheepish look returned to Brynhild's face. "I told the Allfather after I delivered your sentence I would never speak to you again."

"Could that be another of those things about which he doesn't need to know the full details?" Maja asked.

Brynhild smiled. "I think there may be more of those in the future." She surprised Adam by holding out her hand. When he took it, her grip almost brought him to his knees. "I can show you on a map where they buried your brother's body."

"Thank you." He held the door open for her. "I meant what I said. I will take care of her."

She nodded. "I know you will."

Was this it? Was it all finally over? Knight was defeated. Odin had not condemned her to death. She could live in the mortal realm. She was free to bring up her child as a human. It felt like a giant knot had been undone inside Maja's stomach. And yet...

Apart from one brief comment about asking her to marry him, Adam hadn't referred to the future at all. Now, as they traveled from the hospital in Greenwich back to the apartment, he gazed out of the cab window and seemed unaware of her presence. If anything, his thoughts appeared a million miles away. Could his mind be back on business so soon after the momentous events they had endured? It certainly looked that way.

A few days ago, all she had wanted was to be able to

stay here with him. To be able to raise their child together. Now, she wanted more. After all they had been through together, she didn't want half measures. *I want everything.*

Could she say that to him? Explain that she wanted reassurances about the future? She knew he loved her, but after everything that had happened, she needed to feel his arms around her as he told her he would never let her go.

The apartment was curiously quiet when they stepped inside. "Where is Tarek? He should be home from school by now." Maja turned to Adam with a furrowed brow. "And Leo? Why isn't he here?"

In response, he swung her up into his arms, carrying her up the stairs to the master suite. "I asked Sophie to take them out. To give us some peace."

"I'm fine. I really don't need peace..." The words of protest died on her lips as they entered the room. Beautiful arrangements of white roses lined the walls and filled every surface.

"I wanted it to be special, but I thought you'd want to keep it private because of the bruises." Carefully, he set her on her feet and went down on one knee. Withdrawing a small, square box from the inside pocket of his jacket, he opened it. Sunlight glinted on diamonds.

"What are you doing?" The blaze of love in his eyes almost tilted her off balance. She might not know the details of human courtship rituals, but she had a feeling she might be in the middle of one. If so, she needed clarification about her role.

Adam started to laugh. "I should have realized I would have to provide a commentary. This is what mortals do, Maja. When a man loves a woman and wants to spend the rest of his life with her, he asks her to marry him. It's customary to give a ring as a sign that the couple have made a promise to marry."

"And the kneeling?" Maja studied him with her head on one side.

"A sign of respect and humility." His eyes twinkled. "Although most men don't have to explain it to their partners."

"I understand. You can continue now."

"Thank you." His lips twitched as though he was suppressing a smile. "Maja, when our worlds collided, something unique happened. We created a new world. Our own world. From now on, within that world is the only place I want to be. With you. Wherever you go, I'll walk beside you. Whatever you do, I'll support you. Every dream you have, I'll make it come true." His eyes were bright with the same tears that stung her own eyelids. "Because I love you, and I want you to be my wife."

Maja placed a hand on his shoulder. "What do I do now?"

"You give me your answer."

"Oh. My answer is yes. Yes, please." As she tugged at his shoulder to get him to stand, Maja was relieved that she didn't have to rein in her strength. She was no longer stronger than Adam, and she liked it that way. Liked this new imbalance. Loved it when he placed the ring on her finger—it seemed to matter which one—then swung her up into his arms and kissed her until her head spun.

"What happens next?" she asked, when she was able to catch her breath.

"Next, I explain to you how a wedding works, then we get married as soon as we can. Since you don't have any identifying documents, I'll have to pull a few more of those strings that confused you when we first came to America." His smile shone brighter than the diamonds on her finger. "But once that's done, you will be Mrs. Lyon."

Maja shook her head in amazement. "I will be a real person."

Adam held her close. "You always were. I thought you were my fantasy, but it turned out you were my reality all the time."

Epilogue

Daniel Lyon's baptism was a quiet affair, attended only by close family and friends. After the ceremony, they went back to the four-bedroom cabin on the waterfront plot in suburban New York.

Elvira looked around her in surprise at the homey rooms with their bright rugs and comfortable furnishings. "This is not the sort of place in which I pictured you living."

Adam grinned. "It's temporary. We are having a new home built closer to the lake. Although Maja has made me promise it will not be a monument to the glass and chrome industries."

Elvira looked across the room at where Maja, holding her baby son on one arm, was getting a soft drink for Tarek, while talking to Sophie and Brynhild. "Who is she, Adam?"

He raised a brow. "She's my wife, Elvira."

"Oh, very well. Be mysterious if you must. Don't think

it hasn't escaped my attention that Knight was captured just after you came to see me. And at his trial, they said he claimed he was severely beaten by a group of beautiful blonde women. From the details he gave, he could almost have been describing Maja and her sisters."

"Delirium." Adam poured her a glass of champagne as he spoke. "The man was unhinged *and* he had just been attacked. He wasn't expected to live."

"But he did live. He's alive in his prison cell after being found guilty of murder and using weapons of mass destruction." Elvira's eyes were probing his face. "Was letting him live all part of your plan?"

"I don't understand."

"Come now, Adam. Let's not play games. Sooner or later the devil will come for Knight. It might have been easier on him if he'd died." Elvira's expression was bleak. "Satan doesn't like failure."

"I hadn't thought beyond neutralizing the threat." It was true. Making sure the Reaper consortium couldn't do any more harm had been his only goal.

And the world had felt like a better place recently. Adam wasn't going to claim responsibility for a change in the global climate, but the imprisonment of terrorists seemed to have signaled a fresh approach among world leaders. There was a new sense of international responsibility.

In his own life, Adam felt renewed. Taking a step back from business had been a huge relief. The man who once thought the office was all there was had discovered it was only a minor part of his life. He had his priorities right now. His family came first.

"But if I'm honest, I'd have preferred him dead. Maja still has nightmares about him. Even here, in our own little corner of paradise, she worries about security and makes me sleep with a gun in the drawer next to my bed."

He didn't add that it was a major personality change for a Valkyrie. Odin had made Maja human, but part of the price of that had been fear.

"What now?" Elvira's voice drew his attention back to her.

"Are you asking if I'm going to continue being a inter-worldly vigilante?" He laughed. "The answer is a resounding no. This was a one-time-only mission. Coming to terms with Danny's passing is taking time. I have a new Daniel in my life now, and two sons to care for. From now on, I am living a quiet life in the country with my wife and family."

"That sounds like a good ambition to have." She nodded approvingly.

Later, when Daniel was sleeping in his crib and Elvira had left, Sophie took Tarek out to play on the lawn.

"I'm glad to have this time alone with you," Maja told Brynhild. "There is something I have wanted to ask you."

"Is it about how I managed to get away so I could be here today?" Brynhild's smile encompassed both Adam and Maja. "I told the Allfather I was spending time organizing my maps and charts."

Although Maja smiled, Adam was surprised to see a touch of nervousness on her face. "That was not what I wanted to know." She took a breath. "When you came to see me in the hospital to tell me how Odin reacted to the news that I had broken the Valkyrie Code, you said something that intrigued me. You said he told you that he always knew this day would come. What did he mean by that?"

"Yes." Maja kept her gaze fixed on her sister's face. "Does this have something to do with Freyja? Is it the reason why our mother never loved me?"

Adam sat up straighter. "What is this? You've never spoken to me about your mother."

Maja seemed to drag her eyes away from Brynhild with an effort. "There are twelve true Valkyries. We are the daughters of Odin and his wife, Freyja. I am the youngest. But our mother never cared for me the way she loved my sisters."

"You don't know that," Brynhild said. "She is not a demonstrative woman."

Maja's smile was sad. "I do know it. Throughout my entire life, she has scarcely looked at me, let alone spoken to me. Although Freyja is close to her other daughters, she and I are barely acquaintances."

"You are Odin's favorite. Perhaps she felt it was necessary to redress the balance."

"Perhaps. But if there is something more, you can tell me now. I won't be returning to Valhalla," Maja said. "If there is a scandal in my past that affected Freyja's attitude to me, it no longer needs to remain hidden."

Brynhild appeared to consider the matter for a minute. Then she gave a decisive nod. "I always believed you should have been told the truth. You are not Freyja's daughter."

Adam was watching Maja's reaction for signs of hurt, but she remained calm. It was as if Brynhild was confirming something she already knew. "Who was my mother?"

"She was a Dryad named Tansey. She was the first of the new Valkyries. Odin fell in love with her at first sight. It was a difficult time. Freyja felt her position was threatened, particularly when there was a baby on the way." Brynhild smiled reminiscently. "And Tansey was very strong-willed and rebellious. It is easy to see where you get your stubborn streak from."

"What happened to her?"

Brynhild's expression softened. Despite her protestations that she didn't do feelings, now and then the Valkyrie leader displayed her gentler side. "Tansey died soon after you were born. Odin went to Freyja and begged her forgiveness. She agreed to raise you as her child on one condition. All future new Valkyries must be given the status of stepdaughter. That would put them out of reach of Odin's roving eye."

"So Freyja tolerated me but couldn't love me. And Odin favored me because I reminded him of my mother." Maja shook her head. "Yet no one told me. I lived with the scolds and the frowns. I was always the bad Valkyrie. I was told I was a rebel, a troublemaker, that I couldn't be trusted to lead an expedition on my own. But no one ever told me why."

"We thought we could teach you to conform," Brynhild said.

"But you didn't understand me. You didn't love me for who I was." Maja spoke with quiet dignity. "I only got that acceptance when I came to the mortal realm. Adam was the first person who saw the real me."

"I'm sorry." Brynhild's expression was pained.

"It wasn't your fault. It was the life we were forced to live."

Adam moved away, leaving the two sisters alone as they embraced. They didn't know when, or even if, Brynhild would be able to return. He owed Maja's sister a lot. Thanks to her, his brother now had a grave next to his parents in their family plot. Getting Danny's body home from Syria had not been an easy task, but Adam had applied his usual hardheadedness to the task. It helped that he was now the man who had turned the spotlight on the Reaper consortium. Although an air of mystery hung over how he had achieved that, it had given him some leverage with the authorities.

Dusk was falling, leaching the color from the sky as he went into the kitchen and looked out over the lake.

He opened the sliding glass door and called to Tarek and Sophie. It was time for Tarek to come in for his bath. Although there was some good-natured grumbling from him about this arrangement, the boy said goodbye to Sophie and went to the bathroom.

When Sophie and Brynhild had gone, Adam went around the house, locking the doors and closing the drapes. Although they were miles from anywhere, that was another of Knight's legacies. Maja worried that they were vulnerable if it wasn't done properly.

"All done?" Maja was feeding the baby when he returned to the family room.

"All safe." He sat next to her on the sofa, placing an arm around her shoulders.

"It was good to see other people today, but this is what I like best." She leaned against him. "Just us."

He nodded. "Our family of four."

Maja woke with a start, her eyes straining into the darkened corners of the room. Was it a dream that had wakened her? It wasn't the baby. Daniel was sleeping peacefully in the crib he occupied next to the bed.

She lay still, hoping it was nothing. Knowing there had been something. A faint noise reached her ears. Midway between a growl and a whimper. She had never heard Leo make that sound before.

Getting out of bed, she slipped on a robe. She called

the little dog's name as she made her way through the darkened house, but there was no response.

When she reached the kitchen, she paused. The sliding glass door was partly open, the drape that covered it drawn back.

A cold feeling of dread seized her. There was no way Adam would have left this door unlocked. His nightly routine was precise and unfailing. He checked every door and window, locking them and closing the drapes.

She had half turned to call Adam's name when a movement caught her eye. Illuminated by the light from the exhaust hood over the oven, it was a reflection in the glass window of a figure in the kitchen behind her.

If Maja hadn't seen it and dodged the blow, the baseball bat the man swung would have caved in the back of her skull. Instead, it caught her on the shoulder, bringing her to her knees.

Maja lifted her head and found herself staring down the barrel of a pistol. Behind it, Knight Valentine's eyes glittered coldly. Halfway between the man he had been and the Grim Reaper he had become, he wore a hooded cloak pulled up over his skull-like face.

An unpleasant smell pervaded her clean kitchen. It was the scent of unwashed bodies, blocked drains and something more. Like the residual smoky smell after a match had been struck. It was the aroma of hatred.

"Did you think it was over?"

Knight attempted a smile, but there was something very wrong with his face. Maja guessed it was from the beating he had been given by her sisters.

"I thought it was over for you." Even from her kneeling position, she remained defiant. "You stood trial and were found guilty of the terrible crimes you committed."

"You must have forgotten that I have powerful friends."

As Knight spoke, Maja could see he was a wreck, a mere shell of a man. His cloak fell back, revealing that his body was skin and bone, fitted oddly back together after being broken in so many places. His face was gray, the skin stretched tightly over his skull, giving him a skeletal appearance. Even his once-thick hair had thinned.

How had he escaped? Could that powerful friend he spoke of be the devil? Maja couldn't see any other way this walking corpse could get out of a high-security prison without satanic intervention.

We were right to be scared. The locking of doors and hiding of weapons—that was my intuition telling us he would come for us one day.

That day was here.

Maja's thoughts were divided between what was happening here and what was in the other rooms in the house. Adam and Daniel were sleeping peacefully in one room, Tarek in another. Protecting her family was uppermost in her mind.

"And you have a new baby. Another Lyon to continue the name." Knight's lips twisted. "How nice."

This was not going to happen. The man who had destroyed Adam's family once wasn't taking away what they had now.

As Maja contemplated her options, it seemed Leo was thinking the same thing. The little dog, who must have been hiding beneath the kitchen table, launched himself at Knight's ankle with his teeth bared.

Maja used the distraction to throw herself forward. She heard a gunshot and braced for the impact.

It didn't happen.

As she hit the floor, taking Knight with her, she looked up and saw Adam standing in the doorway between the kitchen and the hall in classic combat stance. His legs were apart, arms extended, and he held the gun he had just fired in his right hand, with his left hand supporting it.

Maja took a moment to register what had just happened. It wasn't Knight's gun that had been fired. Adam had killed Knight before his stepfather could shoot.

Shakily, she got to her feet.

As she moved toward Adam, Maja felt something leave the room. The smell was gone and the pervading sense of menace lifted. Her home was free from evil once more. She looked down at Knight's body and thought she could see peace on his face. She saw the man he must once have been.

"How did you know he was here?"

"I woke and you weren't there. When I came to find you and heard you talking to someone, I went back and got the gun."

He placed the weapon on the counter and she walked into his arms. They clung to each other.

"It's really over." Adam smoothed her hair back from her brow. "It never felt like it while he was still alive. I always thought the devil wouldn't let him go."

"Or Knight wouldn't let the devil go. He didn't exist without his master. He couldn't be the best unless he had the devil at his side." She shivered and pressed her face into his chest.

"I need to get the police out here. Hopefully, they can deal with this before Tarek wakes up."

Maja nodded. A soft wail from along the corridor made her smile. "Real life."

"Our life." He kissed her.

"I'll go and see to Daniel. In the meantime—" she pointed at Leo "—you need to thank the real hero of the night."Adam watched her as she walked away from him. He never tired of looking at her, not since the moment she had burst in on him that day in Warda. She was his fantasy come to life.

And now they really did have forever.

* * * * *

If you loved this romantic story, fall in love with these additional titles by Jane Godman:

THE UNFORGETTABLE WOLF
IMMORTAL BILLIONAIRE
OTHERWORLD CHALLENGER
OTHERWORLD RENEGADE
OTHERWORLD PROTECTOR

All available now from Mills & Boon Nocturne.

And don't miss the first two books in Jane Godman's SONS OF STILLWATER *series,* COVERT KISSES *and* THE SOLDIER'S SEDUCTION, *both available now from* Mills & Boon Romantic Suspense.